P9-CAO-686

# Under
## the
# Starry Skies

# Books by Tracie Peterson

**LOVE ON THE SANTA FE**
*Along the Rio Grande*
*Beyond the Desert Sands*
*Under the Starry Skies*

**LADIES OF THE LAKE**
*Destined for You*
*Forever My Own*
*Waiting on Love*

**WILLAMETTE BRIDES**
*Secrets of My Heart*
*The Way of Love*
*Forever by Your Side*

**THE TREASURES OF NOME***
*Forever Hidden*
*Endless Mercy*
*Ever Constant*

**BROOKSTONE BRIDES**
*When You Are Near*
*Wherever You Go*
*What Comes My Way*

**GOLDEN GATE SECRETS**
*In Places Hidden*
*In Dreams Forgotten*
*In Times Gone By*

**HEART OF THE FRONTIER**
*Treasured Grace*
*Beloved Hope*
*Cherished Mercy*

**THE HEART OF ALASKA***
*In the Shadow of Denali*
*Out of the Ashes*
*Under the Midnight Sun*

**SAPPHIRE BRIDES**
*A Treasure Concealed*
*A Beauty Refined*
*A Love Transformed*

**BRIDES OF SEATTLE**
*Steadfast Heart*
*Refining Fire*
*Love Everlasting*

**LONE STAR BRIDES**
*A Sensible Arrangement*
*A Moment in Time*
*A Matter of Heart*

**LAND OF SHINING WATER**
*The Icecutter's Daughter*
*The Quarryman's Bride*
*The Miner's Lady*

**LAND OF THE LONE STAR**
*Chasing the Sun*
*Touching the Sky*
*Taming the Wind*

*All Things Hidden**
*Beyond the Silence**
*House of Secrets*
*Serving Up Love***

*with Kimberley Woodhouse **with Karen Witemeyer, Regina Jennings, and Jen Turano

For a complete list of Tracie's books, visit traciepeterson.com.

LOVE ON THE SANTA FE

# Under the Starry Skies

## TRACIE PETERSON

BETHANYHOUSE

a division of Baker Publishing Group
Minneapolis, Minnesota

© 2022 by Peterson Ink, Inc.

Published by Bethany House Publishers
11400 Hampshire Avenue South
Minneapolis, Minnesota 55438
www.bethanyhouse.com

Bethany House Publishers is a division of
Baker Publishing Group, Grand Rapids, Michigan

Printed in the United States of America

Library of Congress Cataloging-in-Publication Data
Names: Peterson, Tracie, author.
Title: Under the starry skies / Tracie Peterson.
Description: Minneapolis, Minnesota : Bethany House Publishers, a division of
   Baker Publishing Group, [2022] | Series: Love on the Santa Fe
Identifiers: LCCN 2022012421 | ISBN 9780764237355 (trade paper) | ISBN
   9780764237362 (cloth) | ISBN 9780764237379 (large print) | ISBN 9781493439119
   (ebook)
Subjects: LCGFT: Novels.
Classification: LCC PS3566.E7717 U533 2022 | DDC 813/.54—dc23/eng/20220317
LC record available at https://lccn.loc.gov/2022012421

Scripture quotations are from the King James Version of the Bible.

This is a work of historical reconstruction; the appearances of certain historical figures are therefore inevitable. All other characters, however, are products of the author's imagination, and any resemblance to actual persons, living or dead, is coincidental.

Cover design by LOOK Design Studio
Cover photography by Aimee Christenson

Baker Publishing Group publications use paper produced from sustainable forestry practices and post-consumer waste whenever possible.

22  23  24  25  26  27  28      7  6  5  4  3  2  1

# 1

Hello, Mama." Cassie Barton sat down and smiled. "I couldn't keep myself from coming today. I miss you so much." She leaned forward and placed a small bouquet of flowers on her mother's grave. She glanced to the left and sobered. "I miss you too, Papa."

It had only been a few months since her father departed the earth, and she hadn't quite gotten used to his absence, whereas Mama had been gone for seven years.

"It still feels like yesterday, though." Cassie tried to keep tears from her eyes. How she missed them both. They had been the very center of her world.

"It's going to be another hot day," she said, not really caring. "Sometimes I wish I could be with you. Nothing is the same since you went away. I can't help but think of you both all the time. When we sang 'A Shelter in the Time of Storm' at church, I remembered how it was one of your favorites, Mama. Especially the line, 'The Lord's our rock, in Him we hide, a shelter in the time of storm; secure whatever ill betide, a shelter in the time of storm.'

"I remember your strong alto voice." Her smile returned. "And Papa, you would just mouth the words because you couldn't carry a tune. It always made me giggle because everyone around us knew the truth, yet you sang on in silence."

She arranged the flowers between the two graves and got to her feet. "I have so much to do, or I would just sit here with you all day." She paused and glanced heavenward. "I know you're not here, but it somehow comforts me to find you in different places. Every time I'm near a train engine, I think of you, Papa. And when I cook something, I can almost hear you instructing me as you used to do, Mama. You will both be with me always. No matter where I am, I will feel you near."

She wiped tears from her eyes and drew in a deep breath. They were in a better place. But she was alone. Completely alone in this world, despite having a younger sister. A sister who wanted nothing to do with her.

Cassie headed down the hill from the cemetery and past the Mexican grocery store in the Old Town of San Marcial. Why was she still here? Why did she stay?

"God, help me, please. I don't know where I belong."

***

"Well, Miss Cassie, what's it to be today?" Mr. Brewster asked from behind the mercantile counter.

"I need thread," she said, looking at her list. "Four white, two black, and two navy."

The older man gathered the items and placed them in front of her. "Anything else?"

"Have the scissors I ordered come in yet?" She looked up, hoping he'd reply in the affirmative.

"'Fraid not, Miss Cassie." He shook his head. "Not sure why it's taking so long."

Cassie nodded. "I don't suppose it can be helped." She looked back at her list. "Oh, I need a package of needles—the regular sewing needles. I also need a good leather needle."

Mr. Brewster quickly collected the items. "How about fabric?"

"Not today. Most of my work has been mending rather than making." She glanced around the store. "I will need a few things for the kitchen, however."

"Of course. What'd you have in mind?" They moved in unison toward the opposite side of the store, Mr. Brewster on his side of the counter and Cassie on hers.

"I'd like two cans of peaches, some baking powder, and some peppermint oil." She tucked the list in her pocket.

"We got some new saltwater taffy in just yesterday. Came all the way from San Francisco." He grinned, reached for a piece, and handed it to Cassie. "Here, try a sample." He knew all about her sweet tooth.

"If you insist." She unwrapped the wax paper and popped the taffy in her mouth. Immediately, she tasted cherry. "Mmm." It was all she could manage to say, as the taffy seemed to grow larger as she chewed. It was quite delicious.

"It's not too expensive either. Would you like me to put together a bag for you? There's a choice of cherry, lemon, peppermint, and licorice."

She swallowed the taffy. "Licorice? Truly? How odd to make licorice taffy when there are sticks of licorice to be had."

"I suppose enough folks must like the flavor."

She nodded. "Well, give me a small bag of the cherry and lemon."

Mr. Brewster seemed almost gleeful at her decision. "I told myself when it arrived that you'd probably be the first one to buy some, and now here you are."

"Yes, well, I should probably curtail my spending and get home to my work. I have plenty of sewing that needs my attention."

"But it's past work hours, Miss Cassie. You shouldn't work so hard. I know what with your pa gone you have an extra burden to see to yourself, but you know folks in this town care about you. You need never go hungry. Besides, you ought to be going out with some handsome fella. You need a husband, Miss Cassie."

People were always trying to get her hitched to someone, especially now that her father was gone. "Thank you, Mr. Brewster. I appreciate your kind words. I'm doing just fine, however. I like staying busy. I don't miss Papa quite as much that way." She paused for a moment, hesitant to continue. "As for a husband . . . well, I'm not sure God has that in mind for me. But if He does, I'm sure He'll send the right fella my way."

"Of course. Still, there are a lot of Santa Fe fellas here in town who are reliable and single. I'm thinkin' God might surely have one picked out for you."

Cassie let the matter drop. She pushed back an errant strand of blond hair and waited for the older man to figure out what she owed.

Mr. Brewster finished gathering her things and made a tally on his receipt book. "I'll just put this on your account."

"That's fine. I'll settle up with you next week." She started putting her purchases in her basket. "By the way, how's Lydia doing? I saw she wasn't in church last week and heard she had taken a summer cold."

"She did, but she's doing better. You know how it goes with a cold. A good seven days, and you'll generally feel like a new man—or in her case, woman. I reckon by Sunday she'll be back in church, playing the organ and singing at the top of her lungs."

Cassie chuckled. "Your wife has a beautiful voice, and I'm not the only one who missed it last week. Tell her I'm praying for her full recovery."

He nodded. "I will, Miss Cassie. I will."

Heading for the door with her new purchases, Cassie had to

quickly step aside when two young boys burst through the open door. They paused momentarily at the sight of her.

"Hi, Miss Cassie," the first one said. The second quickly joined in. They tipped their caps at her, then sailed on by. "Mr. Brewster! Mr. Brewster!" they yelled in unison.

"Let me guess. You're here about the new baseball cards I got in," the man said. The boys gave enthusiastic nods.

Cassie smiled. They were so excited. She stepped out of the store and started down the boardwalk.

"Hey, Miss Cassie," another little boy called, jumping up from the sandy dirt road onto the boardwalk.

"Hello, Emmett. How was school today?"

"Long. I hate going back to school. I wanted summer to last forever."

"Well, I'm sorry class had to start so soon." She shifted her basket to her left arm, then reached out to ruffle the boy's wavy blond hair. "Are you going to see Mr. Brewster about baseball cards?"

"Nah, my pa says baseball cards are a waste of time." He looked down and kicked at the boardwalk.

"I'm sorry to hear that." Cassie took pity on him. "How does he feel about saltwater taffy?"

The boy's head snapped up. "I don't know. He didn't say."

"Well then, maybe he won't mind if I share a piece with you." She reached into the sack of taffy. "You must promise that you won't let this ruin your dinner."

"I promise."

She handed him a piece of candy and smiled. "Better not tell any of the other children where you got this. I've only got a few."

He nodded. "I won't." He popped the candy in his mouth, and his eyes widened in delight. "This . . . is really . . . good," he said, trying to master the taffy and his words all at once.

"Well, you run along and chew it slow. It'll last a long time if you just keep chewing on it."

He gave another nod and turned to head in the opposite direction. Cassie noted the way he'd thrown back his shoulders. There was a strut to his walk that suggested he was king of the roost. Taffy had a way of making a boy feel like a king.

She laughed. It was a good way to finish off a Friday. She headed down the boardwalk toward home. Fridays used to be a lot more interesting when Papa was alive. Not long before his death, he earned the right to take Saturdays off. Sometimes he might have to cover for someone, but most of the time he was able to be home Saturday and Sunday, which meant Friday night was something of a celebration.

Cassie always tried to have one of his favorite meals ready and waiting. How she missed their pleasant evenings and discussions of all that he'd seen during the week. She loved Papa's stories of driving the train back and forth from San Marcial to El Paso and Albuquerque on the Horny Toad line. It was nicknamed that because of all the horned toads that made their way onto the rails. A lot of them got killed by the trains, but most seemed to sense the danger and stayed back when the big steam engines came roaring through. Her father had told her about seeing so many horned toads that the ground beyond the tracks seemed to move like water. She had always wished she could see that.

She sighed. Now Papa was gone. It had been only five months. The raid of Pancho Villa on Columbus, New Mexico, had coincided with her father's train derailment, and most folks at the Santa Fe Railway believed Villa's men had something to do with the destruction of the rails that caused the accident. Papa and his young fireman, Archie Sullivan, had both been killed, and the town mourned right along with Cassie. Wesley Barton—Bart to his friends—was beloved by the townspeople. Many of the men volunteered to ride out against Villa and his revolutionaries, who were causing problems all along the border.

Thankfully, the army had pledged to stop the insurgent.

Black Jack Pershing, the general in command, assured New Mexicans that he would capture and deal with Villa. So far that hadn't happened, and folks were worried at the growing number of incidents being attributed to Villa. Especially after it was said that Pershing sent a telegram to Washington that read, *Villa is everywhere, but Villa is nowhere.*

"Why, Cassie Barton, are you so lost in your thoughts that you aren't even going to say hello?"

Cassie glanced up and found Myrtle Tyler, her pastor's wife, staring at her. "Oh, Myrtle, I am sorry. I'm afraid I was lost in thoughts of my father and all the problems along the border."

Myrtle patted her arm. "That's quite all right, my dear. I didn't truly take offense." She smiled and glanced into the basket. "I see you've been busy."

"Yes, I've been shopping and delivering mended clothes." Cassie smiled at the older woman. "How about you? It's rumored you have busied yourself baking twelve dozen cookies for the church picnic."

"It's no rumor. If I never make another cookie, it would suit me just fine, but I know how those things get devoured."

"That's what we get for having so many men working in our town."

"Single men," Myrtle amended. "Cassie, you need to find a husband. At thirty-two, you're a very attractive woman and can still bear children. Now that your father is gone, you need a man to protect and provide for you."

"I know. This isn't the first time I've heard you tell this tale. Nor are you the only one encouraging it."

"Well, goodness, it's true. Your younger sister is married with children. You should be as well."

"I remained single to take care of Papa," Cassie reminded her.

"But he's gone," Myrtle said, softening her tone. "And we miss him greatly, but he wouldn't want you to be alone. Why don't you let me talk to John and see if we can figure out who might be a good match?" She chuckled. "As if you didn't know my choice. Brandon DuBarko was like a son to your father. I think the two of you would be fine together."

"Except that he's never shown the slightest indication that he's interested in me that way," Cassie replied. Myrtle opened her mouth to speak, but Cassie continued. "You can do as you like, but just remember that it doesn't mean things will work out. This is 1916, and folks marry for love. If I can't love a fella, I can't marry him. Even if I do love him but he doesn't love me, I *won't* marry him."

Myrtle chuckled and gave a nod. "I'm as much a romantic as can be. I completely agree that marriage should be between two people who mutually love and respect each other. What's life without love?"

Cassie knew the answer to that. It was lonely. It was facing every day without someone at your side. Someone there in the evening to talk to, someone to turn to when you were afraid.

"Well, my dear, I must be going. John and I are expected to dine with the Mackies this evening."

"I hope it's a wonderful time." Cassie embraced her friend.

"Don't forget what I said, Cassie. A husband would fill all the empty places."

"I'm sure he would."

Cassie watched as Myrtle headed down the boardwalk, then stepped into the street to cross. She was the dearest friend Cassie had, even if the woman was old enough to be her mother.

Cassie reached the boot repair shop and made her way inside, still contemplating all that Myrtle had said. Goodness but people were bound and determined to complicate her life.

Careful so as not to upset the entire contents of her basket, she maneuvered the stack of shirts from beneath her mercantile purchases. At the sound of his bell, Mr. White appeared, ready for business. He smiled when he saw Cassie.

"Well, Miss Barton, this is a surprise."

"I have your mended shirts, Mr. White. Good as new." She placed the stack on the counter.

"That's wonderful. I'm sure you did a perfect job."

"Well, you're welcome to inspect them before you pay."

He shook his head. "You have my confidence, Miss Barton. Like your father, I know I can take you at your word."

"Indeed you can."

"How much do I owe you?"

"They were in pretty bad shape. Two dollars and forty-two cents," she replied, hoping he wouldn't be offended.

"Money well spent. I would have spent a lot more if I had to buy them new."

He reached into his till and pulled out two dollars, then fished for some change. "Can I give you a two-cent stamp?"

Cassie nodded. "That's fine."

He counted out two dollars and four dimes, then added the two-cent stamp. "There you are. All legal tender."

Cassie gathered it up and put it in her coin purse. "I need to write my sister a letter, so the stamp will come in handy."

"Thanks a lot, Miss Barton. I'm sure we'll do business again soon. I seem to have a terrible way of things when it comes to tearing up my clothes."

She smiled and headed for the door. "I'm sure to be around," she called over her shoulder.

Cassie hadn't taken two steps out the door when a crowd of young men engulfed her. She lost her balance almost immediately amid the boisterous group of Mexican railroad workers. One of the boys tried to steady her, but it was too late. She went sidewise off the boardwalk, fighting for all she was worth to hold on to her basket and still catch herself as she landed on the hard-packed road.

The minute her hand hit the ground, she knew it was a terrible mistake. Pain shot up her left arm. She reached for her

13

left hand with her right, noting that her basket had flown from her arm during the fall.

"*Lo siento mucho*," one of the boys declared, apologizing.

Cassie tried to answer, but the wind had been knocked out of her. The pain in her hand increased. She couldn't catch her breath. Things were looking worse and worse.

# 2

Brandon DuBarko was just stepping out of the bank when he saw the accident. Cassie Barton lay in the dirt just off the boardwalk while six of the new workers assigned to him huddled around her. A couple of them were gathering things and putting them in a basket. Her basket.

"What's going on?" he asked, crossing the street in long, easy strides.

One of the young men rattled off an explanation in Spanish. "We weren't watching where we were going. We were just joking around about supper and playing pool, and we ran into her."

"But we're trying to help her," another man spoke up. "She dropped her basket."

Brandon knelt beside Cassie. "You all right?"

She shook her head and seemed to struggle for air. Brandon reached under her arms and pulled her up with him as he stood.

"Just take slow, deep breaths. You probably got the wind knocked out of you." He looked back at the young men. "You fellas could have killed her. You know that?"

They all gave remorseful nods. The one Brandon knew as Javier spoke up. "We didn't mean to hurt her, Boss. We were just excited."

Brandon turned to Cassie. "Are you breathing better?"

She nodded. "But I think my hand is broken." She cradled her left hand with her right. "It hurts something fierce."

Brandon frowned. "Boys, Miss Cassie makes her living sewing. If her hand is broken, you're gonna be the ones who pay for it and for her loss of income. Do you understand?"

The young men nodded. Worry etched into their expressions. It was clear they were filled with remorse, and Brandon could tell they hadn't meant to cause her harm.

"I'm gonna take her to the doc and see what he has to say."

Cassie was pale as she continued to cradle her hand. She winced more than once as she sought a comfortable angle.

"Come on," Brandon said, "we'll figure out what's going on. Can you walk?"

Cassie nodded. Her straw hat hung off the back of her head, and she looked far less orderly than usual.

"Hold on a sec." He secured the hat back on her head and gave a nod. "You're all in one piece again."

"Where's my basket?"

"*Está justo aquí, señorita.*" The boy reached out with the basket.

Brandon took it. "I'll take care of it, Cassie. Now, come on."

He took hold of her right arm and headed toward the building that housed the company doctor. The younger men trailed behind them. It was a sad little parade.

"I'm sure sorry about this," he said.

"I should have watched out better."

"No, they were clearly to blame. That bunch is full of energy. They're all decent fellas, but they're new to this. I just got them two days ago."

"They seem respectful enough."

"They are," Brandon admitted. "Good boys. Go to church, believe in God, wanna work to help their families."

She smiled. "That does sound good." She gasped and tightened her grip on her injured hand. "I hope they don't feel too bad."

16

"Well, I meant what I said. If you can't work, they will make up the money."

"Oh, Brandon, they don't have to do that." She looked up at him. "I have some savings to get me by."

"They need to learn," he replied in a firm tone. "A man has to own up to what he's done."

A memory from the past darkened Brandon's mood, but he fought it off. There wasn't time at the moment to focus on himself or the things he regretted.

"Here we are." He ushered her into the building. "Doc?" he called out, glancing around the outer office. There was an open door to the examination rooms, and Brandon let go of Cassie and went in search of help.

He found the doctor checking the wounds of an employee Brandon knew had been injured in the shops the day before. Word traveled fast among the Santa Fe workers, especially when an accident took place.

"Nurse Welch, finish rewrapping the wounds," the doctor instructed when he saw Brandon's face. "Sam, I think you're going to heal up just fine so long as you keep doing what I told you to do."

"Yes, Doc, I will," the younger man promised.

The doctor came to Brandon. "What can I do for you? You get hurt out on the line?"

"No, Cassie Barton got hurt when a bunch of the boys knocked her off the boardwalk just now."

The doctor frowned. "Let's go take a look."

Brandon followed him back to the front room. He prayed that Cassie's injuries weren't too bad. She was a good woman and deserved much better.

The doctor had taken charge of her and was turning the hand first one way and then another by the time Brandon finished his prayer. He could see that the action caused her incredible pain, but he'd never known Cassie to complain about anything.

"I'm pretty sure the wrist is broken as well as your ring and middle fingers. We'll get it all splinted and casted. You'll need at least six weeks for it to heal."

"Six weeks?" she repeated.

"Yes, and that's six weeks of resting it. I don't want you using it for anything. Especially not sewing—even on the machine."

Cassie bit her lower lip. Brandon didn't know if she was trying to fight the pain or trying to keep herself from protesting the doctor's orders.

"She won't, Doc. I'll see that she has what she needs and doesn't feel that she has to sew." Brandon fixed her with an *I mean business* look. They'd been friends long enough that she should know better than to protest.

"You can wait here, Brandon," the doctor said, motioning for Cassie to follow him. "We'll get an x-ray, and I'll have her fixed up pretty quick."

Brandon nodded and took a seat. He'd promised Cassie's father he'd watch over her long before Bart died in the derailment. Bart Barton had taken no chances when it came to Cassie. He worried about her, since she was all alone. Her mother had died a long time back, and her sister had been sent off to boarding school. From what Bart had told him, the younger daughter had nothing to do with the family, and it hurt Cassie quite a bit.

Cassie had remained to care for her father's house. She had cooked and cleaned and watched over him as a faithful daughter should, but Bart worried that she had traded her entire youth for him. And Brandon could see that he was right.

Not that Cassie was that old. She was still a decent-looking woman. Well, more than that. In an understated way, she was quite pretty. The kind of pretty Brandon appreciated. Plenty of the other fellas appreciated it too and had tried to get her attention, but Cassie had felt responsible for caring for her father, and courtship would have gotten in the way.

Brandon admired that about her. He had his own reasons

for staying single, so he knew what it was to feel called to that path. Even knowing it was his lot in life, it wasn't easy to give up on the idea of a wife and family so easily. No doubt Cassie had some of the same doubts and desires that made her choice difficult. Of course, now that her father was dead and her sister married, Cassie was free to do whatever she wanted and was no longer bound to a pledge of singlehood.

He got up and went to the window. It was getting late. Suppertime. He wondered if Cassie had planned anything for her own meal. Maybe he should get them something. He could take her home and see her settled in and then run over to the café and bring back some sandwiches or whatever was easiest. He could even cook for them, if need be. He could fry up a steak without any trouble and throw in a few onions. The thought made him realize just how hungry he was.

A half hour later, Cassie reappeared with the doctor. Her color was a little better, but she looked exhausted. Her hand and wrist were covered in a cast, and her arm had been tied up with a sling.

The doctor handed her a bottle. "Now remember, just a teaspoon when you're ready to sleep. This is strong stuff, so be careful. A lot of folks have a real problem when they take this. They just want more and more."

"I won't take it unless the pain is really bad," she countered. "I'm pretty tough."

The doctor smiled. "I know you are."

"Doc, the boys who caused the accident are paying for this, so when you've figured the bill, let me know. I'll collect from them."

"I'll do that, Brandon. I've told Cassie she's to rest. I hope you'll make sure she follows orders."

Brandon kept his expression serious. "I will. I've already got it figured out." He took Cassie by the arm, then bent to pick up her basket. "If I have to, I'll sit on her."

The doctor laughed, and Cassie glanced up at Brandon with a raised brow.

He found her look amusing but refused to yield. "She will behave or else."

They headed for her little house, and Brandon nodded at the cast. "Did the doc make it less painful?"

"Surprisingly, yes. Having it fixed in place does help with the pain. The sling helps too."

"What's in the bottle he gave you?"

"Laudanum. He wanted to give me a shot of morphine, but I refused. I've seen what that stuff can do to a man."

"It helps with the pain, though."

"Yes, but at what price? A little pain won't cause me near the trouble."

Brandon frowned. "I don't like the idea of you struggling to get through. If you need it, you should take it."

"I don't need it," she assured him.

"Are you hungry?" He thought it best to change the subject. "Once I get you home, I'll grab us some eats from the café or even the Harvey House."

"That would be nice. I had nothing planned out for supper."

"Do you mind eating with me?"

She shook her head. "Not at all. You've shared our table many a time. Why would I mind it now?"

"Well, I haven't shared it since your pa passed on. Folks might talk."

Cassie frowned. "Folks who know us won't, and I don't care what the others say."

They reached her house, and Brandon couldn't help noticing little things that needed attention. The fence could use a coat of paint. There were places around the window that needed more stucco.

"Do you have the key for the door?" he asked.

Cassie shook her head. "It's not locked."

"It should be. You're by yourself now, Cassie. You need to remember that this town is growing all the time and not all the folks here are safe to be around." He reached past her to open the unlocked door.

"I suppose you're right, but I just never think about it."

"Well, start. I made your father a promise, and I can't live up to it if you're doing your best to put yourself at risk."

Cassie shook her head and entered the house without concern. "You're turning into a regular big brother."

Brandon followed her into the house and placed her basket on a small table near the door. "I'll do what I must to make sure I live up to your pa's expectations. He worried about you."

"Well, he's not worrying anymore, Brandon."

She sat in the rocker near the fireplace. The day was still too warm for a fire, but by evening there might be a need. Brandon glanced around for wood. "You have firewood?"

Cassie shook her head. "Haven't needed a fire yet. If I get too chilly, I heat up the cookstove. Pa had coal delivered just before the accident. There's still plenty out back in the shed."

"Winter is coming, and you'll need to bring in some wood. I heard Arnie Mitchell say he was going up into the mountains to cut. I'll talk to him about bringing you a cord. You might as well start stocking up. They say it's going to be a cold, wet winter."

"That sounds reasonable. I'll check and see if I have enough saved up to pay for it and let you know." She leaned back and closed her eyes. "If you're still planning to get us supper, I have some money in the kitchen cupboard."

"I'll pay. It's the least I can do. You just rest, and I'll be back as quick as possible."

"Better take a couple of plates, maybe a bowl or two. There's a tray beside the stove. Take it too. That way wherever you go they won't be fussing around to figure out how to pack it up for you."

"Smart idea."

He went to the kitchen and caught sight of the tray first thing. He put it on the counter, then went to the cupboards that he knew almost as well as his own and fetched down two large dinner plates and two matching bowls. The dishes weren't anything fancy, just solid, serviceable white plates. There had never been anything pretentious about Cassie's kitchen.

"I'll be back as soon as possible," he said, coming back through the living room with the tray in hand.

"Thanks, Bran." She remained with her head reclined and eyes closed.

Brandon paused only a moment to gaze at her. "You want anything in particular?"

"No, anything will do. I'm just hungry and tired. This day has worn me to the bone."

He nodded even though she couldn't see him. "Be back soon."

He headed for the nearest café. There were several in town. As San Marcial had grown and the railroad offices and shops expanded, there were more amenities that made their lives easier. With a town full of single men, restaurants were in high demand.

Millie's was a quiet café with a steady crowd who frequented it—especially on Friday nights. It was already pretty full, but Brandon bypassed the dining room and went straight to the kitchen.

"Brandon, you here to eat?" Millie's husband, Joe Lancaster, asked. He was the main cook and stood at the stove, stirring a big pot.

"Taking food back to Miss Cassie's for supper. She fell off the boardwalk and got hurt today. Broke her wrist and fingers."

Joe frowned. "She won't be able to work, will she?"

"No, but the young men responsible for knocking her down will be paying her each week until she's recovered. They're my boys and felt pretty bad."

"Well, that's good. I'd hate to see Miss Cassie get in a bind." He looked at the tray. "Glad you brought your own dishes. I'll get you set up in a quick minute."

Brandon waited. It wasn't long before Joe came and took up the plates. When he returned them to the tray, they were filled with pork chops, fried potatoes, and corn bread. Next, he took the bowls, and when those were returned, they held apple dumplings.

"That ought to hold the both of you. There's an extra pork chop on your plate," Joe said, grinning.

"What do I owe you?"

"Nothing this time. It's my gift to Miss Cassie. Tell her we sure are sorry she got hurt and that we'll be bringing her some breakfast in the morning. I'm sure once the church ladies find out about it, Cassie won't have to worry about food at all, but until then, we'll lend a hand."

"That's fine for Cassie," Brandon said, reaching into his pocket for change. He put several coins on the counter. "But I didn't take a tumble and expect to pay for my meal." He picked up the tray and drew it close to inhale. "Smells mighty good. I think Cassie will be pleased. I know I will be."

"Well, come back anytime, and let Cassie know I'll be over around eight with her breakfast."

"Will do."

Brandon headed out the back door to avoid the congested dining room. He was glad Cassie had recommended the tray. This was much easier than trying to juggle several plates up his arms.

Cassie had the table set with a lamp, silverware, glasses, and napkins by the time Brandon returned. He looked at her with a frown before placing the tray on the table.

"You were supposed to be resting."

"I didn't figure it was that hard to get the silver and napkins. The glasses are empty. I didn't even pour the lemonade that's in the icebox." She smiled and took a seat at the table. "I'll leave that to you."

He nodded and began to distribute the dishes. "Joe said to tell you he'll be here at eight in the morning with your breakfast."

"How sweet. I hope he doesn't think he has to do that."

"I think he just cares that you have what you need. I told him what happened. Like he said, once the ladies of the church get wind of this, they'll have you fed, clothed, and tucked into bed each night."

Cassie laughed. "They're a good bunch of women. We do like to take care of each other."

Brandon put the tray back beside the stove and headed to the icebox in the corner of the small room. He grabbed the pitcher of lemonade and brought it back to the table. "Do we need anything else?" he asked as he poured the drinks.

Cassie eyed the table, then shook her head. "Can't think of anything, unless you need more sugar for your lemonade. I like it tart."

"So do I."

He returned the pitcher to the icebox, then joined Cassie at the table. "Shall I pray?"

She smiled. "Please."

Brandon stared at her for a moment. He felt almost mesmerized by her expression. She had to be in pain, but her countenance was almost angelic. A part of him wanted to reprimand her and tell her she was welcome to grumble or cry out in pain, but another part was touched by her ability to endure. No doubt the loss of her father had left her in the same, if not deeper, pain, and yet she continued to move forward and bear up under it.

He noticed she was looking at him with concern and cleared his throat. "Let's pray." He bowed his head, pushing aside any further thought of Cassandra Barton and her resolve.

"Amen," Cassie murmured as the prayer concluded.

Brandon couldn't help looking at the empty place where her father would have sat. He'd avoided coming to check on Cassie because the loss was so intense. Still, he hadn't shirked his responsibilities. As promised, he kept an eye on her from afar or through the pastor and his wife.

"Aren't you hungry?" Cassie asked.

Brandon looked up and found her watching him. "I was just thinking of your father. It's hard to sit here and not think of him."

"I understand. I thought I wouldn't think so much of him since moving here. He never lived in this house, so why would I see him everywhere? But the furniture is the same, and even the way I set it up is similar to what we always had in the company house. I see him everywhere."

Brandon nodded. "I'm sorry I haven't come around more. His death has been constantly on my mind."

"I know you loved him very much." She tried to cut her pork chop, but it was impossible. "Do you suppose you could help me?"

He took the knife from her hand. "Sorry, I wasn't even thinking about how difficult that would be." He cut the meat into small pieces and put the bone aside. "There. That ought to do it. Do you need anything else?"

"No, that's fine." She picked up her fork but then hesitated. "Are you still of a mind that Pancho Villa had nothing to do with my father's death?"

The question took Brandon by surprise. "I feel confident he had nothing to do with it." He remembered the man he'd seen watching the accident scene. The man had been hidden atop a hill, but not well enough. He managed to escape before Brandon got there, but he left behind evidence of his presence.

"I doubt you'll convince anyone else." Cassie took a bite of the pork.

"We don't need to talk about that now. I want you to eat and then go to bed. If you need help getting ready, I'll fetch Myrtle for you, but I don't want any argument about it."

Cassie swallowed and nodded. "I wasn't going to give you any."

# 3

O h, Cassie, whatever happened?" Myrtle asked. She had made a beeline for Cassie as soon as church was over and now stood fussing and tsking like a mother hen.

Cassie explained how she'd broken her wrist, and by the time she finished, several of the other church ladies had gathered as well. "Brandon has been a great help. He even rounded up the boys responsible, and they have pledged to pay me the wages I will lose each week. I told Brandon I had some savings and they didn't have to do that, but he insisted it was a lesson they needed to learn. Hopefully in the future they'll be more careful."

"Boys will be boys, but yes, I agree with Brandon," Myrtle replied. "This town is full of wild young men who need civilizing. They are much too rowdy at times."

"That's the way of youth," Sarah Arnold chimed in.

"I'm still thinking about Brandon helping you," Millie Lancaster declared. "Brandon came to the restaurant to get them a meal on the night she got hurt." She gave a conspiratorial grin. "Maybe Cassie can soften Brandon's hard heart—have a beautiful romance with him."

Cassie rolled her gaze heavenward. "I'm too old for such things."

"I'm forty-four," Sarah protested, "and just married a month ago. You're never too old for love and romance."

"Brandon has been like a brother to me. He was like a son to my father." Cassie could see the wheels turning in the heads of her friends. "We're neither one thinking of romance."

"But you could," Millie said, grinning. "Especially with the right encouragement."

Cassie shook her head and grimaced as the dull ache in her hand grew into pain. "I really need to get home. My hand is starting to hurt something fierce."

"Of course," Myrtle said. "Don't you worry about a thing, Cassie. I'll get the ladies together, and we'll bring you meals every day while you're recovering. If Brandon and the boys can pay your wages, we can at least see you fed. If there's anything else you need, you have but to let John or me know."

Cassie smiled and gave a nod. Pastor John and his wife had been the best of friends to her and her father. They had been so attentive after the death of her father, making sure Cassie knew she wasn't alone.

"Thank you. I appreciate that you care so much." She guarded her wrist as Myrtle leaned in to embrace her.

"We're family. Remember what John preached about at your father's funeral? The church isn't a building but a body. The Body of believers make up the true Church, and we will see to the needs of our Body."

Cassie nodded and pulled away, still protecting her hand. "I remember, and I'm very glad to be a part of that." Many had been the times that the cry had gone out for someone in need. Cassie loved that their little church was so mindful of one another's needs.

"We'll be by with supper tonight," Myrtle declared, glancing around the church. "Come, ladies, let's get the other women together and get this figured out." She took off with Sarah and Millie at her side.

Cassie started for home, still holding her hand. Despite using a sling, she felt the need to give the added protection.

"Cassie."

She turned and found Brandon hurrying after her. She wondered what Brandon would think if she told him what the women had said to her about romance and nearly giggled like a schoolgirl.

"Good Sabbath to you, Brandon."

"And to you." He stopped at her side. "I thought I'd check on you and see if you needed anything."

"Well, as a matter of fact, remember how you mentioned Arnie was going to be cutting firewood?" Brandon nodded, and Cassie continued. "Last night was pretty chilly, and I wondered if maybe you could pick up some wood elsewhere. Just enough until we find out if Arnie can cut a cord for me."

"I talked to him. He's leaving for the mountains tomorrow and said he'd be happy to cut wood for you. But yes, I imagine I can get you enough to last until he gets back." They began to walk again. "I'm sorry if you were cold last night."

"It's all right. I just threw on an extra cover. It wasn't easy, but I managed. It's funny how things I once took for granted are now so much more difficult."

"I don't like you having to stay by yourself. What if you fall again? Or need help making a fire? It seems like we ought to be able to find some single young woman to come stay with you while you recover."

"I'm sure I'll be fine, Brandon. It's not that hard to make a fire one-handed or even to pump water."

"You certainly don't need to pump water. I can get you all you need. I'll pump enough today that you won't need any more until tomorrow evening, and then I'll come after work and pump some more. I can bring in wood and coal too. In fact, I'll bring around a couple of the boys who knocked you down. They should be responsible for helping."

"They're good boys, Brandon. I can tell. They were ever so sorry for what they'd done."

"I know, but they need to make restitution other than just giving you money. This way they'll see what their recklessness caused and the way such actions have lingering effects. Sometimes the things we do can't be undone. It's a hard lesson to learn, but if we don't change our ways, we're doomed to repeat our actions."

"You sound quite philosophical today."

He seemed caught off guard and looked away. "Just don't want it happening to someone else."

Cassie hadn't meant to cause him unease. "I understand."

They had reached her little house.

"What are you doing for lunch?" he asked.

"I'm not sure. I do have stuff I can eat, however, so don't worry about me. Fetching the wood is enough."

Brandon nodded and headed back toward the street. "I'll go get it now. Shouldn't be long."

Cassie smiled and made her way into the house. She spied the bottle of laudanum on the counter and gave serious thought to taking a little for the pain.

*No. Once I sit down and rest, the pain will ease. I don't need to use medicine.*

She thought of how awful it had made her feel when she'd taken it Friday night. It had given her such a dizzy spell and terrible dreams. The lack of pain had been nice, but it wasn't worth the fear. She'd rest for a bit and then see how she was feeling.

She'd no sooner taken a seat when someone knocked on her front door. She didn't figure it was Brandon. Surely with an armload of firewood, he'd just come in. Making her way to the door, Cassie reached up with her good hand to smooth her hair and realized she hadn't even taken off her straw hat.

As she approached the screen door, she saw it was Pastor John. "Come in," she called.

"Myrtle sent me. She forgot to invite you for lunch. She was so focused on arranging for your future meals that she didn't consider the present. She has a nice pot roast that's been cooking slow since last night, so there's more than enough food."

"I was just trying to think of something I could fix and feed Brandon as well."

"Brandon is here?" The pastor glanced around.

"No, he's gone to fetch me some firewood. The night was a bit chilly last evening, and I'm out of wood."

"We have some if you need more. When he gets here, bring him along for lunch. I'll let Myrtle know to set another place. He can bring back some wood from our stack afterward."

"That's so kind of you. I'm sure Brandon would prefer Myrtle's roast beef to my attempt to make a cheese sandwich."

Pastor John smiled. "There've been times I would have been more than grateful for a cheese sandwich. We'll expect you shortly." He opened the screen door to leave, and a lizard darted in and scampered across the floor. "Want me to catch him for you?" he asked.

"No, that's all right. I'm sure I can chase him out with the broom. If not, there's Brandon."

The older man nodded. "I'm sure he'd be better at it than me anyway."

He left her with that, and Cassie turned to see if she could spy where the lizard had gone. She saw him just as he disappeared beneath the sofa. She went to the end and pushed the piece forward using her right hand. The sofa slid easily on the tile floor, and once she'd pushed it a little farther, the lizard's hiding spot was revealed.

"Come on, little fella, you don't need to be in the house on such a lovely warm day. You should be outside sunning yourself."

He just looked at her, not moving a muscle. Maybe he thought he was still hidden from view. Cassie went to retrieve her broom.

Trying to sweep with one hand was difficult. In fact, it was almost impossible.

"Phooey." She tried to extend the broom, but that wasn't any easier.

The lizard scampered off to take refuge under the sofa again. Cassie frowned and tried once more to extend the broom with her right hand. It wasn't working at all, and the action was only causing her more pain.

She straightened and tried moving the sofa back into its former position, exposing the lizard. "If you would just head back to the door, we'd both be happier."

Just then Brandon returned with his arms full of wood. Cassie saw him coming up the walkway and hurried to open the screen door. To her surprise, the lizard followed her and scurried out the door just ahead of Brandon's reaching it.

"Goodness but you're strong," Cassie commented, seeing that there were at least ten good-sized logs in his arms.

"I'll get this split for you before I go." He deposited it in the little woodbin beside the fireplace, then frowned. "I suppose I should have dropped it outside. I can't very well split it in here."

"Well, either way, splitting will have to wait. Pastor John and Myrtle have invited us for lunch. She's made a roast, and if I know Myrtle, there's probably something equally good for dessert."

Brandon dusted off his hands over the hearth. "Sounds good to me, and it will keep you from trying to fix something for the both of us."

"You figured out that I'd be concerned about that, eh?" She grinned. Brandon always seemed to know what was on her mind. Even when her father had been alive, Brandon seemed capable of reading her thoughts. If Cassie remained silent about a matter, Brandon would speak up, commenting that she wore her heart on her sleeve, especially when she was worrying about her pa.

"Well, I wasn't going to work too hard. I figured cheese sandwiches were the best I could do." Cassie shrugged. "Myrtle's roast sounds much better."

"Not to speak poorly of your cheese sandwiches, as I don't believe I've ever had them, but I have had Myrtle's roast beef, and it's quite good. So I'm inclined to agree with you."

"Then we should make our way to the parsonage." Cassie opened the screen door, mindful of the lizard.

Brandon joined her and drew the wooden door closed before letting the screen door bang back into place. He offered Cassie his arm, but she shook her head.

"I've gotten accustomed to protecting my left hand with the right. I don't know why. I suppose I'm afraid I'll fall again."

"That's all right. I'm here this time, and if you're holding on to my arm, I'll keep you from falling."

She wrapped her arm around his. "I suppose that makes sense."

They made their way the few blocks to the Tyler house. It was a simple clapboard two-story painted white. Myrtle had done a wonder with potted plants and an herb garden that rivaled all others.

Brandon knocked on the door, and it was only a moment before John appeared with a warm welcome. "Come on in, you two. So glad you could make it, Brandon."

"Thanks for the invitation. It's always a pleasure to share your table. Myrtle makes the best roast around these parts."

"Well, we're ready, so come on into the dining room and have a seat." John led the way and pulled back a chair for Cassie. "Let me help you."

She was grateful for the assistance and took the seat he offered. "I took for granted how easy things were when I had two good hands."

"God knew what He was doing when He made us, but I've also seen the way He's helped folks compensate. When Tim

Marshall lost his arm in that coupling accident, I wasn't sure he would survive, much less learn how to get along with just one arm. But he did. He learned quickly how to manage, and I credit the good Lord for helping him adapt."

Cassie agreed with an enthusiastic nod. "Papa always said that God had a way of compensating folks for loss. He was specifically speaking of losing my mother, but I've found it true overall."

"I thought I heard voices," Myrtle said, bringing a plate of sliced bread to the table. "John, would you bring in the roast?"

John smiled. "With pleasure. But that means I get first pick."

"Nonsense, that privilege goes to our guests." She shook her head and followed him back to the kitchen.

They returned very quickly. John carried a large platter with the roast and a bevy of vegetables fixed around it. Myrtle brought in a gravy boat and a butter dish.

"It's simple fare, but if you finish your meat and vegetables, there's an apple crisp for dessert."

"You'll get no complaints out of me," Brandon promised. "I'm just grateful to be included."

"As am I," Cassie said. "I can't imagine trying to cook right now. It was bad enough trying to chase a lizard from the house. Brooms are not meant to be managed with just one hand."

"I'm sure sorry about letting that little guy in," John said. "Did you get him out?"

Cassie nodded. "He exited without fuss when Brandon returned with the firewood."

"Oh, by the way, Brandon, you're welcome to take some wood from our pile. We've got plenty for the time being."

"Thanks, I'll do that. Arnie's heading up into the mountains to cut wood, but he won't be back for a week or more. The small amount I brought Cassie won't last that long."

"Take all you need. You can borrow our wheelbarrow to

transport it," Myrtle suggested. "But for now, John will say grace, and we'll get to eating before the food gets cold."

They bowed their heads, and Cassie thought about how grateful she was for these people and their kindness. Being with them reminded her of her mother and father whom she missed so much. She missed her sister too. Melissa was far away in Denver with a husband and new twins. Cassie hadn't met any of them.

"Amen," John declared and held out his hand for Cassie's plate. "I'll serve you up. Just tell me what you want and how much."

Cassie pointed out her desires, and when John started to hand her back the plate, Brandon quickly interceded and took it instead.

He set it down in front of her and shook his head. "I didn't mean to be intrusive, but it looked heavy."

"I hadn't even thought about it, but Brandon is right. It was pretty heavy," John admitted.

"Just one more thing I hadn't considered," Cassie replied.

For the rest of the meal, when the plates were passed around, Brandon or Myrtle acted on her behalf, waiting for Cassie's instruction as to how much gravy she wanted or if she desired bread with butter. She only had to feed herself and probably could have gotten help with that as well, if she'd needed it.

"Have you been down to the new dam? They're nearly done," John said after filling his own plate. "Although I can't say I like them calling it Elephant Butte Dam. I think Rio Grande Dam would be better."

Brandon buttered his bread and gave a curt nod. "I've been down there twice since Villa's raid back in March. There's a lot of concern about the safety of the dam with the Mexican revolutionaries crossing the border all the time."

"I heard General Pershing had them on the move." John offered him the jelly dish, but Brandon shook his head.

"We've heard all sorts of things. I think those movie folks from Hollywood enjoy taking their pictures and printing stories about the great Pancho Villa and the general. I heard they show him at the theater before the movie. Some people even cheer Villa on. I think to them it's all a game. Never mind that seventeen Americans lost their lives at Columbus."

John pointed his fork toward Cassie. "Not to mention Villa was probably responsible for killing Cassie's father and poor Archie Sullivan and who knows how many others."

"I don't think they were involved in that," Brandon said, cutting his roast. "I still can't forget that man I saw watching us work to clear things after the accident."

John eyed him for a moment. "I suppose he could have played a part, your stranger, but he certainly couldn't have done it alone. But nevertheless, if the dam is important enough, the government will do what's necessary to protect it and the people who live around it."

"It's supposed to be quite the tourist attraction," Myrtle declared. "I've read in the newspapers that they hope to bring in hundreds of thousands of visitors each year for fishing and swimming and boating. There are to be all sorts of camping sites, as well as resort hotels."

"I know that's the plan," Brandon replied. "I've seen a few of the hotels. They don't look all that luxurious but are supposed to be mostly adequate."

"Goodness, what do they mean by that?" Myrtle asked.

"I guess the basic needs will be met," Brandon replied.

Cassie enjoyed the food as the conversation continued. The beef was so tender that she could cut it with her fork, and Myrtle had used several of her fresh herbs for seasoning.

Myrtle surprised her by bringing up the accident again. "Brandon, you seem so sure that Villa and his men weren't responsible for Bart's and Archie's deaths."

"To be honest, I don't know what to think. Villa and his men were causing all sorts of trouble at the time, and the accident took place not far from Columbus. Since the train derailment was caused by tampering, it could very well have been done by Villa and his men. But I saw someone watching us clear the scene and fix the tracks. It has been bothering me ever since. I just can't help thinking he had something to do with the accident."

Cassie hadn't heard Brandon speak much about her father's accident. She had known it was generally thought Villa was responsible and that Brandon disagreed, but he hadn't gone into detail.

John piped up. "Well, he could have been one of Villa's men left behind to keep track of what was happening. That would be reasonable, wouldn't it? Anyway, General Pershing has promised to capture Villa and make him own up to all he's done."

Brandon shrugged. "I don't have much hope of the general stopping him. Like I said, this seems like more of a game now. Villa has friends in Hollywood and elsewhere. He's working to get folks to see him as a hero, and a lot of folks would be happy to call him one. If his men are responsible for the train derailment, we'll probably never see justice done."

Cassie lowered her head so that no one would see her dismay at the topic. She didn't want her friends to think they couldn't discuss the situation. Still, it hurt so much to think of her poor father and Archie lying dead on the desert ground after being thrown from the train engine. It had only been a few months, and the loss was still fresh.

"I think we should change the subject," Myrtle said. "This talk is rather heavy for a Sunday lunch."

Cassie glanced up to find them all looking at her. Brandon was frowning as if displeased with her, but perhaps it was displeasure with himself. She couldn't be sure, but either way she was glad for the change of subject.

# 4

The following Saturday afternoon, Brandon showed up at Cassie's after work. He brought three of the boys who had been responsible for her accident, and each carried a wedge and a splitting maul. Arnie had brought a cord of wood the evening before, and Brandon was determined to get a good portion of it split for Cassie's convenience.

"This is Javier, Roberto, and Bruno," Brandon said, introducing them to Cassie. "I'll bring the other three with me next time."

"I'm pleased to meet you," Cassie said in Spanish.

Brandon was pleased she'd remembered that the boys spoke very little English, although they were learning quickly.

Explaining their plans, Brandon continued in Spanish for the sake of the boys. "We're going to split wood for a few hours. It shouldn't take too long with all of us working."

"Thank you for your help," she told the boys. "My hand is doing much better now, so I'll have some refreshments for you when you feel like taking a break." She looked to Brandon for approval on that.

He gave a nod. "It's gonna be a while." He pointed the boys toward the woodpile. "Go ahead and get started. You know what to do."

The boys headed off without any further instruction, and Brandon turned to Cassie.

"How are you feeling?"

"Much better. I hardly have any pain. The hand is on the mend." She smiled, and Brandon couldn't help but like the way it lit up her face.

"I'm glad to hear that. You still need to take it easy."

"I know that. You don't have to bother with me. I've done practically nothing all week. The ladies from the church come over nearly every morning and bring me food for lunch and dinner. A couple of them even brought me a few books and magazines to read. Wasn't that nice?"

"It was. I'm glad everyone is looking out for you. That would please your pa."

She lost her smile. "He always said our church was full of good people who knew what it was to be the hands and feet of Jesus."

Brandon nodded. He hadn't meant to steer the conversation into memories of her father, but here they were. He wondered if he should just quit now and get to work. Who knew what might be said if he hung around?

"Brandon, I've been meaning to talk to you about something. I don't know quite how to broach the subject, but since you brought up Papa, I guess I'll just plunge right in."

He shifted the ax in his hand. "What's the problem?"

"No problem, really. It's just that I still have a couple of boxes of my father's clothes. I wanted to offer them to you first. They're in good shape. I took the other things and mended what needed to be fixed, then sent them off to the free bin at the Santa Fe company shops. But these things are fairly new, and I wanted to make sure that since you were Papa's favorite, you'd have first chance to take them. If you don't want them, then maybe you can help me find someone else."

The thought of wearing a dead man's clothes didn't bother

Brandon in the least. "I'll take them. I'll keep what works for me and distribute the others. There are a couple of men who are about your dad's size, and I know they could use them."

"Thank you, Brandon. It seemed senseless to have them just sitting here in my house when they might do someone else some good. I hung on to the tools because I can use them, but his clothes offered me little unless I wanted to remake them. I think sharing them around will be much better. I know Papa would approve."

Brandon found it touching when she referred to Bart as Papa. He could remember her calling him that when they shared meals or when Brandon stopped by for a game of chess or checkers.

He glanced at Cassie. She wore a dress of faded blue with white trim around the sleeves and collar. Someone had helped to part her blond hair in the middle and pull it back on either side to twist into a bun at the nape of her neck. It was all so very simple, and yet it worked perfectly for her. She was the epitome of a lady.

For as long as he'd known the Barton family, Brandon had found Cassandra to be special. She had such a generous nature and kind heart. She was exactly the kind of woman he would have taken for a wife—had his circumstances been different.

"Are you all right?" Cassie asked.

Brandon refocused on the present moment and realized he was frowning. Shaking it off, he motioned with his head toward the woodpile. "Of course. I'd best get to work, though. There's a lot to do."

He didn't wait for her response before joining the boys.

Cassie wondered what had caused Brandon to look so angry. He was always rather brooding, but the way his brows knit together and his eyes narrowed, he looked downright perturbed.

She shrugged. She'd probably never know, given his propensity toward silence.

She made her way inside the house to the rhythm of the boys at work and started looking around the kitchen for what she could serve them. She'd made fresh lemonade earlier in the day, but that hardly seemed enough. They were working very hard on her behalf. Myrtle had brought her a dozen cookies the night before. Cassie quickly did the math. There were four men. That would allow each three cookies. That seemed a fair refreshment along with the lemonade.

She set out four plates and divided up the cookies. Next, she brought the glasses to the table one at a time. When the men were done, she'd get Brandon to pour the lemonade. Handling a full pitcher was still a bit of a trick for her.

While she waited, Cassie picked up a journal Sarah Arnold had given her. Sarah had commented that maybe Cassie would find it interesting to write about her days, since she could do little else. At first Cassie hadn't been the least bit interested, but one evening when she particularly missed her father, she began to write down stories about him and the railroad. She read back over what she'd written.

*Papa's first experience with the railroad came after the Civil War. As a Georgia boy, he witnessed the war from his front yard in Atlanta. He talked of the terrible destruction and the way the Union soldiers had sorely abused the people. Things were so bad that when Papa turned thirteen, he went to work for the railroad. He was big for his age, so no one questioned it when he claimed to be sixteen. At first, he carried water up and down the track as the men worked to repair the devastated lines. He remembered the empty faces of the men who had fought for the South. They were tired and worn from defeat even seven years after the war's end. Some never recovered.*

*Papa said it felt as though God had abandoned the South, but his mama assured him that wasn't true, even though she'd lost her husband to the Battle of Gettysburg. Papa said she had taught him that even when things were at their worst, God was still on His throne and had not forsaken His children. She reminded her son that God's children could be found on both sides of the war and that He must surely have been heartbroken at the sight of them fighting and killing one another, just as an earthly parent might be when their children fought.*

*Grandmother Barton died when Papa was just seventeen, and with no one else to call family, he aligned himself with the railroad and moved west to become a fireman shoveling coal into the firebox of a large steam engine. The work, he said, was what he imagined it was like for the poor soul who had to keep the fires of hell.*

Cassie picked up her pen and continued the story.

*Papa didn't like working as a fireman, so he began to learn about driving the train. He had a good mentor, Joe Wilcox. Joe became a father to Papa. He showed Papa not only how to drive a train but also how to be an honorable man. By the time Papa applied to work for the Santa Fe, his reputation was set and well-known among railroad men. Wesley "Bart" Barton was esteemed up and down the rails no matter the company who owned them.*

She put down the pen and reread what she'd written. The words brought a smile to her lips. Papa was so admired by his fellow workers that they were even willing to bend the rules for him. She picked up the pen again.

*When Papa was set to take the test to become an engineer, he learned that part of the test was written. He was very nearly illiterate, having had to quit school at thirteen. He could read just enough to get by, but writing down answers to questions was an entirely different story. Joe Wilcox knew about the problem and proposed a compromise to the Santa Fe officials: give Bart Barton an oral test. Let someone read the questions to him and let him answer them aloud. This would prove that he had studied and learned the rules and regulations. In the meantime, Joe read the entire engineer's handbook aloud to Papa night after night, or during the day if their hours were altered by train traffic. By the time they received approval for Papa's unconventional test, he was ready and passed with the highest score of anyone who had ever taken the test. He was so thankful to Joe for his creative suggestion.*

Cassie continued writing until she noticed it was getting dark in the house. She put away her journal and had started lighting lamps when a knock sounded on the front door. No doubt that would be Brandon and the boys.

She welcomed them into the house and suggested they take a seat at the table. "Brandon, if you would pour the lemonade, I'll bring in the cookies."

He followed her into the kitchen. Without a word, he took the pitcher from the icebox and followed her back to the table.

"I'm only good for one plate at a time." She smiled at the boys, who looked grateful for the refreshment.

By the time Brandon finished filling the glasses, Cassie had retrieved the last plate. She put it in front of Brandon, then took a seat at the end of the table.

"I hope you like these cookies. Myrtle Tyler made them, and she always does such a good job."

"Aren't you joining us?" Brandon asked.

Cassie shook her head. "I wasn't out there working hard. I was just in here writing."

"*¿Qué estabas escribiendo?*" Javier asked.

"I was writing about my father and his stories about working on the railroad," she explained.

Bruno laughed. "I have stories about working on the railroad. They aren't pleasant." The other boys joined in the laughter.

"I'd love to hear your stories. I've heard so many interesting stories from my father and his friends." She got an idea. "The railroad might enjoy a book of stories about their workers." She looked at Brandon. "Don't you think that would be fun? The folks who ride the trains might even enjoy that."

"Could be." Brandon picked up his glass. "At least writing will keep you out of trouble." He gave her a side glance, and his eyes seemed to twinkle even though he didn't smile. He rarely smiled.

The boys promised they would stop by and tell her all sorts of stories about their exploits and mistakes on the railroad, but for now they were headed to play pool down the road. They bid her and Brandon good evening and left without further ado.

Brandon sat in silence, nursing a second glass of lemonade. He looked tired—weary, really—and Cassie felt sorry for him.

"I have plenty of food for supper if you want to share it with me. Sarah Arnold made chicken and dumplings, and Millie Lancaster brought over a fresh loaf of bread and half a peach pie."

Brandon's brow raised at this. "Do you have cream for the pie?"

Cassie laughed. "Of course. What's peach pie without cream?"

This brought out one of his rare smiles. It wasn't a full smile, but for Brandon, it was something special. Cassie couldn't help but be pleased.

"All right, I'll stay."

"I'll need to warm the chicken and dumplings." Cassie got up and started for the kitchen. "You just rest. You've done enough today, working on the line and then cutting my firewood. The least I can do is warm up food."

"Are you sure it won't be too hard for you?"

She paused at the entry to the kitchen. "Not at all. You just enjoy your lemonade."

After putting more coal in the stove, Cassie went to the icebox and pulled out the bowl Sarah had brought. She was getting better at managing with one hand. She poured the contents of the bowl into a frying pan, which had proven much easier than a pot because of its wider opening. She stirred the dumplings, then set aside the spoon and went to retrieve the pie. She had already decided she would warm it as well. Given it was in a pie tin, she had only to slide it into the oven and wait for things to heat up.

It wasn't long before she filled their bowls with the chicken and dumplings and took them one by one to the table. She followed this with Millie's bread and the butter she'd been given by one of the other congregants. She brought silverware, then added linen napkins just to make the meal special.

"I have the pie warming in the oven." She reached for her chair, but Brandon jumped up to help her.

"Let me." He took hold of the chair and waited for her to be seated before scooting her closer to the table.

"Thank you. Things really are getting easier. I keep figuring out ways to help myself."

"Just remember, the doc said you weren't to be doing much of anything for six weeks."

She frowned and looked him full in the eye. "Brandon DuBarko, you know me better than most, so you know I can't just sit around for six weeks. That's why I started writing down some of Papa's stories."

"I can't see that writing is going to cause you any problems, but there's plenty else that might." His voice was gruff, but she could hear the concern he had for her.

"Look, I've yielded everything else. Myrtle has arranged for my house cleaning, my laundry, and my meals. You've taken up everything on the outside of the house, so there's nothing left for me to worry about. That should make you happy enough. You needn't treat me like a child."

Brandon took a seat. "Sorry, Cassie. I didn't mean to get bossy."

She sighed and gave him a smile. "It's just your nature, so you're forgiven. Now, let's eat. I'm starving. Would you ask a blessing?"

Brandon nodded and bowed his head. "Heavenly Father, we thank you for this food and ask that you bless it to our bodies. Please heal Cassie's wrist and fingers and take away any pain that she might have. Amen."

"Thank you." Cassie felt a moment's nostalgia. Papa had often asked Brandon to pray over a meal. It seemed like only yesterday that they had all shared supper together, laughing and talking in rapid-fire conversation. The talk was of the Elephant Butte Dam and the railroad's desire to see the name changed to that of the nearby town. However, given that they couldn't agree whether to spell it *Engle* or *Engel*, it seemed foolhardy to try to impose that name on the dam. Papa had commented how typical it was of a roomful of officials to try to rewrite history when they couldn't even agree on how a name should be spelled.

"You look like you have something on your mind," Brandon observed as he buttered a slice of bread. To Cassie's surprise, he handed the bread to her.

"Thank you." She put the bread on her dessert plate. "I was just thinking about the last time we were gathered here with Papa, and the conversation we had regarding the railroad wanting to rename the new dam."

"Funny you should mention the dam. I was going to ask if you'd like to join me on a little trip down there. I have some track to check on, and I thought it might be fun to look things over while I'm there."

"I'd really like that, Brandon." She picked up her spoon. "I've long wanted to see it. Papa was going to take me, but then . . . well . . ." She let her words fade into silence.

Brandon acted as if there were nothing amiss. "I'll be heading down there on Tuesday. If you don't think it will be too difficult for you, I'd be happy to escort you."

"I think I can manage." She looked at him for a long moment. His wavy brown hair needed a cut. She used to cut her father's hair, but it was straight and simple to manage. She wondered if she could handle cutting Brandon's hair. She realized she was still staring at him and quickly lowered her gaze to the food.

"Then I'll pick you up around noon," he said.

She nodded and began to eat. It would be fun to go on a little trip to the reservoir. She hadn't been outside of San Marcial in a very long time.

The next day at church, Cassie shared her planned adventure with the ladies who had been taking such good care of her.

"You're going with Brandon?" Sarah asked.

"Yes, he has to go down there for work and thought I might like to see the dam."

"It sounds to me like he has other interests. Perhaps romantic ones," Sarah teased.

"I'd be careful if I were you," another of the ladies said. "I've heard Brandon is a hardened man with a dark side. He has no interest in a wife and family. My husband says his heart is stone."

Cassie was surprised by the statement. "How would Sam know what Brandon's heart is like?" She asked the question before giving it any real thought.

The woman shrugged. "I certainly can't say, but maybe Brandon declared it so."

"He does seem to have quite the wall built around him," Myrtle admitted. "Although if anyone could knock a hole in that wall, it would be Cassie. Brandon was very close to her father, and I'm sure he mourns the loss as much as the rest of us."

The ladies nodded.

"I would think Brandon is ready for someone to love—especially someone he esteems as much as he does Cassie. I've always thought they would make the perfect couple," Sarah said with a smile.

"Just don't force anything, Cassie. I would enjoy seeing the two of you together, but Brandon seems like a troubled soul at times. There's something going on in that head of his that I can't figure out." Myrtle glanced toward where Brandon stood speaking to her husband. "John probably knows, as they talk all the time, but he would never tell me. He's very good about honoring a person's secrets."

"Do you think Brandon has a secret?" Cassie couldn't help but ask.

Myrtle gave her a thoughtful look. "Don't we all?"

# 5

Monday afternoon seemed a perfect time for Cassie to visit her clients and let them know about her hand and that she wouldn't be able to sew anything for another five weeks. Most had already heard and were fine with the delay in schedule. A couple of the wives who had ordered new dresses or clothes for their children showed their disappointment but understood. After all, what could they do but cancel the order and find another seamstress? There were a few other capable women in town who offered their services, and Cassie couldn't help but worry that she'd lose her clientele, but it wasn't as if she had a choice.

By the time she finished making the rounds, it was nearly five o'clock. Brandon had mentioned stopping by with the other three boys who'd caused her accident. They were going to make sure she didn't need anything, so she wasn't surprised to see them waiting outside, studying her picket fence.

"Afternoon, Brandon." She smiled, then glanced at the other three and gave a nod. "Boys."

"Hola, señorita Cassie," one of the trio said.

"That's Angel," Brandon introduced in Spanish. "This is Maximo, but folks call him Max. And the last is Zorro."

"Ah, the Fox," Cassie said, smiling.

"Sí, I am crafty like the fox," the young man replied with a grin as big as the outdoors.

"We've come to see how you are and what you might need done. I've already determined this fence needs painting and a few repairs on the pickets. We can do it on Saturday after work. Right now, the boys are heading back to be with their families for the evening."

"Saturday works for me. I don't plan on being anywhere else." She glanced at the boys. "I'll try to have some refreshments."

Brandon spoke to the trio and dismissed them. They bid Cassie farewell and hurried off toward Old Town.

"They are such good boys. I'm sure their families are proud of them," Cassie said, switching back to English.

Brandon gave a nod and met her gaze. "They're coming along well in their duties. They are all quick learners. I've been impressed with this bunch."

"How nice. It makes me wonder just how far they'll get. You know, my father started with the railroad when he was just thirteen."

"I was the same age as some of these boys when I began working for the railroad. It worked out much better for me than attending college."

"But I thought you told Papa that you attended college and loved learning."

He shrugged. "It had its good points, to be sure, but the physical work is more satisfying to me. My father was an intellectual and felt that only men of book learning and scholarly debate were of any value. I'm glad to prove him wrong."

"I've never heard you speak of your father before. Were you close?"

Brandon frowned and shook his head. "We weren't, and I'm sorry I brought him up. I'd just as soon we forget about him."

Cassie was shocked by his abrupt dismissal of the topic.

He sounded almost angry, as if she had somehow caused him distress. For a long moment, she had no idea what to say or do.

Supper came to mind, and she thought perhaps it would work as a way to smooth things over. "Are you hungry? Millie and Joe brought me quite a few leftovers from the restaurant yesterday. There's a big pot of beef stew, dinner rolls, fried fish, and cake. Oh, and several ears of corn."

"Sounds good." He still seemed rather upset. "Look, I'm sorry for being angry."

She shrugged. "Things happen. It's not my place to force your confession. Let's just eat and enjoy a quiet evening. No more questions." She headed to the house and opened the door.

"I thought you were going to start locking up," Brandon muttered behind her.

"I keep forgetting. I've gone so long without doing it that it seems completely strange to do it now. But if it makes you feel better, Bran, I promise to try."

He said nothing, and Cassie feared she'd made him mad again. She couldn't help but think of the things the church ladies had said about him. For all the time he'd spent in her father's house, Cassie knew very little about Brandon.

"It's kind of chilly in here. Would you like me to make a fire?" Brandon offered.

"Maybe later. I'll soon have the kitchen stove heated up, and there will be plenty of warmth from it. Do you want the stew or the fish? Or both?" She glanced over her shoulder.

"Stew, please. I've never been all that fond of fish."

She nodded. "Stew it is. It shouldn't take too long. There are still embers in the stove, so I'm sure it will heat up fast."

"I'll help you. What do you need?"

"If you want to get some kindling and get a real fire started, I can add the coal in a few minutes."

Brandon nodded and left the kitchen. He returned soon enough with some of the kindling he and the boys had chopped on Saturday. With the skill of one who'd done it thousands of times, he got the fire going without difficulty, and rather than turn the job over to Cassie, who was busy getting the stew into a pot, Brandon went ahead and added the coal.

Half an hour later, they were sitting down to supper with large bowls of beef stew and thickly sliced bread. Cassie offered grace and then gave Brandon the nod to dig in. She kept her gaze fixed on the food, almost wary of upsetting him again. Myrtle had said he had a wall around his heart, and Cassie wondered if his father had helped put it there. She didn't feel like she should ask, but it kept her mind occupied.

When the coffee was ready, Cassie retrieved a couple of mugs and then the pot. Brandon quickly took it from her and poured them both a cup before returning the pot to the stove. Cassie added cream to her coffee, but Brandon drank his black.

"Would you like some cake?" she asked, motioning to the plate of lemon sponge.

"Sure."

He had been unusually quiet throughout the meal, but Cassie pretended all was well.

"Look, I want to say something," he began without warning.

"You know you can talk about anything." She focused on slicing the cake.

"I didn't mean to sound so gruff earlier. You didn't do any-thing to deserve my bad attitude. It's just that . . . well, my father and I weren't close. There were a lot of problems be-tween us."

She handed him a plate of cake. "Brandon, you don't owe me an explanation."

"I feel like I do. You and I have been friends for a long time."

"No, you and my father were friends for a long time. I feel like you and I are only just getting to know each other."

He gave her a surprised look. "Really? We've shared many a supper table and conversation."

"I know, but you wouldn't have been here except for my father. It's not like you were here to talk to me." She took a piece of cake for herself. "You've been like extended family to me all these years, but even then, I've not known you all that well, not like Papa did. He always spoke of you like a son. He thought so highly of you, and I'm sorry your own father didn't."

Brandon's frown deepened. "Your pa was a special sort of man. He knew how to be a good father."

"He would have argued with you on that point. After my mother died, he didn't know what to do with my little sister. She was only thirteen, and losing our mother was more than she could bear. She cried so much that we both feared she'd make herself sick. When it was suggested that we send her to boarding school with one of the Santa Fe officials' daughters, I think Papa was so relieved that he didn't consider the consequences."

"Consequences?"

"Of Melissa being gone all the time. We heard so little from her, even though we got regular progress reports from the school. During holiday breaks and summers, she always wanted to remain in Denver with her best friend, Abigail. We now know it was Abigail's big brother Terrance who actually held Melissa's interest, but I digress." Cassie shrugged. "The fact of the matter is that Papa felt he was a terrible father. Melissa looked so much like our mother, and Papa's grief was so deep. He could hardly bear the loss himself. How was he to comfort a child?"

"I know he missed your mother a great deal."

"Yes, and he blamed himself for not realizing she was sick. But who could have known she had a bad heart? Even the doctor didn't realize it until it was too late. I was with her when the attack came. It happened so fast that there wasn't even a single word spoken between us."

"I'm so sorry."

"I regret it, to be sure. Just as I regret losing Papa. We always made sure to tell each other *I love you* when we parted. I am glad for that. But even so, we couldn't have known he would die that day. He was there and then gone. No warning."

"And all because a Mexican rebel decided to raid the United States." Brandon shook his head.

Cassie frowned. "You don't think the man on the hilltop was responsible?"

"What John said gave me pause. It could have been someone from Villa's crew left behind to observe the scene," Brandon admitted.

"So it could have been Villa or one of his men after all?"

He shrugged. "Sure, though Villa was supposedly long gone, back to Mexican soil, by then."

"So it could have been Villa, but then again it might not have been." She sighed. "I guess I just can't see worrying about it either way. My father is still dead, and that's all that matters to me."

"Don't you want to get the man or men responsible for what happened? Make them pay?"

She considered that for a moment. "It won't bring him back, but yes, I suppose I want justice."

"I want more than that," Brandon replied. "Your father deserves more than that. He deserves for his killer to hang. If it's not Villa, then I want to know who I saw and determine if he is the guilty party."

They were at a stalemate, and there was nothing to be gained by challenging him on the matter. Cassie focused instead on her cake. Maybe in time they would learn the truth of it, but for now she chose to accept the possibility that she would never know who had tampered with the track and caused her father's train to derail.

Brandon was just finishing up instructions for the things he'd need to take to the dam when word came that there had been bandits in the area of Engle. They had caused problems on the rail line. Soldiers had been summoned, and additional repairs would need to be made. The increased danger made it impossible to take Cassie along.

"I'll need to let Miss Barton know the trip is off," Brandon told his supervisor, Bud Wilkes, after hearing the news. "I was going to take her along."

Wilkes grinned. "I hear you've been spending a lot of time with her."

"My new boys caused the accident that left her with a broken wrist and fingers. Since she sews for a living, I've made the boys share a portion of their salary to make up her loss. They were quite willing and all took responsibility, I'm happy to say."

"And that's the only reason you've been keeping her company?" the older man asked, still grinning.

Brandon wanted to slap the smile from his face, and yet Wilkes had done nothing wrong. He was grateful for the interruption when one of the office boys brought yet another message.

"I've got to take care of this," Wilkes said, reading the message. "Once you've told Miss Barton, be sure you take your boys and head down to get those tracks repaired. I can't pull off any of the other section workers."

"Will do. We'll see that everything is back in good working order."

Brandon called Javier to join him and then let the boy know what was going on. "Get the others and join me on the southbound freight. They're loading most of our stuff in the front boxcar. We can ride there with it. We'll be gone until the job is done, so bring your bedroll in case they don't have space for us with the dam builders."

Javier gave a nod and rushed off to find the other boys while Brandon made his way to Cassie's house. The early September day showed definite signs of being cooler. Autumn was soon to be upon them, and finally temperatures would be bearable—even pleasant.

Cassie opened the door to her house after Brandon's single knock. She was dressed for travel in a dark blue traveling suit.

"I wasn't expecting you quite this early."

"I'm afraid there's bad news. I can't take you to the dam today. There's been trouble down there—bandits—and it wouldn't be safe."

"Are you still going?" Cassie asked, her apprehension apparent.

"I am. We have to make repairs to the tracks they tore up."

"Villa?"

"Possibly. There's no way to know for sure."

"I wish you didn't have to go," she said.

He could hear the worry in her voice. She was probably remembering her father and what had happened to him when he ventured into a troubled area.

"We'll be all right. They've sent for soldiers to provide protection. I just think it would be best for you to remain here. San Marcial won't be attacked. Of that I'm sure."

"How can you be so certain? Columbus was attacked."

She made a good point. Brandon reached out and squeezed her shoulder. "If there is even the slightest threat, go stay with the Tylers. They'll most likely seek safety at the shops if the town comes under attack."

"I'll be fine, Brandon. I promise I'll go to them."

"Good. That will give me one less thing to worry about."

She looked puzzled. "You never have to worry over me. I'm old enough to take care of myself."

He said nothing. What could he say? She was right. He had no say over her and no real reason to make her one of his concerns. Except that he had promised her father he would look after her and see to her needs if anything ever happened to him.

Cassie kept thinking about what Brandon had said long after he'd gone. To keep her mind occupied, she decided to go to the store. Mr. Brewster had sent word that her new shears were in, and besides that, she was contemplating another purchase.

"What is it you're looking for, Cassie?" Mr. Brewster asked as she moved around the shop.

"I've been writing a lot lately, and I'll soon need another journal. Do you have any?"

"I think so. Hold on. I'll look." He disappeared behind the counter and returned a moment later with two red books. "Here we go. These are what I have."

Cassie examined them. "They'll be perfect. I'll take them both."

"Goodness, you do have a lot of writing planned."

"I'm writing down stories about the Santa Fe and its workers. The boys have been telling me stories about their work on the line or in the shops, and my father always shared so many adventures and thoughts. I figure there are plenty of other men who might do the same. I want to put it all together in a book."

"Well, isn't that something," Mr. Brewster declared. "I'd like to read that myself."

"See there? I thought the same thing. I want to know their stories, so other folks might like to know them too." She smiled, feeling a great sense of satisfaction. "Maybe the railroad would want to have a copy."

"I'll bet they'd even want to sell copies, Miss Cassie. You just never know what this might bring about. Folks all over the country might want to read about workin' on the Santa Fe."

She nodded. "I've thought about that too. I guess we'll put it in God's hands and see what happens."

# 6

Brandon's crew spent most of the day repairing and replacing ties and rails that had been damaged near Engle. Brandon admired the strength of these boys. They were young and inexperienced, but strong and capable. They made him proud.

That night they unrolled their sleeping bags and slept around three small fires. Most of the boys were asleep the second they lay their heads on the bedrolls, but Brandon couldn't help thinking of the problems they might face in the area if renegades and bandits continued their courses of action. They were causing problems all along the border and up as far as Elephant Butte Dam. If there was a constant threat of such activities, it was going to put an end to the planned celebrations for the opening of the new dam come October.

He worried about what might happen if the Mexican revolutionaries continued to battle it out not only amongst their fellow Mexicans but with Americans as well. It seemed they recognized no boundaries or borders. Brandon didn't intend to spend his life repairing their damage. Somehow, the army or the governments needed to figure out what they could do to resolve problems at the border between the United States and Mexico.

Not only that, but the Great War was raging on and on in Europe, and Brandon had a feeling it was only a matter of time until America had no choice but to join. People were suffering horrific tortures, and the United States couldn't continue to ignore that.

But so many felt it wasn't their war—that this was a fight between Queen Victoria's offspring, and Americans had no need to be involved. However, the entire matter was rapidly getting out of hand, and now all of Europe and Russia was involved. If America went to war, Brandon couldn't help but wonder what he would do. The railroads needed to continue to run, and his skills were needed. He was also older than the common soldier. Usually much younger men were desired for their agility, trainability, and lack of fear.

Brandon shook his head. He wasn't going to solve the problems of the world tonight. Not even the parts that involved him. He knew it was best to let it all wait for another day. He needed to sleep in order to function in the morning.

As he relaxed and gazed up into the skies, he let go of the struggles of the day and his concerns for the future and instead studied the constellations overhead. When he'd been at school, he had taken a class on astronomy. It had been a fascinating study of the heavens. He had very much enjoyed it and remembered coming home to share information with his mother and father. Mother had been interested, especially when Brandon had taken her outside to show her the Big Dipper and the North Star. Father had chided him for getting caught up in the foolishness of such a thing. Astronomy wasn't a real science, as far as he was concerned. There would never be anything useful done with such studies.

But there was. Brandon had heard predictions that with the success of the Wright brothers and their airplane, man would one day be able to fly into the heavens and land on other planets. He tried to imagine how such a thing might be. It didn't strike him as impossible—after all, many people had found it impossible to believe in train travel from one side of the United States to the other. Yet here they were in 1916 with the ability to go from coast to coast. A trip that had once taken months was reduced to a fraction of the time.

With thoughts of stars and travel floating through his mind, Brandon drifted to sleep.

He awoke the following morning before it was light. The stars were fading from the sky, but he thought immediately of the section of Scripture where God showed Abram the stars and talked about how he'd one day have descendants just as numerous. The thought must have amazed the old man since he had no offspring at the time.

Brandon stretched, then stood. It would soon be dawn. He shook a couple of the boys awake. "Time to get up."

They moaned and sat up as Brandon bent to tie up his bedroll. He washed his face and went with his men to the dam workers' mess building, where they ate a hearty breakfast. It wasn't long before they were back on the line, jacking rails and replacing ties. The work was hard, but the boys were used to it, and they had come together as a real team. Brandon was pleased with the way they looked out for each other and weren't afraid to volunteer.

That night, with another day's work behind them, Brandon wired the shop in San Marcial to report that they would complete the job by the end of the week and be home on Saturday. He wondered if the boys were still going to be willing to help with Cassie's fence. It could wait, but Brandon didn't want to put off the job. He cared about Cassie having what she needed. She'd been on his mind a great deal, and he was concerned that she might be suffering without him close at hand to help.

"Boss?" Javier asked, coming to sit by the fire where Brandon was settling in for the night.

"What do you need?"

"I just wondered if it was true that you went to a university back east?"

Javier was the oldest of the bunch at twenty years of age, and Brandon couldn't help but wonder at his interest.

"I did. I had done well in high school and graduated when I was just sixteen, so my father felt I needed to attend higher education."

"But you work for the railroad. What happened?"

Brandon shrugged. "I like physical labor better than book learning, I guess." That wasn't exactly true, but how could he tell Javier that his father had ruined learning for him?

"I wanted to go to the university, but my family needs me to work," Javier said, clearly trying to hide the disappointment from his voice. Brandon heard it all the same. "We have a very large family. I have fourteen siblings, and my grandparents live with us, as well as my mother's sister. My father has cattle, but there's not enough money, so my brothers and I have taken jobs."

"It's admirable that you would make the sacrifice to help your family rather than seek out your own desires. You're a better man than most."

Javier stared into the fire. "I feel so bad that we caused Miss Cassie's accident because she reminds me of my Aunt Rosa. She was crippled when a horse trampled her. She sews for the family and sometimes makes things to sell. She's good like Miss Cassie—always making people feel better."

"Miss Cassie does have a way about her," Brandon admitted.

"I think you two will be very happy together," Javier said, getting to his feet. "I'd better get my bedroll spread."

Brandon wasn't sure what to say about Javier's comment regarding Cassie, so he said nothing. It seemed strange, however, that Javier would put them together like that. He hardly knew anything about either of them. Certainly, he knew nothing of their history.

The other boys gathered around the three fires once again. None of the fires was all that large, but they were effectively positioned so that the boys had plenty of warmth through the night. Brandon spread his bedroll carefully, making sure there were no snakes seeking comfort there. Long ago he'd learned that when the desert nights turned chilly, snakes often sought comfort where they could. He'd once found a rattlesnake curled up in his things, cozy and warm. Of course, when Brandon and the snake came face-to-face, neither was willing to accommodate the other.

As he stretched out, he thought again of Javier and his question about attending a university. Brandon's father had been an intellectual. He owned a newspaper and intended for Brandon to take it over one day. Had his father been less of an abusive tyrant, Brandon might have enjoyed that. He had loved learning, and reading had been one of his favorite pastimes, but given his father also took delight in such things, Brandon had gone out of his way to rid his life of them. There was a fear in him that perhaps education and a love of the intellectual things of life had given his father an ugly temperament. Ernest DuBarko cared nothing for people, only for knowledge and arguing its points.

Brandon's frown deepened. His father had been a belittling dictator who treated his employees like slaves and his family even worse. Many times Brandon had watched his father battle the household servants and even his wife as if he were a soldier in combat. His tongue was as sharp as any sword, and when that failed to impress, he would use other weapons. Striking blows was something Ernest DuBarko seemed to enjoy.

The memories were haunting. Brandon shook them off and rolled over toward the fire. He stared for a long time into the flames. He had his father's temperament. It was only by the grace of God that he contained it and had learned to refine it. Cassie's father had played an important role in that. Bart had taught him how much of a waste a bad temper could be. Arguments and fights seldom resolved anything adequately. Brandon learned to reason and to question rather than rest on his own certainty. He'd become a gentleman in his behavior rather than a ruthless bully. Still, it wasn't enough to redeem him from the past.

Brandon drew in a deep breath and let it out slowly. He closed his eyes and prayed for peace. Several Bible verses came to mind, but one in particular settled on his soul.

*"Be not hasty in thy spirit to be angry: for anger resteth in the bosom of fools."*

Cassie had shared supper with the Arnolds earlier that evening and gathered several great stories from Adam, Sarah's husband. He had worked in the Santa Fe shops most of his life. First in Topeka, then Albuquerque, and now in San Marcial. He preferred the little town to the big cities.

Writing down the anecdotes he shared, Cassie couldn't stop smiling. He told of tricks they played on newcomers, usually young men who were barely out of knee pants, as Adam put it. There had been one young man in particular who had so little knowledge of life and working for a living that he had been particularly easy to fool.

"I sent him for a left-handed hammer," Adam related. "I said I was left-handed and couldn't work with a right-handed one." He grinned at Sarah. "I told him to go see the supervisor if he couldn't find one. That boy searched high and low. He didn't want to have to go to the big boss. Mr. Payne could be pretty stern, and most of the new boys were afraid of him. But sure enough, even though he went from man to man in the shop, there were no left-handed crescent hammers to be had. The kid went to Mr. Payne, who just rolled his eyes and went to the tool bench. He handed the boy a hammer and told him there was no right or left with them. They could be used in either hand." Adam, who'd been chuckling throughout the story, began to roar with laughter. "You should have seen the kid's face as he concentrated on that. He brought me back the wrench and told me what Mr. Payne had said, but he still didn't understand that we'd been funnin' him."

His amusement at his own trick made Cassie and Sarah laugh. Even now the story brought him a great amount of pleasure. That was what Cassie hoped all of the stories would do for folks—bring them pleasure.

Of course, there were stories that were heartfelt and sad as well. One of the men she'd interviewed talked about when her father died. He was a brakeman on the train that derailed. He was knocked out during the accident but managed to come to not long after. He found her father and the young fireman who'd been working at his side, Archie Sullivan. He was the one who had found a couple of blankets to wrap the bodies for transport back to San Marcial. He was still young, and seeing death for the first time had a profound effect on him. He'd cried on the train back to town. When they arrived and some of the men came to get the bodies, he'd tried to hide his tears out of embarrassment, but the other men told him not to be ashamed.

"They told me that those two men were worth all my tears and theirs as well. It wasn't even a moment before every man there had tears in his eyes. I felt such a sense of camaraderie. We were truly of one heart and mind in that moment. Brothers. Real brothers."

Cassie teared up now just putting the story down in her journal. There was something so powerful about the bond between these men. They worked at a variety of jobs doing completely different tasks, but they were all working for the same common goal—to keep the railroad running.

After an hour, she closed her journal and rubbed her right hand against her thigh. It ached from the long spell of writing and cramped with pain. She looked at her left hand. The cast rendered it useless, but at least she didn't have to keep it in a sling anymore. Just four more weeks. Four weeks, and she'd be able to get the cast off and go back to work.

She slid open the drawer of her desk to put the journal away, and her eyes landed on a photograph. It was her sister's wedding photo. Two years ago, Melissa had married Terrance Bridgestone in a small private ceremony in Denver. The photo showed an elaborately gowned bride and perfectly tailored groom. They stood at a table with the bride looking happily at the camera while the groom looked at his bride.

Cassie pulled out the photo and gazed at it for a long time. *We weren't even invited.*

She and her father had first heard about the wedding from a newspaper article that Pastor John saw in the Denver society pages. Papa had been deeply hurt by the fact that the article said the bride had no living family. No doubt this had been mistakenly presumed, but it devastated Cassie to think her sister might have told people she was alone in the world.

Melissa had no interest in having her family at her wedding. That much was clear. She knew how to reach Cassie. Knew that she and Papa would have come to Denver to be a part of her big day. Cassie presumed this was exactly the reason Melissa hadn't let them know.

"Why don't you want me in your life?" Cassie whispered.

They had been so close when Melissa was little. For the first few months after their mother's death, Cassie had been the one who was there for Melissa. She'd often held her sister close through the night when bad dreams left Melissa in tears. Cassie had been the one to teach her sister from home when she refused to go to school. She had taught Melissa to fashion her hair and walk like a lady.

But none of it mattered. Melissa wanted nothing more to do with Cassie.

Swallowing the lump in her throat, Cassie put the photograph facedown in the drawer. It was best just to forget about that part of her life.

# 7

Friday arrived, and women from the church hosted a quilting party at the Brewster house. Anne Brewster was soon to marry, and the ladies had come together to quilt a large double wedding ring quilt that Lydia Brewster had pieced together for her daughter.

Cassie knew she wouldn't be of any use, but Myrtle encouraged her to come and join in the fun. "Fellowship is good for the soul," Myrtle had insisted.

She was right, and Cassie was glad she'd joined them. Anne Brewster was a quiet, reserved creature who did not share her parents' enthusiasm for meeting and befriending others. Anne usually had her nose in a book, and her mother had told the ladies it was a wonder she had stopped reading long enough to even meet a young man, much less agree to marry him.

Cassie chuckled with the other ladies, but Anne's face had reddened, as she was clearly embarrassed.

"Anne, you mustn't mind us," Myrtle soothed. "We're all very excited for you and can't help teasing you, for you are young and just starting out in life, and we're at the other end."

"Speak for yourself, Myrtle. I don't feel that old," eighty-year-old Granny Lancaster declared.

Again, the group of ladies broke into laughter, and this time Anne smiled.

Cassie had always been soft-spoken and slow to insert her opinion, but she wasn't as painfully shy as Anne. She felt sorry for the girl and was determined to offer her friendship, even if they were a dozen years apart in age.

As the women gathered around the quilt frame to continue what Lydia had begun, Cassie sat down by Anne.

"You mustn't let them upset you, Anne. They mean well, and they're so excited for you to become a bride."

Anne glanced up. "I know. It's just hard to be the center of attention."

Cassie nodded. "I hate it as well. I'm not at all comfortable being the focus of everyone's thoughts. It makes me feel like I'm one of those circus performers walking a tightrope."

"Yes!" Anne declared. "Exactly that. You know they're all watching and will see your every step."

It was clear the young woman was starting to relax a bit, so Cassie continued. "I don't believe I've met your intended. He works for the Santa Fe, I know that much."

"Russell Westmore. He works in the offices. He's a supervisor," Anne replied.

"How did you meet?"

She looked down at her hands, which were folded quite properly in her lap. "I worked for a time as a secretary in the offices. Russell supervised clerks in another part of the building, but we often encountered each other. One day, I came around my desk at the same time he barreled into the office, calling for one of the other girls. He knocked me back against my desk, which sent him spiraling into a nearby chair." Anne smiled, remembering that day. "Instead of being embarrassed or jumping back up, he just straightened and said, 'I'm ever so sorry, Miss Brewster. I was looking for Miss Reynolds.' He was just so matter-of-fact, as if the collision had never happened."

Cassie laughed. She'd heard the story from Myrtle, but it was nicer to have Anne tell it. "That will definitely be something special you can tell your children one day."

Anne blushed just a bit. "I was shocked that he knew my name, but I was even more surprised when he asked me to join him for dinner the following evening." She lowered her head as if the memory were too much.

Unwilling to lose her now, Cassie pressed on. "And what about your wedding dress? I heard you sent all the way to New York for it."

"We did. Mother's sister lives there, and she offered to purchase the gown for me. I'm her only niece, and she wanted to do something special."

"That is very special indeed."

"Mother wanted to hire you to make it. She's been worried that you're offended we got the dress elsewhere."

"Oh, I could never be offended by that." Cassie held up her arm. "And if I were working on it, we'd all be in a mess, for I can't sew for another few weeks."

Anne nodded. "I suppose that would be bad, even if the wedding is in October."

"Yes, wedding dresses take a lot of time."

"What are you girls chatting about?" Mrs. Brewster asked.

"Anne was telling me about her wedding dress," Cassie said with a smile.

The older woman frowned. "I hope you aren't offended that we didn't ask you to make it."

Cassie laughed. "No, I was just saying it would have been awful if you had because I can't sew for a few more weeks and might not have finished it."

"Oh, that's true." Mrs. Brewster nodded, looking at Myrtle. "God certainly made provision for that."

"As He does everything," Myrtle replied. "It's always amusing that we are so amazed when God works out the details in our lives before we even know to ask. Here sits Cassie with a broken wrist. Then there's Anne, who was in need of a wedding dress, and her aunt decided to purchase her one from New York. God set things in motion before Cassie even got hurt."

"I wish he'd prevented my getting hurt at all," Cassie murmured.

"I do too," Myrtle agreed, "but then there might not have been a reason to put you and Brandon together so much, and frankly, John says it's been the best thing to happen to Brandon. Since your father died, he seemed rather lost." She put her hand to her mouth for a moment, then dropped it and shook her index finger at the ladies. "Do not repeat that I said that. I apologize for sharing a confidence."

"It's not like we didn't know Brandon and Mr. Barton were close." Lydia Brewster shrugged.

"We know they were like family," Sarah added.

"They were close," Cassie agreed. "And Brandon has been a good friend to watch over me."

"Maybe God is bringing the two of you together for an entirely different purpose," Sarah said, grinning. "Maybe we'll have two fall weddings."

Cassie shook her head. "Then you should rethink the matter. Brandon is just a good friend, and really more my father's friend than mine. He's just helping me with the household chores I cannot manage right now. He's organized the boys responsible for my accident, and they've been such good help."

"I heard you're keeping a book of stories," Granny Lancaster chimed in. "What do you plan to do with it?"

"I hope it might be published one day. I love hearing stories about life on the railroad, and I think others would enjoy reading them."

"Why don't you come to supper on Tuesday? Say, five thirty," Sarah suggested. "Adam would love to tell you more of his stories. He's had some interesting experiences, to say the least. He's quite good at storytelling and makes you feel as if you were right there."

"I'd like that." Cassie hoped she'd remember. "Would you remind me again on Sunday?"

"Of course." Sarah gave her a wink. "Maybe I should invite Brandon as well."

The other ladies chuckled and cheered her on. Cassie just rolled her eyes.

It was nearly four o'clock in the afternoon when the ladies decided to call it quits. Most needed to get home to tend to supper for their husbands. Cassie knew she had plenty of leftovers to eat, so when Myrtle invited her to stay for dinner, she declined.

"I have more than enough to eat at the house, and I'm quite tired. But thank you so much. You all have taken such good care of my needs."

"As God intended the Body to do for one another," Myrtle replied.

Cassie made her way home and was surprised to find a letter from her sister awaiting her. Melissa hadn't sent any kind of correspondence since the twins were born in May. Even then, the note hadn't been from her—it had been written by her friend Abigail for the purpose of announcing the birth of Annabella and Lily Mae Bridgestone on May thirtieth.

The impersonal announcement had left Cassie feeling completely disregarded, but of course that was nothing new. Cassie had written Melissa every week while she'd been away in school and then once a month after she'd graduated and announced she was staying in Denver with Abigail's family. Melissa eventually sent them the photograph of her and Terrance in their wedding clothes but didn't bother to write a letter to go along with it to explain why she had chosen to leave Cassie and their father out of her happy occasion.

Cassie worked to get a fire going in the stove. It was yet another thing that wasn't easily managed one-handed. She would never again take for granted the joys of having two working hands.

Finally, when she had the coffee on the stove to percolate, Cassie sat down and opened the letter. When she unfolded the single page, she found a photograph of the twins. Such darling little babes propped up on a large ruffled pillow. She studied it for a long time before remembering the letter.

*Dear Cassie,*

*Since you continue to ask me why I won't write to you, I thought I would send this photograph of Annabella and Lily Mae and explain that I am far too busy to spend time letter writing. My life has importance that I'm sure you do not understand. Suffice it to say, I care too much about my dear daughters to abandon them for more mundane projects.*

*Melissa*

Cassie reread the harsh words again. She had never expected such cold words from her sister. Melissa had totally depended on Cassie after their mother died, and they had been quite close. Cassie had argued with her father when he made the decision to send Melissa away to boarding school, reminding him that she was only fourteen and still needed to be close to her family. But he was determined, especially since one of the workers for the Santa Fe offices was sending his daughter away too.

It had been a hot summer evening when Mr. and Mrs. Stanley had come to the house to explain they were sending their daughter Mimi to an illustrious girls' boarding school in Denver and wondered if perhaps Mr. Barton would consider sending

Melissa, since the girls were good friends. They hoped this would help their daughter better adjust to the change.

Papa had given it very little thought before agreeing. Cassie tried to explain to him that sending Melissa away would be a mistake. She wasn't over losing their mother, and the separation would be yet another loss to deal with, but he felt it would be better this way. She wouldn't be in the same house where their mother had died. She wouldn't have the daily reminders.

Melissa had cried and begged not to be sent away, but their father's mind was made up. Cassie had done her best to keep a constant flow of letters going to her sister, the only comfort she could provide.

Surprisingly, for as much as she hadn't wanted to go, Melissa was just as adamant about remaining in Denver after her first few months of attendance. When the holiday break came at Christmas, she told them she would stay with her new friend Abigail and the socially elite Bridgestone family. She hadn't asked or sought permission of any kind. She had simply made it clear this was how it would be. When summer came and Cassie looked forward to her sister's return, Melissa wrote their father to say that Mrs. Bridgestone wanted to take her with them to Europe as a companion for Abigail. They pledged to handle all of her expenses and needed clothing. Papa hadn't given it a single night's consideration. He asked Cassie to write up a letter he could sign, giving his permission and wishing them all safe travels.

Cassie had received several postcards from her sister as she moved through Europe. She had envied Melissa's good fortune but hated the lack of any real communication between them. It only got worse as Melissa grew older, until finally letters only came when the schoolmistress forced the issue.

Looking at the photograph, Cassie could only imagine what it was like to be a mother to twins. The tiny girls looked so angelic in their long white gowns. Cassie wondered which was

Annabella and which was Lily Mae. She was still contemplating this when a knock sounded on her front door.

She set down the picture and letter and went to answer it. Brandon stood on the other side, hat in hand.

"Come in," she encouraged, pushing back the door.

"I figured I'd come by and see if you need anything."

"A friend." She hadn't meant to say that aloud, but now that she had, Cassie knew that no one but Brandon would fit the bill.

"What's wrong?"

She shrugged. "I have a letter from Melissa. It was short and to the point and held not even the briefest hint of love." She headed to where she'd left the letter and picture. "There was also a photo of the twins." She picked it up and handed it to Brandon, who had followed. He glanced at the photograph as Cassie continued. "She was harsh. After not writing for months, she chose only to say that she was much too busy being a mother to spend time writing to me."

"I'm sorry, Cassie." He gave her back the picture.

Cassie glanced at the photograph before setting it aside. "I suppose her daughters shall be great beauties, as she is and Mama was. I took after Papa." She gave a laugh that lacked any sense of amusement. "Plain and simple Cassandra."

"I like your looks. You have a simplicity about you that draws out those big blue eyes. You're all sweetness and innocence, and I prefer that to haughty and aloof."

Cassie felt her cheeks grow hot. "I wasn't trying to get praise. I'm sorry if it sounded that way." She headed for the kitchen. "Would you like something to eat? Coffee will be ready soon." She opened the icebox. "I have ham and beans and some corn bread."

"Cassie, I didn't think you were looking for praise. I just wanted to say what I felt was true." Brandon's gaze pierced her façade of indifference. "You remind me of my ma. She was a sweet and gentle woman. She dressed in a simple style despite my father always suggesting she buy better, fancier clothes. He was always after her to change up her hair and be more fashionable. But I thought she was perfect the way she was, and I think you're perfect too."

Cassie wasn't at all sure what to say. She looked back into the icebox. "Thank you."

"Ma was a woman of few words, like you. She never used ten words when two would do. My father, on the other hand, was a word man. Owning a newspaper made him care about such things. I suppose that's why he wanted his wife to be dressed in clothes by the latest designers."

Pulling out the ham and beans, Cassie looked up to meet his gaze. "I wish I could have known her. She sounds like a wonderful woman. Were you close?"

This time it was his turn to look away. "I only brought it up because of your sister making you feel bad. She has no right to be mean to you."

It was obvious he didn't want to talk about his mother, and that was something Cassie could understand. Sometimes talking about the dead only left you longing for them all the more.

"I've not understood Melissa in years. We were so close at one time, but no longer. I suppose going away to school, despite the pleasure of having one of Denver's most elite families take you in as their own, was bound to change her. Change us and the relationship too."

Cassie tried to pour the bowl of ham and beans into a pot, but she couldn't make it work. Brandon stepped up and took charge of the situation. He had the pot on the stove quicker than Cassie could have ever managed. Then he checked the fire and added more coal before guiding Cassie from the kitchen to the dining room.

"It'll take a while for that to heat up. Why don't you let me keep an eye on it, and you can go write your sister a letter? Maybe sending you that photograph is her way of trying to break down the walls between you."

Cassie thought of how Myrtle had mentioned Brandon having a wall around his heart. It was certainly more apparent when it came to talking about his family. He did it so seldom, and when he realized what he was doing, he was quick to put an end to it and change the subject.

"I do wish you'd tell me more about your family," Cassie urged.

He paused at the archway into the kitchen and stared at her as if trying to decide something important. His furrowed forehead suggested it wasn't an easy contemplation.

"I'm sorry," Cassie said, backpedaling. "Obviously, I've caused you discomfort. That wasn't my intention. My motive was actually a selfish one."

His expression softened. "How so?"

"My heart is still smarting from my sister's severe words. I suppose I was looking for something else to think about rather than answering her letter. It honestly wasn't meant to make you feel uncomfortable."

"I understand." He turned his attention back to the kitchen and said nothing more.

Cassie frowned and stared at the floor. It was clear he didn't want to talk about his family, but why?

# 8

Cassie had never been one for window shopping, but after three weeks in a cast, she had little else with which to entertain herself.

Several new hats struck her fancy, but she knew she'd never buy them. First, they were quite expensive, and second, wherever would she wear them? She imagined showing up in church with the wide-brimmed straw hat trimmed in ostrich feathers and a black-and-white-striped ribbon. For those who were used to her simple attire, it was sure to shock.

Moving on to the next shop, she paused to look at the clocks and watches displayed in the window. This was a newer shop run by an older man from California whose son had been transferred with the Santa Fe to San Marcial. The old man repaired clocks and watches and sold a few on the side. The railroad was very strict about its timepieces and was sure to keep the man in work.

"Cassie!"

She turned to find the pastor's wife hurrying toward her. "Myrtle, where are you headed in such a rush?"

"I just heard from the constable that there's been more unrest down south. They believe Pancho Villa and his men have torn up a sizable piece of track and attacked one of the little Mexican towns."

"Here on our side of the border?" Cassie asked. The US-Mexican border was only a hundred fifty miles away, and now that distance seemed shorter and shorter.

"Yes. In fact, there was some concern they were headed this way with plans to attack Albuquerque." Myrtle bobbed her head. "I can't help but be alarmed. You know they have pledged to wreak havoc on the dam and all the towns in between. They want to petition the government to return this land to Mexico."

Cassie shook her head. "They've long talked about taking back it and the other land they lost, but it won't happen. My father and Brandon used to discuss it, and they felt confident that since we achieved statehood, Congress will never be swayed to return this region to Mexico."

"That doesn't stop people from trying. Look what's happening in Europe. There are battles upon battles for the return of land, as well as the desire to claim new territory."

Cassie couldn't argue with that. "I suppose anything is possible, but concerning our backyard, I don't think we have much to worry about. Brandon told me they sent more troops to guard the dam, and I'm sure if it becomes necessary, they will send the army to protect us as well."

The first drops of rain began to fall, causing Myrtle to forget about Pancho Villa. "Goodness, I must get home before I'm drenched. I didn't think to bring an umbrella when I went out this morning."

"Neither did I." Cassie wasn't all that concerned, but she encouraged her friend nevertheless. "Go now, and we can finish our discussion another time."

"I'll see you at church on Sunday," the older woman said, pressing past Cassie to make a dash for her home.

Cassie watched her go, unable to keep the frown from her

face. What if Myrtle's fears were rational? What if the revolutionaries attacked San Marcial? They weren't that far away. Not really.

The Santa Fe whistle blew, signaling the end of the shift. If Brandon was in town, he'd be sure to come check on her. He'd been so good to see to her needs and make certain she didn't want for anything. Cassie had to admit she had grown quite accustomed to his company and would miss him after she was healed and the cast came off.

She started for home, contemplating what she might offer to feed Brandon. Millie and Joe Lancaster had brought her a nice arrangement of food just yesterday. She had cabbage rolls, roasted pork, fresh dinner rolls, and apple strudel. The latter was compliments of Granny Lancaster. Cassie was certain there was enough for both of them.

She hadn't quite reached her house when the rain slowed to a sprinkle and Brandon appeared. He was filthy from a hard day's work but didn't seem to notice as he approached.

"What are you doing?" he asked.

"I was bored and decided to take a walk in town. Living this life of ease where everyone does everything for me isn't at all appealing. How am I to entertain myself?" She gave him a big smile.

He shrugged. "I suppose you could read or write more of your stories."

"Which brings something to mind. Mr. Brewster said he received a broken typewriter that the Santa Fe was throwing away. He's fixing it up and wondered if I'd like to have it. I told him I would. Do you suppose when it's repaired you might be willing to fetch it for me?"

"Of course. Something like that is much too heavy for you to carry with a broken wrist. Just let me know."

"I will." She turned for the house. "Do you want to join me for supper? Joe brought me some food from the restaurant."

"I'd like that, but first I've got to clean up. I was just going to Brewster's because I realized I was out of hand soap."

"I've got plenty. The women were more than generous with bringing me things they thought I could use. I must have six bars of soap."

"Thanks, that'd be great."

They stopped at Cassie's door while she took out her key. "See? I've locked up just as you told me to do."

"I'm glad. There's been more trouble on the line."

"I heard." She unlocked the door and stepped inside. "Myrtle was just telling me. She was quite upset and fears the revolutionaries are coming our way. Is it that bad, Brandon?" She took off her hat and shook the rain onto the little rug in front of the door. She hung the straw hat up to dry and turned to look at him. "Is it?"

"It's bad enough." His serious expression left her feeling anxious.

She went and found one of the extra bars of soap and brought it back to him. "What should I do, then?"

"Keep your eyes open and your doors locked. If there's trouble, the railroad guards will get word to the constable, and I'm sure he'll see that everyone in town knows. If there's immediate danger, go to the Santa Fe shops. The fellas will see to your protection. Maybe even put you on a train."

"To where? I have no place to go. I have no one."

He frowned. "Despite your sister's attitude, you could always make your way to her. She'd have to take you in."

"I don't know about that." She shrugged. "Melissa hasn't wanted to have anything to do with me in years. I'm not convinced she would care."

His frown deepened. "Well, for now just go to the Tylers' or the shops. One way or another, you'll be looked after until I can get to you."

She nodded. "Thank you, Brandon. I appreciate that you care."

For several seconds he just stared at her, and Cassie had to admit he was quite handsome—not at all hard to gaze upon. She wondered why she'd never thought of him this way in the past. He was big and rugged, with wavy brown hair cut short. His face was clean-shaven—well, usually. Right now there was a bit of scruff. He'd probably shaved early that morning, however.

"I'd better go clean up. I'll be back as soon as I can," he told her and then left.

Cassie watched until he disappeared from sight. She closed the door, still wondering about this man who had been a part of her life for nearly as long as they'd been in San Marcial.

Cyrus McCutchen sat nursing his beer in a Mexican saloon. He'd been out of prison since March and still hadn't found a decent position. He'd worked his share of low-paying labor jobs, but nothing that really appealed or benefitted. What he really wanted was revenge. Revenge for being sent to jail. Revenge against the people and the company that had wronged him.

The Santa Fe Railway had sent him to prison for stealing some expensive tools, and Brandon DuBarko was the person Cyrus most wanted to punish now that Bart Barton was dead. He'd managed to accomplish that back in March and had even gotten the deed blamed on Pancho Villa. Taking care of DuBarko wouldn't be as easy, but because Brandon and Bart had been responsible for catching his thievery and seeing him sent to prison, Cyrus wouldn't stop at punishing just one of them. He would see them both dead for what they had done to him.

He tossed back the rest of his warm beer and slid the mug to the bartender. "Make it cold," he demanded of the squat Mexican man.

"Sí, señor." The bartender hurried off to another room as half a dozen men entered and made their way to Cyrus.

"*Jefe*," one of the men said in greeting. It was akin to calling Cyrus *boss*, which he had more than earned with this motley group.

"What did you learn?" Cyrus asked.

"The newspaper has an article about the tracks we tore up." He motioned for one of the other men to come forward, then took a newspaper from him and offered it to Cyrus. "They think it's Villa." He gave a smile that didn't reach his cold, dark eyes.

The bartender reappeared with another beer. Cyrus sampled it before glancing at the newspaper article. At least the beer was cold.

Cyrus scanned the paper, learning that additional National Guard troops were being called up to protect the railroad. He'd anticipated this and even had a plan. He and his gang were going to pretend to be lending a hand. They'd dress as regular cowboys from the area ranches, and if stopped by any of the soldiers, they'd claim to be helping watch over the rails and herds. He doubted anyone would worry overmuch about a group of American and Mexican cowboys. Then, when the soldiers were out of sight, they'd do as they pleased.

The other men ordered beer while Cyrus continued to check out what else was happening in the area. There was a small announcement that mentioned the formal opening of the dam on October 14. The article noted that there was still an argument over the name of the dam. Elephant Butte Dam seemed to be the favored title, but there were powerful folks who wanted it called Engle Dam. Some even demanded it be named after the country's much respected symbol—Eagle Dam.

Eagles or elephants, Cyrus couldn't care less. Neither did his men. They were all of one mindset, and that was to wreak havoc on the Santa Fe. Each man in his gang had been fired from the railroad for a variety of reasons. They all had records and had been in jail, and none of them cared about being "reformed." So far, they'd torn up the tracks in a few different places, but he knew the others wouldn't be satisfied with that for long.

"So what's our next plan, jefe?"

Cyrus put the paper aside and picked up his beer. He could hardly tell his men at this point that the only thing on his mind was revenge. Revenge wouldn't fill their pockets with gold and silver. His hatred of DuBarko wouldn't motivate them to do his bidding.

"Well, jefe? What are we going to do?"

Cyrus smiled and raised his mug. "A little drinking. A little gambling. And a little fun with the ladies."

Brandon cleared away the supper dishes and helped Cassie with the washing and drying. He was amazed at her ability to manage so well for herself. He thought about the first time he'd met her—she'd been just a girl. She was mousy and shy, so soft-spoken that he could hardly understand her. She had mentioned recently that she'd gotten her looks from her father, but Brandon couldn't make the comparison. She had a natural beauty to her that was simple and yet refined. Cassie was content to downplay her appearance, which might have made her all the more attractive.

"So do you?" Cassie asked.

Brandon looked at her. "Sorry, what?"

"I asked if you thought America would go to war."

"There are a lot of folks who wish we would, and an equal number who are glad Wilson has kept us out of it. I think he'll be reelected as president for it."

"It's a worrisome thing, nevertheless. Do you suppose you would have to go if America did decide to join?"

"Hard to say. I have a vital job here, and I am kind of old.

Most soldiers are in their late teens and twenties. Men my age are usually the officers directing them. I don't qualify to be an officer, so I tend to think I wouldn't be called to join up."

"I wouldn't want you to go,"

She said it in such a way that Brandon couldn't help but be intrigued. "Why's that?"

Cassie shrugged and put away the last of the plates. "You're the one I count on to keep me informed and to . . . well, watch over me. I know that probably sounds silly to you, but Papa always said I could count on you if he wasn't around."

Brandon nodded.

"Papa said you were the most trustworthy man he knew and that you would never take advantage of me." She smiled and met his gaze. "That always made me feel safe, because Papa was gone a lot, as you well know. You were usually closer at hand, even when you were off fixing track."

"Not so much these days. We've lost a lot of men. Most have moved out of the area altogether. The young ones don't like to stick around long. Railroading isn't for the faint of heart. That accident last month scared off a lot of them."

"The one where the brakeman was caught between cars?" she asked.

"Yeah, I had a whole section crew in the yard when it happened. Most were young, and that was too much for them to handle."

"That would have been too much for most men to handle. Long-term railroaders are a hardened bunch. They develop a shell of protection that keeps them from feeling things that would destroy other men."

"It doesn't keep us from feeling. It just helps temper us to bear it."

"Yes, that's the word Papa used to use. I remember asking him once what *tempering* meant, and he told me that when steel was tempered, they would heat it up to just under the point of melting, then cool it off. He said it purified its characteristics and lessened the chances of brittleness that might cause it to break. He told me God did that with us—allowing us to go through things that almost brought us to that melting point, but then He'd cool things off. He doesn't want to destroy us, just temper us."

Brandon remembered having that very conversation with Wesley Barton. "He made a good point. The comparison was more than accurate, it was inspired. It's hard to go through the bad times, but when you know they have a good purpose . . . it eases the pain a bit."

She set aside her dish towel. "Coffee?"

"Sure. Let me get it, though. You've done enough. Maybe too much. I specifically remember the doc saying he didn't want you doing much of anything."

Cassie laughed. The pleasant sound seemed to fill the room like music. Brandon couldn't understand the feelings stirring inside. He fetched the coffeepot from the stove while Cassie grabbed the mugs.

Earlier in the evening, Brandon had made a fire in the hearth, so he motioned in that direction. "Wanna sit in front of the fire?"

"All right." She tucked the mugs against herself with her left arm and grabbed the cream with her right hand. "You lead— I'll follow."

He didn't know why, but her words pierced his heart. What was happening to him? It couldn't be love. He was immune to that emotion. At least, he'd always figured himself to be after watching the destruction of his mother and father's marriage. Still, he felt a tenderness growing toward Cassie that he couldn't explain. What if it was love?

He shook his head. It was just his promise to keep an eye on her, that was all. She was special to him because Bart had been special. It was nothing more.

# 9

Cassie decided October 6 would be a celebration day on her calendar. That was the day the doctor removed her cast and declared her free to go about her business. Her hand felt a little strange now that it was out of the cast, but the doctor assured her she wouldn't even remember it in another day or two.

At home she made stacks of her sewing, setting the items that needed her immediate attention in one pile. She would do her best to finish those within the week. There was nothing all that complicated, and she knew the owners would be ever so grateful to have their clothes returned. Most were railroad workers who didn't have that many articles of clothing to begin with.

She glanced at her desk, where her new typewriter and stacks of handwritten journals sat. She would love to return to typing up the stories. While the cast had been on, she had managed to type one-handed, but it hadn't been easy. She had never learned to type properly but thought she might talk to one of the secretaries at the Santa Fe offices and see if someone could teach her. She really liked the little contraption. Typing seemed such a wonderful way to put a story on paper.

"Cassie, are you in?" Myrtle Tyler called from the screen door.

"Come on in. I was just sorting through my sewing." Cassie turned as the older woman entered the house. "See?" She held up her arm. "The cast came off a little while ago."

"I heard that it had. You know how news travels in this town."

"I'm surprised you didn't hear my squeals of delight. I'm so glad to have that horrible thing off."

"Well, that horrible thing was necessary to heal your bones, so don't think too badly of it." Myrtle chuckled. "I don't have much time, so I'll get right to the point. You know the celebration to open the dam is coming up on the fourteenth."

"Yes." Cassie motioned to a chair, but Myrtle shook her head. "What about it?"

"They are encouraging as many people as possible to attend and give a good show of how popular the recreational aspects of the lake and dam are going to be. John and I have decided to go camping there and join in the celebration. We wondered if you'd like to come along. We have a large tent and all the supplies we'll need, so you wouldn't have to bring anything. We even have an extra sleeping bag."

"Oh, that does sound like fun."

Myrtle nodded with great enthusiasm. "We also plan to hike and fish, and Mr. Carlson at the Santa Fe has a boat he's bringing in from Missouri, where he used to live. He left it there with his brother—New Mexico is not exactly known for its lakes. Anyway, he's having it brought here on the train and taken directly to the dam. He's offered to take us out in it, and I'm sure he'd extend that invitation to include you."

Cassie imagined the fun of boating on the newly made lake. She'd never been on a boat in her life. "I would love to join you. When?"

"We're going early on the thirteenth. I'm sure there will be a lot of other folks heading down then as well, but Mr. Carlson assured us seats on the passenger train. I'll let him know you are going to join us."

"Oh, that does sound like such a wonderful diversion. I haven't been away from San Marcial in ages. The last time was years ago, when I went with my father to the capital when we became a state."

"It's the same for us, so I'm looking forward to it."

"Is there anything you'd like me to bring? Something I can bake or cook ahead of time?"

Myrtle thought on this for a moment. "Cookies. Why don't you bake a few dozen cookies, and then I won't have to? Maybe make those cocoa ones with the frosting."

"Consider it done." Cassie flexed her left hand. "Now that the cast is gone, I feel I can do anything."

Hours later, the Santa Fe whistle blasted the end of the first shift. Cassie wondered if Brandon would show up for supper. He'd been coming so regularly that she put out a place for him.

As if on a pre-agreed schedule, Sarah and Lydia showed up just as Cassie pulled two pans of cookies out of the oven.

"Ladies, you're just in time for cookies."

"And we've brought you supper," Sarah declared, then gave a squeal. "Oh, look! Your cast is gone."

"Yes." Cassie held up her arm. "Just today."

"I'll bet that feels so much better."

"It does." Cassie reached for the supper basket Lydia held. "This smells delicious."

"It's just simple baked chicken and carrots. And a few potatoes. I made a gravy for it," Lydia added.

"And this is my crumb cake," Sarah said, setting the towel-wrapped bundle aside. "Now I have to rush home and get our supper out of the oven." She leaned over and kissed Cassie's cheek in an unexpected display of affection. "Enjoy."

"I will." Cassie handed them each a cookie. "Here's something to munch on as you go. It shouldn't ruin your dinner."

Cassie thanked them again and bid them good-bye. Throughout her ordeal, she had felt so cared for and loved. The ladies of the church were truly amazing.

She left the food in the warming box on the stove, certain it would be perfect for supper. In the meantime, she finished making cookies. The idea of the trip intrigued her. She had never traveled just for the fun of it. This would be a new adventure for her.

She pulled out the final batch of cookies and placed the pan in the partially open window to cool. The night air had grown chilly, and the smell of woodsmoke fires filtered into the house and mingled with the aroma of roasted chicken and carrots. What a perfect evening.

She went to the cupboard and pulled out a jar of pickled jalapeños, knowing Brandon loved them. Would he come for supper? Surely he would.

Deciding a little flair would be fun, she went to the linen box and pulled out a tablecloth. She set the table with her best dishes and smiled at the result. Her mother's china gleamed in the lamplight. Someday, Cassie vowed, she'd get some real crystal glasses for lemonade and water. Wouldn't that be pretty?

It was nearly five thirty when Brandon finally showed up. Cassie had almost begun to think he'd found somewhere else to eat. But he'd cleaned up, and his hair was still damp and clinging to his neck in little curls.

"You're rather late this evening," she said lightly, noting he'd changed from work clothes to a simple button-down shirt and trousers. He hadn't bothered to do up the top button of the shirt nor don a tie, and he had rolled up the sleeves, adding to his casual appearance.

"I was extra dirty. It took longer to clean up than I'd figured."

"Are you hungry?" She used her hands as she talked, wondering when he'd notice her missing cast.

"Famished. I feel like I could eat a toad—maybe ten."

She laughed. "How about chicken? Sarah Arnold and Lydia Brewster brought dinner tonight. I'm going to miss everyone making such a fuss over me."

"Why should they stop?"

She held up her arm. "Because I'm able to fend for myself again."

"You got the cast off!" His voice was enthusiastic even if he didn't show it with a smile.

"I did, and the doctor said I'm perfectly healed. I've been sorting through my sewing all afternoon to figure out what to do first. I want to get the oldest stuff done by the end of next week."

"You don't have to overdo it. You probably should take it easy to begin with. It has been six weeks since you used that hand."

She held out a chair for him. "I know that. Now sit. I'll serve you tonight, and you won't even have to help with the dishes."

"I don't mind," he said, taking a seat.

Cassie brought the food to the already-set table. Last of all, she brought some iced lemonade she'd just made that afternoon. She put a glass in front of Brandon and then took hers to her seat. "You can have coffee too. I was just excited to have some fresh lemonade. The train brought in a big supply of lemons today, and Mr. Brewster made sure I knew about it. Along with a new shipment of taffy." She laughed. "You know me and my sweet tooth."

He nodded and reached for the platter of chicken. "I do, but this is more my style right now."

"I even opened a jar of pickled jalapeños. I know they're your favorite."

"They are. Shall I pray?"

She nodded, then bowed her head.

Brandon offered a short prayer. "Lord, we thank you for this food and for Cassie healing up. I'm particularly glad for that. Amen."

Cassie couldn't help but smile at his being so happy for her healing. "Doc said I was as good as new and shouldn't have a bit of trouble. My wrist feels a little odd, but I think it will be fine. Besides, most of the sewing I do requires the right hand for the detail. The left hand just comes behind, helping." She gave a little laugh and then added chicken and vegetables to her plate.

Brandon ate in silence. It was clear he was half-starved. The men worked so hard at the railroad.

"Were you on the line most of the day?"

He shook his head. "Actually, no. The boys were, but I had to interview a bunch of kids for the section gang."

"Any good prospects?"

"A few. Mexicans, mostly. Of course, if we go to war, all of the young men will be snapped up for action."

Cassie frowned. "I hope the war ends soon. I don't want us to get involved."

"I feel the same, but I'm betting no one cares how I feel about it."

"The newspaper makes it sound like it's getting worse. There was an article about a battle by some river in France that's raged on all summer. Or at least most of it. And it's still going on."

"The River Somme," Brandon replied. "Thousands, if not hundreds of thousands, have lost their lives. England hopes they can defeat Germany—after all, they're fighting the Russians on another front, so their troops are divided."

"I just wish the war would end. I'm so afraid if it doesn't, America will be forced to enter it."

Brandon nodded. "It doesn't look good. It's been going on for quite a while, and there is no end in sight."

Cassie sighed and gazed down at her half-eaten food. She

found her appetite was stifled at the thought of so many people dying.

Brandon continued eating while Cassie moved her food from one side of her plate to the other. She tried to keep her mind occupied with something hopeful, but it wasn't easy.

"Do you plan to go to the opening of the dam?" she finally asked.

"I doubt it. It's on a Saturday, but I'm sure to be working at least half the day. What about you?"

"The Tylers invited me to go down on the thirteenth and camp. I've never done that before. Myrtle said we would hike and fish and maybe even go out on the lake in a boat. I've never done any of those things, save hiking."

"You've never gone fishing?"

She shook her head and forced a smile. "No, Papa was always too busy with work, and Mama and Melissa had no interest in such things. To be honest, neither did I, but now it sounds exciting to me. I don't know what all it entails, but I'm looking forward to it."

"I'm sure you'll have fun, and I think you'll be perfectly safe. They plan to have a lot of soldiers around. They still can't figure out who's been causing problems on the lines. I've had so many calls to repair the tracks that we know some group of hoodlums is causing the damage. The question is who might be behind it."

"I thought everyone figured it was Pancho Villa. Since he declared his own war on America back in March, most things that go wrong get blamed on him and his revolutionaries."

"Yes, and with good reason. They have access and hold a grudge against the US for taking land they believe belongs to Mexico."

Cassie sighed. "I do wish we'd find a way to be at peace with him. Just as I wish there would be peace in Europe. I see absolutely nothing to gain by fighting and killing folks. Violence is never the answer."

Brandon put down his fork with a frown. "Sometimes things happen that can't be avoided. Killing isn't the desired solution, but there are times when it's the only way to stop the wrong being done."

"I can't imagine that ever being the right situation. After all, God commands us not to kill." She put her fork aside as well and dabbed her mouth with a linen napkin. She got up and began to collect her dishes. "It may be that society justifies death, but I'm sure God doesn't."

Brandon rose from the table. "I'm sorry, I need to go. I just remembered something I have to do."

"Are you sure you don't want dessert? I have crumb cake."

"No, but thank you for dinner."

He turned and left before she could say anything else.

How strange that he should suddenly remember something he had to do. Brandon was always very meticulous about his duties. She'd never seen him forget any detail.

Cassie wasn't sure what had caused him to leave in such a hurry, but she had to admit she'd grown weary of company anyway. Pondering such negative things had been a mistake. She'd still been so happy after talking to Myrtle, but discussing the war and Pancho Villa just served as a reminder that the future looked rather grim.

She was definitely out of sorts at the thought of America involving itself in the European war—and at the thought that there might well be war of a different kind going on in their own state. She had heard all of the horror stories about the attack on Columbus. She'd paid little attention to them at first, because her father had been killed during that same time. All of her focus had gone to him and to plans for his burial. She had sent a telegram to Melissa to let her know so she could come to the funeral. That was when she'd learned that Melissa was due to have twins in the next few weeks. She could hardly attend a funeral hundreds of miles from her home.

But with all of that behind her, Cassie had heard details about the raid on Columbus, the people who'd died, and the destruction of property. It was said unthinkable things happened to some of the women. What a horrible ordeal.

Cassie added wood to the fire and gazed into the flames. What if it happened in San Marcial? What if it happened elsewhere along the line? It was said that things were happening every day that proved Villa and his men were active in this region.

She thought of what Brandon had said. *"Killing isn't the desired solution, but there are times when it's the only way to stop the wrong being done."*

How she prayed that wasn't the solution for them this time.

Brandon walked back to his house, glad the skies were turning dark. He had no desire to make small talk with anyone. He felt deeply troubled by the conversation he'd had with Cassie, and yet he couldn't begin to explain it to her. There was no explaining it.

"Boss, we're back. We got those tracks fixed up in record time. George said we're getting to be almost as good as you."

Brandon nodded at Javier, who was coming from the shops. "Well, if George inspected your work and said that, I believe it." Brandon had trained George as well, and now the younger man had his own section gang to watch over. For the jobs they'd been doing this week, the teams had combined.

"We've had the best teacher. Even George said that."

Brandon shrugged. "Maybe."

"You never smile. Don't you have anything good to smile about?"

"A lot of folks go around life laughing and grinning like idiots. There's too much that requires serious thought, so I can't see smiling about it."

Javier shrugged. "Did you give Miss Cassie our money?"

Brandon had forgotten all about it. "It slipped my mind. I'll give it to her tomorrow after work. It'll be the last time. She got her cast off today. She'll soon be back to making her own wages again. I have to say, I'm proud of you boys for honoring your word to help her."

"It was our fault. We needed to do the right thing. I wrote to my mother when I sent her money and told her why it wasn't as much as I hoped. She wrote back to tell me how proud she was of me." Javier grinned from ear to ear.

The young man was clearly pleased with himself. Brandon couldn't remember a time when he'd felt that kind of pride in himself. He was always finding fault with his own accomplishments. He'd never be good enough. Especially after failing so miserably.

"There's nothing as good as makin' your mama proud," Javier said.

Brandon couldn't help remembering the last time he'd seen his mother. She had encouraged the same thing, suggesting he leave town and go as far from the sorrows of his youth as possible. She had looked with such love upon her only son. He could almost feel her hand touching his face.

"*I love you, Bran,*" she had whispered. "*Make me proud.*"

And he had tried. But within three years, she was gone.

He hadn't even known she'd taken ill. His aunt, with whom his mother lived, sent only the briefest telegram upon her death. Brandon found it almost impossible to forgive himself for not being there in her final hours.

But that was the least of the things he couldn't forgive . . . nor forget.

# 10

Cassie stood watching the bevy of travelers step from the train. Only two days earlier, she'd received a telegram from Melissa stating that she and Terrance were coming for the ceremonies to open the dam. They would arrive on the afternoon of the fourteenth. Unfortunately, excess rain had caused the ceremonies to be postponed until the nineteenth of October. Perhaps that would allow Cassie and Melissa some much-needed time to catch up.

It seemed curious that they would come for the celebration, but Cassie was grateful. She had longed to see Melissa. After all, it had been what felt like a lifetime. She wondered if she'd even recognize her sister. Of course, Cassie had her sister's wedding picture, and Melissa looked very much like their mother.

She craned her neck, trying to see around a tall gentleman directly in front of her. She had little success. Perhaps it would be better to wait inside. They would have to pass through the depot to reach the street. Cassie had started to step away when she spied Melissa.

A gasp escaped her at the sight of her younger sister. She was dressed in an impeccably neat navy traveling suit with black piping. A high-necked, lace-edged blouse peeked out from beneath this with an ivory cameo at the base of Melissa's neck. She was the spitting image of their mother.

"Melissa!" Cassie called and pushed her way through the crowd.

Melissa stopped and stared at Cassie as she approached. She looked for a moment as if she had no recollection of who Cassie even was. The thought stopped Cassie midstep.

"Melissa, it's me. Cassie."

Her sister frowned. "Good grief, I know who you are." She looked to the man at her side. "Terry, this is my sister, Cassandra."

Cassie extended her hand, uncertain whether that was the appropriate way to greet her brother-in-law. "I'm glad to finally meet you."

"As am I, Miss Cassandra," the tall man replied. He hesitated, then shook Cassie's hand. He looked almost as apprehensive as Cassie felt.

"Please call me Cassie." She glanced around, thinking perhaps a nurse might be following with the children. "Where are the babies?"

"They're too young to travel," her sister snapped. She looked at Cassie as if she'd lost her mind. "We left them at home with their nanny."

"Oh, I see. I didn't think you'd want to be away from them. I thought maybe you would bring them and their nurse. But nevertheless, I'm so glad you're here."

She reached out to hug her sister, but Melissa turned away. "It was a terribly long journey. Terry and I are staying at the Grand Hotel and must arrange for the bags."

"I'll go see to that right now," her husband said. "Why don't you wait for me inside? I think it's going to start raining again."

Melissa nodded and, without even commenting to Cassie, headed inside the depot to wait. Well-dressed men crowded every corner, but they parted and bowed as Melissa made her way into the building. She walked like a stately queen attending to her court. It was clear the men appreciated her looks and sophistication.

Cassie followed her, completely confused by her sister's attitude both in receiving her and in acting the grand dame. Melissa had definitely taken on the role of socialite, and Cassie wasn't sure she liked it.

"We'll be here a couple of days," Melissa said. "Then we'll head down to the celebration and afterward take the train directly to Albuquerque. I won't be stopping back in San Marcial."

"I plan to be at the celebration. I won't head down until the eighteenth, but once I'm there, perhaps we can attend together."

"No, that won't be possible. Terry has an interest in one of the resorts there. He'll be with other officials, and I will be at his side. We have many meetings and important people with whom business is to be done."

"I see." Cassie tried to hide her disappointment. "Well, we can still spend time together here. I'd love to have you both over for dinner."

"I don't believe there will be time for that either. We already have a dinner request from Mr. Mackie with the Santa Fe."

"Maybe you could spend tomorrow evening with me."

"No," Melissa announced. "However, I would appreciate some time tomorrow morning. I'd like to walk up to the cemetery and see where you laid our father to rest."

Cassie buried her disappointment regarding dinner. "Of course, I'd like that very much. When would you like to go?"

"Let's say ten. I'm sure I will be inclined to sleep in. This travel has exhausted me."

"Should I come by the hotel for you?" Cassie hated that everything felt so formal between them. She wasn't sure if it was just because Melissa was tired or if there was something else.

Terry returned. "I have arranged for the luggage. They will

bring everything over. The hotel is just a couple of blocks away. The stretch of our legs will do us good."

"That's fine," Melissa replied. She looked at Cassie. "Yes, come for me at the hotel."

Cassie watched them go, feeling frozen in place. Melissa was nothing like Cassie remembered. She was haughty and aloof with no trace of the tender girl who had left for Colorado six years before. Her very attitude suggested she thought herself better than those around her, and she looked at Cassie as if she were a stranger. Had she not read Cassie's letters? Melissa so rarely wrote that Cassie couldn't be sure.

There was a great emptiness in Cassie's heart. She headed home, pondering all that had happened. She couldn't understand it, but perhaps it was just the years. After all, they had parted when Melissa was only fourteen. There was such pain in her departure. Had it changed her that much? What about the love they had shared? Even though Cassie had been much older than Melissa, they had loved each other. Cassie had cared for Melissa as if she were her own.

"It makes no sense," Cassie muttered.

Myrtle Tyler joined her as she walked. "You look as if you just lost your last friend."

Cassie had no idea where the woman had come from, but she was glad for her company. "My sister has come to town, but it's as if we don't even know each other."

"How long has it been since you saw her?"

"Six years."

"Why so long? You could have taken the train up to Denver to see her."

"Father never wanted to make the trip. I considered going by myself, but there always seemed to be another pressing matter that needed my attention. I should have gone, I suppose." Cassie shook her head. The entire situation gave her great sorrow. She had missed her little sister, but it seemed Melissa had not missed Cassie. "She wants to see our father's grave in the morning."

"Maybe she'll be more like herself after a good long rest. She did just become a mother not long ago, and to twins. That's quite a job to keep up with."

Cassie nodded. "I hadn't considered that. I presumed she had servants to do all the work. It wouldn't surprise me, however, if she spends a great deal of time with her babies."

"There. It's probably nothing but the fact that she's tired. Are you looking forward to our little escape?" Myrtle asked, changing the subject.

"I am." Cassie pushed aside her worries over Melissa. "I've baked several batches of cookies to take along. I also bought some warm woolen socks and splurged on a new pair of boots. I haven't had a new pair in a great many years. I intend to spend the next few days breaking them in."

"Very good. I think we shall have a wonderful time. There is a disappointment, however. John said that President Wilson isn't coming. It was deemed too dangerous, given all the problems he is facing right now, as well as the unrest here in New Mexico."

Cassie hadn't really cared if the president came or not. She knew she wouldn't be one of the few to share his company. Melissa and her husband came to mind. No doubt they would have been introduced to President Wilson. Was Melissa terribly disappointed?

Cassie bit her lower lip and kept silent while Myrtle rambled on about something to do with their trip. Until this matter was settled with her sister, she wouldn't be able to rest nor enjoy the planned trip.

The next morning at ten o'clock exactly, Cassie arrived at the Grand Hotel. Melissa was already waiting in the lobby, where several other people were talking or sitting. Melissa stood off to one side, looking rather bored.

"How are you feeling today?" Cassie hoped the night's rest had restored Melissa to the person she'd once been.

"I slept well, thank you. Let's go." Melissa led the way out the door.

Cassie noted her sister was wearing a stylish walking suit. The base color was ecru with dark burgundy to band the sleeves at the wrist and cover the lapels. There was burgundy braiding on the side, with gold buttons to decorate each side of the skirt. The same buttons trimmed the suit jacket. A wide-brimmed straw hat sat atop her head. It too was trimmed with burgundy and gold. She wore ecru-colored gloves and boots to finish off the outfit.

Perhaps a compliment would put her sister in a positive state of mind. "You look so nice, Melissa," Cassie said, "and thankfully the rains have stopped."

"Yes." She offered nothing more.

They crossed Main Street and headed to the left. After a couple of blocks, Cassie pointed down the street. "Do you see down there—the white picket fence? That's where I live. After Papa died, I had to leave the Santa Fe house."

"They put you from the house just because our father was no longer able to work for them? How rude."

"If I'd taken a job with the Santa Fe, I'm sure I could have stayed, but they probably would have wanted me to take a smaller house anyway since that house was designed for a family."

Melissa opened her mouth as if to reply, then snapped it closed and stared straight ahead.

Cassie shrugged and glanced down at her simple blouse and skirt. She'd worn a colorful Mexican shawl to fight off the morning chill. She would have looked like one of the Mexican townsfolk except for her pale skin and blond hair.

A thought spread a sense of dread through her. What if Melissa was so used to a fashionable life with the privileged that she was ashamed of Cassie? Goodness, that hadn't even occurred to her before now. Cassie felt an immediate sense of regret. It would make sense, since Melissa was used to moving through elite circles in life. The people with whom she spent her days were worth thousands, even millions, of dollars. They had beautiful homes and clothing. Their manners were impeccable and refined. Cassie was just the daughter of a simple railroad engineer for the Santa Fe.

Melissa seemed to have no difficulty remembering the way to the cemetery. She didn't ask for Cassie's help with directions nor follow her lead. She just kept pace with Cassie as they might have done when they were younger. Cassie tried pointing out things here and there along the way, but Melissa said nothing. Her silence was maddening.

They passed the Old Town stores and Mexican adobe houses. There were some women outside hanging clothes on lines. It was a good sign that the rains were done for a while.

Cassie reached the cemetery gate first. Melissa seemed distracted by the various headstones. Perhaps she was trying to figure out which one belonged to their father.

"Papa is on the far east side," Cassie said, pointing to her right. "By Mama."

Melissa nodded. This time she let Cassie lead the way. When they reached the headstone of Wesley Barton, Cassie stepped to the side, allowing her sister to stand directly in front of the plain stone.

*Wesley Barton*
*B—1859 D—1916*

"I suppose you wonder about my wanting to come here," Melissa said as if she were speaking to no one in particular.

"Not at all. It makes perfect sense that you would want to visit Papa's grave and say good-bye. I'm sure it was hard for you, not being able to be here for the funeral."

Melissa turned to face Cassie. "I didn't come here to say good-bye. I came to see if perhaps the hatred I felt for both of you would somehow be diminished. I'm sorry to say it hasn't lessened it at all."

Cassie felt as if she'd been slapped. She took a step back. "Hatred?"

Melissa's eyes narrowed. "Yes. Did you think I wouldn't hate you both for sending me away when I was already suffering such loss that I wanted to die?"

"I didn't want Papa to send you away. You knew that. I told you that."

"Words. Nothing more than words." Melissa shook her head. "You both wanted me gone. I looked too much like Mama. I was too much of a reminder—even to myself. The older I grew, the more I took on her features. It was like a constant reminder of my loss."

"It was to Papa as well. I know that's why he let you go to school in Denver."

"He didn't let me go. He pushed me out the door. He abandoned me and left me to make it on my own. And I did. I have done quite well for myself. Who would have ever expected a poor engineer's daughter to marry into one of Denver's finest families?"

"I hope you married for love and not just social standing," Cassie said, letting her anger get the best of her.

Melissa gave her a withering stare. "Of course I married for love. Love was the thing missing in my life. It became my full-time mission to find it."

"I always loved you, Melissa. I always will—even now when you've hurt me so deeply by suggesting I pushed you away and abandoned you. I wrote you every week, knowing you must be scared and lonely." Cassie hugged the shawl to her body. "I tried to talk Papa out of sending you away. I fought for you."

"Not hard enough." Melissa looked down at the grave. "He couldn't have loved me." Her voice softened. "He might as well have sent me off to die."

"I'm sorry." Cassie wished she could embrace her sister but knew Melissa would reject any show of affection on Cassie's part. "I'm so sorry."

Melissa straightened and walked away. She headed back to the gate and the road that led to the cemetery.

"Wait, Melissa, please." Cassie hurried to catch up.

Melissa stopped and turned. "What do you want?"

"I want to know what I can do to make it up to you. I don't want to go through life with you hating me. We're sisters. We're all we have—just each other."

"I have Terrance and his entire family. They took me in when you threw me away. They have loved me ever since. They were faithful where you were not. You failed me, Cassandra."

"Then I'm sorry. I did my best."

"You did nothing."

Cassie shook her head. "What was I supposed to do?"

Melissa lifted her chin in a haughty expression. "You could have left our father and come with me. But you didn't. That probably never even occurred to you, did it?"

"No, I suppose it didn't. You were going to a boarding school. It didn't come to mind that I should move to Denver and live there while you lived at school. I did, however, tell you how much I was looking forward to your Christmas break. I told you how I planned to come to Denver to get you. We would ride the train together back to San Marcial, and then I would ride with you again when you had to return. We could have had a nice few weeks together, but you chose not to come."

"And Papa said nothing to reverse that decision. He couldn't agree fast enough for me to stay away. You could have come then. You could have rebuked our father and come to Denver to spend the holidays with me—perhaps even stayed the entire break."

"I didn't have that kind of money."

"There was always an excuse, I'm sure." Melissa shook her head. "Love would have found a way."

She walked away, leaving Cassie to feel as though she'd been punched in the gut. Tears came to her eyes and streamed down her face. How could Melissa believe so sincerely that Cassie didn't love her? It wasn't true. It wasn't.

Cassie buried her face in her hands and crumpled to the dirt at the edge of the cemetery. She cried for the loss of her sister. She hadn't realized the depth of Melissa's anger. She had allowed that Melissa was mad at their father, but never once did Cassie believe it extended to her. It was a devastating awakening.

*How could she hate me? We're sisters.*

# 11

Brandon had followed Cassie and a woman who could only be her sister, Melissa, at a distance. He couldn't say why, but something about the situation bothered him, and he found himself drawn to follow. Seeing Melissa storm off and Cassie fall to the ground left him no doubt it was God's prompting and not just his own feelings.

"Cassie?" He leaned down. She continued to sob so hard that Brandon wasn't even sure she'd heard him.

Careful so as not to hurt her, Brandon lifted her into his arms and carried her to a nearby bench. He set her on the wrought iron and slipped in beside her. He put his arm around her and pulled her against him. She continued to cry, and he didn't try to stop her.

It was hard to imagine what Melissa could have said that caused Cassie such pain. It was possible, he supposed, that coming to her father's grave had brought out her sadness at losing him, but Cassie wasn't that kind of person.

He wondered what, if anything, he could do to help. He remembered times when his mother had cried, and he'd tried to comfort her as well. He'd been about as successful then as he was now.

Of course, his mother's tears had often been brought on by

his father's cruelty. Ernest DuBarko thought nothing of belittling her until she was reduced to fits of tears. Brandon frowned. His father had been a cruel man. He found power in making others feel small.

Memories Brandon seldom allowed came to the front of his mind. He could see his father and mother at the dinner table, Father reprimanding Mother for something she'd failed to provide. Brandon had commented that it wasn't that big of a problem.

*"Son, there are times when you will have to chastise and punish your wife for her failings. You'd best learn now what is needed in order to be the man of the house."* Without warning, he'd backhanded Brandon's mother.

It wasn't the first time. Brandon had been thirteen when a resigning maid told him in private that his father had beaten his mother that day while he was at school. Brandon was always mature for his age, but he had been mortified to imagine such goings-on. Although he had often heard his father railing at Mother, he hadn't known he beat her.

Brandon went to his mother and asked her if it was true. She told him it was and that she intended to leave, but every time she tried, Brandon's father found out about it and threatened to keep Brandon from her.

Brandon had been thoroughly disgusted by his father's threat. He'd had his fair share of spankings and punishments and knew Father could be very harsh. But imagining him beating Mother was more than he could bear. He immediately tried to think of a way to counter the problem and decided head on was best.

But that had been far from the way to deal with it. Father had sent him off to a boarding school while he continued to treat his wife as he pleased.

Brandon graduated early and was ready to go to college at the age of sixteen. His father took complete control of that decision and made arrangements for his son. Given Brandon was still underage, he had little say in the matter.

He remembered the shock of returning home on one of his breaks from college. His mother looked to have aged twenty years. She wasn't at all the jovial soul he had once known. That night at dinner, he understood why. His father was ruthless. He chided and berated Mother, gradually getting angrier. He was drinking more than he used to, but when Brandon commented on it, he told him a man should be able to drink as he pleased in his own house.

*"You're a dim-witted fool, son. The gardener has more brains than you. What are they teaching you at that college? Or aren't you able to learn?"*

Brandon was eighteen and starting to feel the strength of manhood. His father's demeaning remarks almost made him laugh. His instructors had told Brandon how smart he was and how he showed great capability. His perfect grades proved he was not only able to learn but to master even the most difficult of classes. So when his father later made a condescending comment that Brandon must not be taking classes of consequence, Brandon wrote out a difficult mathematics problem and challenged his father to solve it.

Father had been infuriated and struck out at Brandon, but before he could strike his son's face, Brandon had caught his father's arm and held it back. Two years of being on the college rowing team had made him strong.

*"Release me, you ungrateful wretch. A son who won't receive correction is a disgrace to his father."*

Mother unfortunately took that opportunity to enter the room. She hurried to put herself between the two men. That was her first mistake. Trying to bring reason between them was the second. She paid the price for her interference and spent a week in bed after Brandon's father had finished with her.

"I'm sorry," Cassie said, interrupting his thoughts. She

searched her pocket for something. "I thought I had a hand-kerchief."

Brandon handed her his blue-and-white bandanna as those painful memories faded. "Here, use this. It's greasy. Sorry I don't have anything clean."

She took it and wiped her eyes and nose. "It doesn't matter, I'm sure I look a sight."

"What happened?" He kept his voice low and gentle.

"I hardly know where to start." She handed him back the handkerchief.

Brandon tucked it back in his bibbed overalls. "Well, if you don't want to talk to me, I understand."

"No, it isn't that at all. You're probably the only one I would talk to. I'm not close enough to anyone else." She looked at him for a moment, then lowered her head. "Melissa and her husband are in town for a couple of days, and then they're heading down to the opening of the dam. They will, of course, keep company with the railroad superintendent and his officials. I suggested she and I could share some time there, but she refused."

Cassie sat back against the wrought-iron bench, not even seeming to notice that Brandon had his arm draped casually over the top.

"I invited her to dinner yesterday, but they already had plans. So she asked me to walk to the cemetery this morning to see where we buried Papa. I thought it a very nice thing to do, sisters visiting their father's grave together. I had it in mind that she must have been very sad to miss Papa's funeral, but nothing could be further from the truth."

There didn't seem to be anything to say, so Brandon remained silent and stared straight ahead.

"I will never forget what she said when I showed her the grave." Cassie paused and shook her head. "Melissa said, 'I came to see if perhaps the hatred I felt for both of you would somehow be diminished.'"

Brandon couldn't help turning to look at Cassie, shocked by this.

She met his gaze. "She hates me. She hates me because of what our father did. She hates him, which I can understand—to a point. But she hates me, as well. I, who only ever did what I could to offer her comfort. How could she hate me?"

The question begged an answer, but Brandon had none. "I don't know. Maybe just by association."

"She said I could have come to her. She made it sound as if I should have followed her to Denver to watch over her. Believe me, I thought of visiting, but I had so many responsibilities here. I was already sewing for the town and keeping house for Papa. I thought she'd come back to us on her time away from school. I had no idea she was staying in Denver to spite us. I was so naïve, Brandon. All this time, I presumed she loved me. Loved me as I did her."

"Sometimes anger kills love. You've told me before that your father forced the situation. She didn't want to go to Denver."

"No, she didn't. Father honestly hoped that being away from San Marcial would offer healing for Melissa as well as himself. He missed Mama as much as Melissa did, and he couldn't bear that she looked more and more like her every day."

"That was hardly her fault."

"I know that. I told him as much. I suppose I never told Melissa." She gave a long and heavy sigh. "What can I do now, Brandon? How do I win back her love?"

"Maybe you can't. Sometimes situations are such that for-giveness doesn't come. Not for a long time, if at all."

"But she's a Christian, and in the book of Matthew, Jesus says we must forgive others or our Father in heaven won't for-give us," Cassie protested halfheartedly. "I'll seek her out and beg her forgiveness. Wouldn't that show her my sincere desire to make things right?"

Brandon stiffened and pulled his arm away. "That's a hard verse to live up to."

She blinked at him for a moment. "I'm sorry. I've clearly offended you, and I had no desire to do so. I just can't imagine hating my sister for any reason. Not even her hatred of me causes me to feel that for her. She will always have my deepest love, until my dying day. I just never imagined . . . never realized I had earned her hate."

"Cassie, you did nothing wrong, did you?"

"I don't believe so, but I should have gone to Denver to see her. Maybe then this hatred wouldn't have had six years to fester and burn."

"Are you at fault for anything else? Bart told me you didn't want her to go but that he felt it was the best thing for everyone."

Cassie clenched her hands together. "No. It might have been the best thing for him, but it wasn't best for Melissa or me. I see that now more clearly than before. Melissa felt we had abandoned her—thrown her away. She felt punished for her mourning and for looking like our mother." Tears came again. "Oh, Brandon, how that must have hurt her. Just when she needed us most, we put her from us. I wish I'd done things differently. I wish I could have made certain she knew she was loved. I must find a way to make her see that now."

"It's something she'll have to come to in time, Cassie. You won't be able to make her see it."

"But I have to fix this. I can't leave it undone." She took hold of his hand. "Don't you see?"

Brandon met her eyes. "Cass, sometimes even God can't fix things—not unless everyone involved wants it fixed. God doesn't force a person to accept love. Not His and certainly not anybody else's."

"But God can soften their hearts with understanding. He can help Melissa know the truth. We can start fresh, then. So long as she's drawing breath, I have to try to salvage our sisterhood. She's all I have left, Brandon. I have no one else."

"You've always got me," he said without thinking. He got to his feet, knowing he shouldn't have said such a thing. What would she think? "I mean . . . I promised your father I'd always be there for you, Cassie. You won't ever have to worry about being alone. It's important for you to know that." He was rambling and couldn't seem to stop. "Your pa wanted you to be safe and cared for. Long before he died, knowing he held a dangerous job, he asked me to look after you. I made him a promise."

She nodded. "I know that. I know you care, and I'm grateful. I couldn't have talked to just anyone about this." She gave him a smile. "You mean the world to me, Brandon."

He momentarily froze in place. Feelings that he hadn't realized even existed reared up to remind him that he too needed someone—needed love. But how could he ever offer his love to anyone, much less take theirs? The past could not be wiped away. Not for him.

"We haven't got any money, jefe." One of Cyrus's gang gave him an accusing look.

"We've never had any money." Cyrus leaned back in his chair and put his feet up on the table. They'd been staying with one of the men's ancient grandparents while they tried to figure out how they could best benefit themselves.

"The boys and me think we could rustle some cattle."

"That is one thought." Cyrus looked around the tiny room. Most of the men stayed outside during the day and then came inside to lie side by side on the floor to sleep at night. It wasn't a good situation, to be sure, but with the nights having turned chilly, it suited them better than sleeping outside. "I've got a better one. Get the boys together. We're going to have a talk."

The man nodded and headed outside. Cyrus followed at a slower pace and found his gang assembled like a pack of hungry dogs over a kill. He smiled. They had been cooperative and encouraging at the idea of causing trouble for the Santa Fe, but hunger and boredom made it impossible for this brood to give complete loyalty.

"I have a plan, and it's going to benefit us greatly."

"I hope it gets us a lot of money," Juan, the self-appointed leader of the pack, announced.

"It would be foolish to consider any other plan." Cyrus leaned back against a tethering rail. "Look, the opening of the dam is in a few days. There are going to be all sorts of grand and wealthy folks attending this shindig. Most are staying at the facilities offered nearby. The resort-type places are going to be full to the brim with uppity visitors from Washington and elsewhere. As I hear it, everyone, including the staff, is going to attend the celebration speech. While that's happening, we can slip in and ransack their rooms. Maybe even the stores they've set up there. I heard that most of Engle is planning to attend. It might behoove us to pay attention to some places in town as well. We could leave a couple of boys in town and the rest could come with me to the dam."

There were comments of approval as the men spoke amongst themselves while nodding in Cyrus's direction.

"I figure we can get a haul in goods as well as cash from the stores, and maybe jewelry and other things from the hotel rooms. But we'll need a good plan, and we've only got a short time. The place is going to be crawling with soldiers and the railroad's hired peacekeepers, so we'll have to avoid them and look like we fit in. I suggest we send a few men to scout out the surrounding area. Find us some hiding spots in case we get in trouble and need to disappear. We can also use those spots for hiding the goods for a time."

"Frank and I already know the area. We can handle that job," Juan offered.

Cyrus nodded. "Sounds good. The rest of us can go down to Engle, take a look at what's available, and make a plan on how to best cover the area. We'll slip over to the dam and check that out as well."

"What if the soldiers stop us?"

"We'll clean up before we go. Cut our hair, trim up our mustaches and beards." Cyrus had neither, but many of his men did and looked like the scum they were. "Wear your best clothes."

"These are my best clothes," Juan announced, laughing.

Cyrus smiled. "The point is, we need to look like we're just like any other visitor. There will be a great many people from all over the state coming to this, and some are just regular folks. Not to mention the workers will all be there as well. They're being honored too. We'll try to blend in the best we can. They're going to be much too busy guarding the dam and the officials to worry about the hotels or stores."

"I like the sound of it," Frank declared, giving the man beside him a jab.

"Good." Cyrus felt a sense of satisfaction. This could finally get them a bit of financial security, after which he could focus on his revenge.

And, if not, there was always cattle rustling.

# 12

The weather was perfect for camping, fishing, and a dedication ceremony. There wasn't a cloud in the sky as Cassie stood at the edge of the spillway with at least a thousand other people while A. A. Jones spoke of the statistics that surrounded the dam.

Because of the risk and other duties that demanded his attention, President Wilson sent Mr. Jones as his representative. Also in attendance were Brigadier General George Bell Jr. and Brigadier General Morton, commanders of the 10th and 11th Divisions of the army. With them were companies of soldiers and a marching band from the 23rd United States Infantry.

Cassie had heard Mr. Jones announce earlier that there were over three hundred fifty delegates from the International Irrigation Congress, as well as the International Farm Congress. These, along with hundreds of other guests, were stretched out along the spillway, across the top of the concrete dam, and along the lake. Mr. Jones had a special spot on a platform that someone had built over the spillway so he would be easily visible and better heard.

He rambled on and on about the importance of the dam as the largest irrigation system in the United States, providing farmers and ranchers with much-needed water and reclaiming many thousands of acres of desert land.

Cassie was more than a little impressed with the mammoth structure. She'd never in her life seen anything like it and marveled at what simple men could construct.

"It's quite the deal, isn't it?" Myrtle commented after the speeches concluded and they had begun their walk back to the campsite they'd chosen.

"I'm very impressed," Cassie replied.

"As am I," John agreed. "I've seen dams before but never this close. It's going to be such a blessing to the people. Hopefully it will help stop some of the flooding we get."

"Wouldn't the dam have to be above us on the river to do that?" Myrtle asked. "The floods in San Marcial are usually due to the heavy rains and flash floods they get to the north of us."

"You're right, of course. But it will help the flooding to the south." John put his arm around his wife. "I told the O'Briens we'd meet them after the ceremony." He looked at Cassie. "You're welcome to join us."

"I think I'll just take a walk. They're allowing folks to walk across the top of the dam, and I'd like to try it." She did up the buttons on her traveling suit. It was her very best outfit, and she was glad she'd chosen to wear it, as the other women at the celebration seemed so gloriously attired. Had she worn her day-to-day clothes, they would no doubt have thought her unworthy to share their company. At least this way she only got the occasional upturned nose.

She turned and headed through the crowds to the walkway at the top of the dam. Hundreds of people had the same idea, and it wasn't easy to maneuver through the people, but little by little Cassie managed to make her way to look out over the lake side of the dam. It was so beautiful. The blue water and sky made a picturesque scene one might find in a painting. For several moments, she just stood and enjoyed the landscape and light breeze.

"Miss Barton?"

She looked up and saw her sister's husband, Terrance Bridge-stone. "Please call me Cassie. You are my brother-in-law, after all."

He smiled. "Yes, of course, and you must call me Terry."

"I'd like that." She looked beyond him. "Where's Melissa?"

"She was tired and went back to our room. I wanted to look around. We are invested in the recreational aspect of the area."

"How nice. I hope it goes well for you."

"It looks as if it will." He gazed out at the lake. "I, uh, wonder if we might talk."

People pushed in all around them. Most were talking about how amazing the dam was and how beautiful the area would one day be. "I would like that, but I suggest we go somewhere else. Otherwise, I doubt we'll be able to hear one another."

"Of course." He offered her his arm. "Let me make way for us."

They pushed through the crowd and with some difficulty finally found themselves on the gravel road that led away from the dam. There were still hundreds of people around them, but at least they had a little more room to move.

Terry took them to the pathway near the lake. It was a beautiful walkway for those who wanted to stroll along the lakeside and enjoy the day. Cassie had already taken it several times.

"This is a lovely place, don't you think?" she said.

Terry slowed his pace. "I do. I like it very much. Before seeing it, I found it hard to believe what they had created out here in the middle of all this scrub and desert. And naming it after elephants in a place that has never seen the likes made it all the more unusual."

"It's named for that elephant-shaped rock behind the dam. I'm not sure who named it that, but apparently they had seen an elephant." Cassie smiled. She wasn't sure what her brother-in-law wanted to talk about, but she figured it was time to get started. "What did you want to discuss?" She let go of his arm. "I wouldn't want you to be too long away from Melissa."

He nodded and stopped. "I just wanted to better know you. You seem quite congenial."

"I suppose Melissa made me out to be coldhearted and indifferent, but I assure you I am anything but." Cassie folded her hands. "I was shocked to learn that she hates me."

He nodded. "When I first met her, she was so filled with rage that she wouldn't even discuss her family. After a few years, she finally confided in me. She told me she wasn't wanted or loved, and that her father couldn't bear the sight of her."

"Well, that's true, in part. It was hard for him. She is the spitting image of our mother, who died so suddenly. She had a heart condition. The doctor said she'd most likely had it for many years, and we just didn't know. We were all very close before she died."

"And afterward?" Terry asked.

"I took care of Melissa. She was only thirteen and so heart-broken. A girl that age still needs her mother. What am I saying? I was twenty-five, and I still needed Mama." Cassie shook her head and wrapped her arms around her middle. "I did my best to comfort Melissa. She couldn't bear the idea of going back to school, so I taught her at home for a time. I held her when she cried and sometimes cried with her. I always tried to be there for her and offer her comfort. Helping her gave me comfort."

"She never told me this."

"No, I don't imagine so. I'm sure the heartbreak of being sent off to boarding school erased all of those memories."

"How did it happen that your father sent her to Denver?"

"One of the local families had a daughter who was friends with Melissa. They were sending their daughter to the school in Denver and asked Father to allow Melissa to accompany her so that their daughter wouldn't be lonely. He thought it a wonderful idea. I know he was thinking only of himself. No matter what I did or how I tried to help her, Melissa continued to mourn. Papa couldn't bear it. He sent her away to preserve his own sanity, I believe.

"I begged him not to let her go. I told him she needed us and that we needed her. But he said it would do her good to have a different environment—one in which Mama had never been—so there would be no haunting memories lurking in the shadows."

Cassie paused and looked into Terry's eyes. "After speaking to Melissa at our father's grave the other day, I have to admit one thing: she was abandoned. Especially by our father, but even by me, to a degree. I wrote her every week, but I never went to see her. There wasn't a lot of money for such things. I could have gotten a free pass on the train because of Father's working for the railroad, but I would never have been able to afford a hotel for long. Still, I suppose I should have tried."

"You could have stayed with us," Terry countered. "We had plenty of room."

Cassie shook her head. "That was only later, and it never even came to mind. I would have never had the nerve to ask if I might stay with your family, perfect strangers. That wasn't the way I was raised. Worse still, Melissa never encouraged me to come. She so rarely wrote to me, and when she did, it was usually to tell us that she was going to spend her time away from school with your family. It hurt that she didn't want to come home. I missed her so much. I miss her still."

"I'm sorry. I was convinced by Melissa that you wanted nothing to do with her. My own mother pitied her greatly. She often commented to my sister and me that we needed to offer extra friendship and love to Melissa. My mother and father are devout Christians, and not just in the sense of using church for social importance. When they were young, before Father received his inheritance, they were missionaries. They went with another group of believers to China."

"How fascinating." Cassie couldn't begin to imagine.

"My mother taught us a deep, abiding love of God and shared that with her friends and neighbors as well. She saw Melissa as yet another person God had put in her path."

"I'm glad Melissa had that. She so needed a mother's care, and to know she had a godly woman in her life gives me great joy. I'd love to meet your mother one day."

"I think she'd enjoy meeting you, Cassie." He gazed out at the lake.

People continue to pass by, chattering about the ceremony and the dam. Cassie had very nearly forgotten where she was. She was completely caught up in Terry's story.

"I'm glad too that Melissa has you," Cassie finally said, since Terry remained silent. "I was so sad when she wrote to tell us she'd married. I would have loved to have been there, but I understand it was a very small private affair. Sometimes those are best."

Terry's brows drew together in a look of confusion. "Our wedding had over three hundred people in attendance. My father spent thousands on the occasion. It was the social event of the year, and anything but small and private. Did Melissa tell you that was what it was?"

Cassie nodded, feeling a deep sorrow that her sister had felt the need to lie. "She told me that exactly. She didn't tell us prior to the occasion but rather afterward. She sent me a photograph on a postcard of you and her in wedding clothes. It was such a charming picture. You were about to kiss her, and she was holding her bouquet and looking at the camera. I could see by the twinkle in her eyes that she was truly happy."

"We had those photos made for one hundred of our friends. No expense was spared on the wedding." He shook his head. "I'm sorry she lied to you. She lied to me as well. She told me she had invited you and your father, and you had both refused."

"Never! I would have done anything to be there." Cassie

dropped the hold she had on herself. "I never abandoned her like that. I didn't." Tears came to her eyes. "I couldn't make our father change his mind about sending her away. She assumed I wanted her to go, but I wrote hundreds of letters to her that clearly told another story. If she read those letters, she knew that I loved her dearly. And if she didn't read them . . ."

"I'm sorry for you both. I know this break can't be what God wants for the two of you. Please be patient, Cassie. I'll do what I can to encourage her to change her heart toward you."

Cassie pulled a handkerchief from her purse and dabbed her eyes. She couldn't imagine the lies Melissa had told. Why would she do such a thing?

Terry put his hand on her arm. "Cassie, try not to judge her too harshly. She was just a child. No doubt this was how she decided to protect her heart, and once the lies began, she found herself believing them. She convinced herself that no one loved her. Satan often causes doubt to rise up between people to separate them. We need to let God put this back together again."

"From the way she acted that day at the cemetery, it will take a miracle," Cassie said, squaring her shoulders.

Terry smiled. "It's a good thing God's in the miracle business, then, isn't it?"

"It's been such a lovely time down here on the lake," Myrtle said as John put another log on the fire. The railroad had brought in carloads of firewood for the campers to buy, and John had smartly purchased some the day they arrived. Now it was nearly gone.

Cassie sat gazing into the flames. "It has been interesting, to say the least." She had told Myrtle and John of her discussion with Terry Bridgestone. "I can't say it's been relaxing or refreshing, but definitely informative."

Myrtle chuckled. "I think the relaxing aspect will come when we return home. Sometimes that's the way it is with traveling."

"It's true," John agreed. "I've walked more on this trip than I ever would at home. I'll bet I've put in a hundred miles just walking around the area, talking to this person and that."

"Did you ever hear anything more about someone wanting to attack the dam?" Myrtle asked.

John used a stick to stir up the fire and arrange the logs. "Only that the army was doing regular patrols around the dam. Oh, and one of the officials said that he'd been told Pancho Villa planned to dynamite the dam and flood the entire area. He just laughed at the idea, saying it would take a railroad car full of dynamite to blast through the dam's thickness."

"Goodness, I don't think I'd want to be around to see such a sight." Myrtle offered some of Cassie's cookies to her husband as he came to sit back down with the ladies.

"Nor would I." He took some cookies, and then Myrtle turned and offered them to Cassie.

"These have been so good," Myrtle said. "I'm glad you were able to bake them for us."

Cassie took a cookie and smiled. "It was the least I could do. I've enjoyed our trip. I'm glad I came and was able to talk to Terry. It would have been nice to see Brandon."

"Did I hear my name mentioned?" Brandon strode into their camp at that moment and plopped down on the ground beside Cassie. "I had a dickens of a time finding you guys. John, your instructions on how to get here sent me to two other camps before I found yours."

John laughed. "Well, giving directions has never been my strong suit."

"Nor following them," Myrtle declared. "We were once on a trip through Kansas with written instructions, and we still managed to get lost."

That made John laugh all the more.

Myrtle handed Cassie the cookies again. "Better see if he wants a few of these. I'll check if there's any coffee left."

"That's okay, Myrtle. The cookies are enough. It seems I've been eating all day. I joined in on several cookouts," Brandon said, taking a couple of the cookies.

"Maybe that's what we should have done," John said. "Just wander around and invite ourselves in where food was to be had."

"Was there any trouble today?" Cassie asked. "We heard there was a threat of someone coming to blow up the dam."

"There's been a threat of that since it began construction," Brandon replied. "But everything was quiet today where the dam was concerned. However, there were a lot of thefts. Apparently someone or several someones went through the lodges and hotels and stole whatever they could. No one is sure who is behind it, but it adds up to quite a take."

"How awful." Myrtle shook her head. "What's wrong with a soul that they feel they must steal from others?"

"Could be nothing more than hunger, Myrtle," John replied. He looked at Brandon. "Are folks sticking around to see if their property can be found?"

"No, most filed their claims with the police and will no doubt have had the really expensive stuff insured. I suppose except for pieces that are old heirlooms, the jewelry doesn't matter. Of course, cash and various goods were reported missing, but I suppose those who have plenty aren't overly concerned. A lot of the officials have already started back for their homes. With an abundance of private railcars, they have their hotels with them on the rails. I don't know if anyone broke into those cars. I have my doubts, given the army patrolling the tracks as they watched over the dam."

"I think it would be fun to ride in one of those private cars. I've heard they're quite grand." Cassie smiled. "Maybe someday, eh?"

"You can never tell, my dear. I'm sure they're very nice." Myrtle stretched her legs out toward the fire. "You could just climb aboard and travel from one part of the country to another and never leave the train."

"When are you heading home?" Brandon asked.

"Tomorrow morning. I'm sure the train will be packed with folks," John answered, "but I figure I've been gone long enough."

"Me too. I still have a lot of sewing to catch up on." Cassie finished her cookie and stood. "I'm going to take a walk." Given there were campfires and other camps all along the lake, she didn't feel the least bit concerned about being alone.

"May I join you?" Brandon asked, getting to his feet. "I actually came over to suggest a walk."

Cassie smiled. "I'd like that. I have a lot to tell you. I talked with my brother-in-law today, and it was most enlightening."

"Don't be gone too long. We plan to go to bed soon, and given your spot in the tent is on the far side, you'll have to climb over us if you return late," Myrtle reminded her.

"We won't be long," Brandon promised. "I have to leave later tonight on a special freight."

John waved them on. "Then you'd best get to courting that girl. You're running out of time."

Cassie felt her cheeks grow hot. She hated that John had implied this was anything more than two friends taking a casual walk. She hoped it hadn't put Brandon off.

For what seemed a long while, neither said a word as they walked. A group of folks around one of the campfires was singing songs while a young man accompanied them on the guitar. At another campfire, two children were begging their parents to be allowed to stay up later. Cassie smiled. It was all so homey.

"Everyone seems so content. I suppose such a celebratory day has left them all in good spirits, and these folks probably had nothing worth stealing."

Brandon turned to glance at the gathering. "They do look like they're having fun. I always find that being out under the night sky causes folks to feel a sense of freedom—of returning to the old days, when things were much simpler."

Cassie wished she could have a family who enjoyed themselves the way these seemed to. She longed for that close relationship but knew it probably wasn't going to come to her any time soon.

"So what did your brother-in-law have to say?"

"He told me things Melissa had said. Brandon, she was so upset by Papa sending her away that she actually made up stories and lies. At first I was hurt by it, but now I just feel sorry for her."

"Why? She knew better."

"About some of it, yes."

"And you wrote to her, showing love and compassion."

"I did, but she was already so wounded that it didn't matter. I don't even know if she read the letters. One thing I learned is that Terry and his parents are strong Christians. His folks were even missionaries in China. Can you imagine going thousands of miles from home to share the Gospel with people who know nothing about Jesus?"

"No, I honestly can't. I know what it is to leave home for another part of the same country—your own country—but I can't imagine leaving all you know and love for a strange place."

"I can't either." She gave a bit of a laugh. "I've moved around a bit, but people mostly spoke the same language and shared many of the same customs. I will say, however, I enjoyed learning Spanish when we moved here. I suppose I might be able to learn Chinese."

"Is that what you want to do with your life? Go to China and be a missionary?"

"Goodness, no. I don't feel called to that at all. You?"

"Not me. I've got too many skeletons to bury." Brandon sounded momentarily sad. "Like you, I don't feel called to it."

"I remember once Pastor John talked about people trying to place themselves in God's service—particularly in places where they weren't called to serve—just because it seemed exciting or even glamorous. He warned us against that. Do you remember?"

"I do. It was an impactful service." Brandon stopped and looked out toward the black water of the lake. For a long time he was silent, but then he turned to Cassie. "We'd best get back. I need to head down to the train."

As they started back toward the Tylers' camp, Brandon remained silent, and Cassie wondered if he was concerned with John's insinuation that they were courting. She figured she'd better make sure before they parted company.

"Are you upset about John's joke about our courting?"

"I'm not upset. Why do you ask?"

"Well, you grew so quiet."

Brandon looked at the trail they were on. "I've just got a lot on my mind."

"Are you worried about someone attacking and robbing us?"

"Not exactly. There will always be the threat of someone attacking someone, but I'm not really worried about it. The folks responsible for the thefts today are no doubt long gone. I guess I'm just tired."

She smiled again, feeling a sense of relief. "Me too. It's been a long couple of days, and I'll be glad to sleep in my bed again."

He nodded as they reached the Tylers' camp.

Cassie stopped and turned to face him. "Will you be home tonight, or do you have to be out somewhere on the rail?"

"I'll be home."

"Good. Try to get a good night's sleep. That will help eliminate some of those things you've got on your mind. And remember, if you ever want to talk about what's bothering you, that's what I'm here for. You always listen to me, and I can do the same for you."

He looked at her for a long moment, then nodded. "Good night, Cassie."

Brandon rode in an empty boxcar all the way back to San Marcial. He was glad for the lack of company as he considered his future. Cassie was ever present in his mind. He was coming to care for her more than he had thought possible. During all those years of friendship with her father, he'd never once thought about having a relationship with Bart's daughter. Now that was all he could think about.

But the past stood as a huge roadblock. There were things back there that couldn't be resolved. Problems that had the potential to destroy his future.

"That's what happens when you run away from the past and the mistakes you made," Brandon muttered to the darkness.

# 13

re you sure you don't mind riding the train alone, my
dear?" Myrtle asked Cassie for the third time. At breakfast, they'd learned that friends of theirs were camping
farther down the lakeside, so the Tylers had changed their plans
at the last minute to stay an extra day at the dam.

"I don't mind at all." Cassie gave Myrtle a reassuring pat. "I
will sit in the ladies' car and be just fine. There are quite a few
women heading back alone while the men stay to work." She
kissed the older woman's cheek. "I'll see you Sunday."

At the train station, Cassie asked the conductor about the
location of the ladies' car and learned it was the last car before a
series of private railcars. She'd nearly reached it when she heard
a woman cry out. She glanced at the car to her right and saw an
older, very well-dressed woman fussing over her gown's bodice.

"What am I to do? Oh, this is a tragedy. We sent all of our
clothes on to Santa Fe."

Cassie could see that the woman had torn her dress, and she
made her way over. "I could mend that for you before we reach
San Marcial." The Worth gown could be repaired, although it
would take a little creative genius to keep the restoration from
being visible.

The older woman gave her a startled look. A maid hurried

forward and placed herself between Cassie and the older woman. "This is the Duchess of Canton. You mustn't address Her Grace without her seeking to speak with you."

Cassie looked at the uniformed woman. "I apologize. I'm unfamiliar with the customs of aristocracy. I saw that she was distressed and offered to repair the gown. I make my living as a seamstress."

"It's quite all right, Miriam. Ask the young lady her name."

"Her Grace would like to know your name."

"Cassandra Barton." Cassie smiled, hoping it would put everyone at ease, although meeting nobility made her nervous.

"Miss Barton," the older woman said, giving a nod. "Are you truly capable of repairing this gown?"

"I am . . ." Cassie looked at the woman and then to the maid.

The maid leaned toward her. "Your Grace."

Cassie nodded. "I am, Your Grace."

The older woman nodded. "Then I suppose I shall take a chance. Come on board. Miriam, retrieve your sewing kit."

A uniformed man appeared and helped the duchess up the stairs and into the private car. Miriam motioned for Cassie to follow her.

After Cassie had just talked the night before about wishing she could ride in a private car, it seemed like a dream come true. The train car was unlike anything she had ever seen. The lavish furnishings looked nothing like what she'd expect on a train. The main room was paneled with gleaming wood, and gold trim furthered the rich effect. There was even a chandelier with crystal prisms dangling down. The chairs and settees looked to be of the finest woods upholstered in sateen and velvet.

"You may sit here while Miriam helps me change into a dressing gown," the duchess instructed.

Cassie met her gaze and smiled. She didn't know if that was an appropriate response, but it was all that came to mind. Hopefully she hadn't offended the duchess.

It wasn't long before Miriam came with a sewing basket and led Cassie to a small desk. "I hope you will find whatever you need." She placed the basket on the desktop. "Will this work for you? There's a dining table in the next car if you need more room."

"No, this is fine."

Cassie opened the basket and began to search through it. She found thread that she thought would match and a pincushion with pins and needles. She took them out and set them on the desk, then reached back inside for the scissors. "I think this will do."

She heard the conductor call for final board, and a thought came to mind as the same uniformed man who'd helped the duchess on board began lowering the windows. "Do you have a dress bag?"

"For travel?" the maid questioned.

"Yes, I worry with the windows down that soot might get on the dress."

The maid nodded. "I'll see what's available after I finish helping Her Grace." She left Cassie and made her way from the room.

The whistle sounded, and the train jerked to life. Cassie sat looking out the window as the train picked up speed. The people and station soon gave way to arid land and the Rio Grande ribboning its way through the desert. It would be so good to be home once again. She knew there were people who loved to travel the world. The duchess was probably just such a person, but Cassie preferred home.

It was only a few more minutes before Miriam reappeared. She brought the beautiful Worth gown and a bedsheet.

"I couldn't find a garment carrier, so I thought perhaps this sheet would do."

"It'll be fine." Cassie helped her wrap the sheet around the skirt of the gown before she started to examine the damage.

The bodice was an intricacy of layers. At the base lay delicate peach-colored lace sewn over silk. This was banded on either side by silk that was drawn at the waist, giving the bodice a V effect. The bands disappeared into the pleated silk waistband of a flowery print whose background was powder blue. The flowers were predominantly the same color peach as the lace with bits of yellow at their centers and green foliage entwined through the powder blue. The lace and banded edge were the main areas of Cassie's concern, although she had great admiration for the rest of the gown. It was sheer perfection.

The silk foundation looked to be intact, so Cassie began to carefully pin the lace. She would do the mending in layers just as the gown had been created. Hopefully, with the fact that there were multiple layers, she would be able to make it look as if her repairs were just one more layer.

The duchess, wearing a dressing gown, joined her and took a seat near the desk. "Do you think you can manage the restoration?"

"I do," Cassie replied. "I've studied the way the bodice is put together, and I believe I can fix it in such a way that it will look like it was always meant to be this way." She smiled at the older woman.

"I do hope so. I should have known better than to allow our things to be sent ahead."

"I assure you I'll have this fixed in no time at all."

Forty minutes later, Cassie held up the finished product. The duchess came to inspect the gown and marveled at the intricate work Cassie had managed. She fingered the newly made repairs, then stepped back to observe it from afar.

"You were right. It looks as if it were always intended to be that way. Miriam, come help me dress."

The duchess went to her dressing room, and Miriam followed with the dress in hand. Cassie began putting away the various things she'd used. She was pleased with the result and knew the duchess was as well. It gave her a great sense of accomplishment.

When the duchess next appeared, she was once again regally clothed and looked like the grand lady she was.

"You have done a most remarkable job. Are you married?"

Cassie found it a strange question but answered nevertheless. "No, I'm not."

"I wonder if you would care to join my household. Usually, I leave these things to my steward, but in his absence and seeing the remarkable things you are capable of accomplishing, I would like to offer you a position."

"I'm honored, Your Grace. However, I don't wish to leave San Marcial. I have a job sewing there for the people."

"But I could use a woman of your talents. Can you not reconsider?"

Cassie smiled. "I have to say it was a great honor to work on a Worth gown and to meet a duchess. This has been more exciting to me than seeing the dam."

The duchess chuckled. "You are quite outspoken."

"I'm sorry if I've offended. I've never been a talkative woman, but I cannot hide my delight in this occasion."

"I am most happy we have met, Miss Barton. You are indeed far from talkative, but you are full of grace and charm. I do wish I could persuade you to return to England with me. My peers would be positively envious. Are you certain you won't reconsider?"

"You flatter me, but again, I must refuse. San Marcial is my home. I just buried my father a few months ago and feel it only right to remain. Besides that, it is where I am most needed. I'm certain you must have an entire staff of seamstresses to care for you."

"Yes, well, that much is true, but none who have your talent. Your touch on this gown was like that of its creator. I marvel at such skill. You are more artist than mere seamstress."

Cassie blushed. "You are very gracious, and I am glad I was able to assist you."

She could feel the train slowing and knew they were no doubt close to San Marcial. "I will be leaving your company now, as we've reached my home, but I am glad God chose to put us together for this time."

"As am I, my dear Miss Barton. However, there is one thing I will not allow. You will not refuse my paying for your work."

Cassie had barely stepped from the train with twenty dollars in hand when she spied her sister and brother-in-law. She was still so shocked at the amount of money the duchess had given her that she very nearly missed recognizing them.

Melissa had said they would go directly to Albuquerque and not return to San Marcial, which was why Cassie was surprised to find them here. She wondered if it would cause a scene if she went to speak to her sister, but they seemed in such a hurry to get out of the depot that it was impossible for Cassie to reach them.

Outside, she saw them making their way to the Grand Hotel. She wondered what was going on but didn't feel she had a right to intrude. Perhaps they'd send her word that they were in town.

"I doubt it," she murmured to herself.

She took up her small carpetbag and made her way home. Her experience with the duchess faded from memory at the reminder that her sister had lied to her husband about Cassie and their father. Why had she done that? Had she not merited enough sympathy with the truth?

It was impossible not to ponder her conversation with Terry for the rest of the afternoon. Cassie tried to lose herself in sewing, but no matter how she tried to forget about their discussion, she always came back to the fact that her sister had lied and told him that her family didn't want to come to their wedding. It made her angry.

*Well, at least he knows the truth. Perhaps he'll confront her.*

But Cassie wanted to confront Melissa herself. She wanted to ask about the lies she'd told. She wanted to know if her sister had ever read the letters—if she'd ever even tried to think about how hard their separation had been for someone other than herself.

By evening, Cassie had had more than enough contemplation. She grabbed her shawl and made her way to the hotel. She was going to speak to Melissa whether her little sister wanted such a conversation or not.

"Good evening, señorita Barton," the man behind the desk said.

"Good evening, Manuel. My sister is staying here, and I would like to see her. She's registered under Terrance Bridgestone."

"Ah yes, they are in room ten. Top of the stairs and to the right. It's at the end of the hallway. Mr. Bridgestone is out for the evening, but Mrs. Bridgestone stayed in."

"Thank you." She was glad Terry was elsewhere. Perhaps Melissa would be more forthcoming with answers if she didn't fear her husband overhearing.

Cassie made her way upstairs and down the hall. She paused for a moment, then raised her hand to knock. It was only a few moments before her sister answered the door. It looked as if she had been crying.

"What's wrong?" Cassie asked, unable to hide her concern.

"You're what's wrong," Melissa replied. "What do you want? Haven't you caused enough trouble?"

"What did I do?"

Melissa stepped back. "Come inside. I'll not have my business known to the entire hotel, although I fear they probably already know."

Cassie came into the room, and Melissa closed the door behind her. "Please tell me what I've done." The room was warm, so Cassie discarded her shawl.

"You told Terry I lied to him."

"Well, you did. I didn't know you had, but he mentioned that you said Papa and I refused to come to the wedding, and I couldn't let that stand. You knew better."

Melissa began to pace. "We've had a terrible fight because of you."

"I am sorry about that, but it hurts me that in all this time, you've never considered anyone's feelings but your own. I can give grace for the fact that you were a child when Papa sent you away, but you are grown now. I demand you give me my due. I was just as devastated at losing you as you were at losing us. I felt just as much frustration with Papa. As I've already told you, I begged him to let you stay. His refusal is his sin alone."

Melissa said nothing. She continued pacing back and forth, chewing on her lower lip. Cassie wondered if she was trying to keep herself from speaking.

"I would have come," Cassie continued. "I would have been happy to come and see you marry. Terry seems to love you very much."

"Yes," Melissa said, stopping abruptly. "At least he did. Now he's put out with me. He says he doesn't know if he can trust me to tell him the truth, since I've fooled him all these years."

"Why did you lie to him? Were you afraid you might lose him if he knew you weren't truly abandoned?"

Melissa met her gaze and shrugged. "I don't know. I've asked myself that question. I suppose your reason is as good as any. Maybe I wanted his pity. I definitely wanted his love. And his family's too. If you've cost me that, I'll never forgive you."

Cassie wanted to be angry with her, but Melissa suddenly seemed like a child again. "It won't be me who has cost you anything. This is all by your own hand, Melissa. Lies always have a way of catching up with us."

Her sister plopped down on the edge of the bed. She looked at Cassie and shook her head. "I don't know what to do. He's so angry. He had a meeting tonight, but I know he'll hardly be able to keep his mind on business."

Cassie moved closer to the bed. "Why didn't you invite us to the wedding?"

For several long moments, Melissa said nothing. When she finally did speak again, tears fell anew. "I was afraid you would say no. I couldn't bear the idea of being cast away twice."

Taking a seat beside her sister, Cassie put her arm around Melissa's shoulder. "I never cast you away. Not even once. I cried for weeks after you left. I never quite got over it."

"You cried?" Melissa asked, tears streaming down her face.

"Of course, Melissa, I loved you. I love you still. You're my sister, and for a time you were like my own child. You have the twins now, so you must know how that feels. I wanted only good things for you, and you seemed so much happier in Denver. Don't you think it hurt me to know you didn't need me anymore?"

Melissa looked at her. "I never even thought about that."

Cassie fought back her own tears. "It was devastating. Papa was gone all the time because he couldn't bear to be home. I sat in our old house night after night, day after day, alone. I had even given up the man I thought I might love to care for you, and then you were gone and so was he. I had no one."

"What man?"

Cassie shook her head. "It doesn't matter now, but I was courting Justin Beecher. A young man who worked as a clerk at the Santa Fe."

"He was tall and thin with a mustache, wasn't he?" Melissa asked.

"Yes."

"I remember him. Mama liked him because he made her laugh. He made all of us laugh. I didn't know you were thinking of marriage."

Cassie nodded. "He asked me to marry him right after Mama died. He was moving away to a job in California and wanted us to go as husband and wife."

"But you couldn't leave . . . because of me."

"And Papa. I needed you all as much as you needed me."

"I didn't know, Cassie. I swear I didn't."

"I know. There was no reason to tell you. If Justin had loved me as he said he did, he would have known I needed to stay. He would have found a way to make a home here in San Marcial so I could be there for you and Papa. And maybe if I had loved him as much as I should have, I would have found a way to make it all work."

"I'm sorry."

"I just want you to understand that you have always been loved and missed. Even Papa loved you, he was just too lost in his grief to show it. He was never the same after losing Mama. When he died last spring, it was a grief to me, but I'd seen him so little in the last few years that the separation was nothing new. This time I just knew he would never be coming back. But, Melissa, I used to think that might happen anyway. I think San Marcial made him too sad, and I know he often thought of leaving here."

"It seems we were both abandoned by Papa."

"Yes. However, that's all in the past. We cannot allow it to dictate our future. Melissa, I want to be close to you again. I want to know your children. I want to be Auntie to them."

"I want that too." Melissa fell into Cassie's embrace. "I'm so sorry. Can you forgive me?"

"Of course, God would want me to do nothing less, and my heart declares the same. Can you forgive me?"

Melissa nodded and whispered against Cassie's ear. "Yes."

They held each other close, and that was how Terry found them when he returned to the hotel room. They were startled by his appearance but stood and smiled as they continued to hold on to each other.

"It would seem my prayers have been answered," he said, returning their smiles.

# 14

Cyrus paid for his breakfast, walked out of the El Paso café, and started for the livery. One thing he'd made sure of after their robberies at the dam celebration was that each man in the gang got a decent mount with a bill of sale. Afterward, they made careful copies of those bills and sold their stolen horses in a variety of locations, keeping only the legitimately purchased ones. Cyrus had told the men that the way to ensure getting caught was to have stolen articles on them and no proof of purchase. Mounts were especially vulnerable because you couldn't disguise or hide them, yet in the vast desert lands, they were sorely needed.

They had worried about being caught robbing resorts and shops on the day of the dam's dedication, but in truth, no one had seen or cared. There were so many people coming and going, both at the dam and in the surrounding areas. The loot had been stashed, the food eaten, and cash spent, but they were running out fast. It was expensive to keep a gang of men and their horses fed and sheltered. Sooner or later, they would have to sell some of the things they'd taken, and that wouldn't be easy around here. Maybe Cyrus could take a train to California or even Kansas City. Somewhere far enough away that the property wouldn't be recognized. Maybe he'd even stay away for a while.

Over the month since the grand opening of the dam, Cyrus had given a lot of thought to what they'd do next. They had torn up a bit of track here and there, but nothing all that impressive. Damaged track did cause problems and expense to the Santa Fe, but it didn't get him revenge against Brandon DuBarko, and that was what he wanted more than anything. And that was the reason he couldn't leave. At least not for long.

Cyrus entered the livery, and a boy came running. "You want your horse, Mr. Mac?" the young Mexican boy asked. He always called Cyrus Mr. Mac because he had difficulty pronouncing his last name.

Flipping the boy a coin, Cyrus gave a nod. "Make it quick." The boy hurried out to the corral.

Even if he couldn't leave the area until he got his revenge on DuBarko, maybe it was time to leave the gang to themselves. They could easily go make their own trouble. A couple of the boys had talked about heading to Mexico. Maybe it was time to divvy up what was left from their haul and go their separate ways.

"Jefe." Juan walked into the livery. "You ready to leave El Paso?"

"I'm considering it."

Juan frowned. "Were you gonna go without us?"

"No, just restless and wanted to go for a ride. You're welcome to come along. We've got some decisions to make, so it might be good if you rode with me."

Juan nodded, and when the boy returned with Cyrus's horse, saddled and ready to go, Juan ordered him to retrieve his mount.

Cyrus led his horse toward the door. "I'll wait out here for you."

They rode for a while without exchanging any thoughts, and

then Cyrus slowed his horse and looked at Juan. "What do you think our next move should be?"

"Something that will bring in a lot of money. The boys are restless. Some want to return to Mexico to see their families. The white men want to go to wherever they can make money easily."

"We'd all like that, I'm sure." In the distance, Cyrus heard a train whistle and stopped his mount altogether. "The only person with big money in these parts is the railroad paymaster. Once a month they have a courier come in with the payroll. Might be we could relieve him of it before it reaches San Marcial."

Juan nodded. "That makes sense."

"Then we could all go our separate ways for a time. I have a job that needs to be done, and it's probably best to do it alone. Killing DuBarko won't be quite as easy as it was with Barton. As an engineer, I knew he'd be on the train. DuBarko isn't usually on the trains unless he's transporting men and equipment from one place to another, but it's never anything routine."

He quieted in order to think about their plans. If they were going to get the payroll, he would have to take care of Brandon first. There'd be no sticking around after the company's money was taken. Cyrus's presence in San Marcial would be noted, and people would talk. Because of the past, they'd presume he was the one responsible, since he'd stolen from the Santa Fe before and got sent to prison for it.

A thought came to mind, and he smiled. "Let's get back and talk to the men."

It was nearly dark before Juan managed to round up all the men. They met at one of the local pool halls, as it was one of their favorite places. No one seemed to notice them or care that they were drinking and talking amongst themselves.

"I have an idea for making some real money." Cyrus lowered

his voice. "We're going to steal the train's payroll." He had their attention now. "I don't know the shipment schedule anymore. After all this time, I know very little about how they're doing anything, but I intend to get back in."

"How you gonna do that, jefe? They sent you to prison." Juan looked skeptical.

"Everyone loves a repentant sinner." Cyrus grinned. "I'll go and tell them I'm a reformed man—that I found religion in prison and that I want to make amends for my sins. I'll ask them to take me back on. I'll offer to work for them and let them take money out of my wages to make up for what I stole."

"That should convince them," one of the men commented.

"Exactly. I think they'll be impressed. Once I'm in, I can learn what the schedule is with the payroll and how we can best rob them of their money."

"And what about DuBarko? We know you want revenge on him," another of the men asked.

"He's still working for the Santa Fe. Being there will give me a better opportunity to get my revenge. You don't need to feel obligated to go with me. I know several of you were planning to go back to Mexico and your families, and that's perfectly fine. But if you want to help me with this, we'll leave first thing in the morning."

The newspaper announced that Wilson had narrowly held his presidency. The opposing party was demanding a recount of the votes. Brandon was curious as to how things would turn out. There had been many who thought Wilson would lose the election. Those folks wanted to go to war and help their European family and allies. Brandon had hoped the war would be done by now. Far too many people were losing their lives.

150

Scanning the front page, Brandon saw an article that immediately caught his attention.

*Villa Captures Parral, Chihuahua*

That was hundreds of miles away. If Villa had captured that city, he could hardly be destroying railroad track in New Mexico. Brandon frowned and read further. It was clear that Villa was busy on the other side of the border. He wasn't in the United States, and, from the sounds of it, hadn't been in some time.

The thought was perplexing. Everyone had been certain that Villa was responsible for everything. Since the raid on Columbus in March, Villa had been blamed for every missing chicken, torn-up track, and death along the Rio Grande. Brandon had thought it silly to blame one man and his group of revolutionaries for everything, especially when no one had seen them. Not even the army had been able to figure out where Villa had gone.

Out of habit, Brandon walked by Cassie's house. He liked to check up on her and make sure everything was all right. Since her bones had mended, he didn't have a real excuse to stop by. Unless he admitted to the feelings he'd begun to have for her, and he wasn't about to do that.

To his surprise, the laughter of several men rang out from Cassie's house. He decided if she already had company, it couldn't hurt to impose himself and see what was happening. He'd just tell her that he had returned from down south. He could offer her his newspaper, even though he hadn't finished reading it. He could ask if she needed anything done. There were three perfectly good excuses for stopping by.

Music started inside the house, and someone began to sing an old Mexican folk song. Brandon knocked on the front door but doubted anyone would hear him. When no one responded, he let himself in and immediately joined the celebration.

"Brandon, how nice to see you," Cassie said, raising her voice to be heard. "Come join us. We're having our own little fiesta. Some of your boys wanted to tell me more of their stories, so they brought quite the arrangement of food."

"Boss!" Javier said, jumping up. "When did you get back to town?"

The music stopped, and everyone's gaze went to Brandon.

"Just a little while ago." He had been busy down near one of the stops on the main line, discussing the possibility of a spur line to connect with another town.

"We're having a fiesta," Max said. "Come and join us."

All around the room, agreements and comments in Spanish filled the air, and Brandon nodded. "I'll stay. Sure."

The boys wanted to know what Brandon had found in his inspections. He let them know about the newspaper article regarding Villa.

"We probably won't have any more tracks torn up for a while," Zorro declared. "Maybe not ever, if they stay in Mexico."

"Well, that's the problem." Brandon shook his head. "We're still having vandalism, and Villa took that village days ago, which means he's probably been in Mexico for weeks, if not months."

The men all seemed to get it at once. "Then who is tearing up the tracks?" Javier asked.

"That's the question." Brandon filled his plate with food and made his way to where Cassie sat at her desk. There was an empty chair beside her, so he took it and placed his plate next to her journal.

Cassie nodded toward the newspaper still tucked under Brandon's arm. "Was there anything in there about the thefts that took place on the day of the celebration at Elephant Butte Dam?"

"I didn't see anything. The only thing I've seen on it was a few weeks ago, not long after it happened. They think it was a coordinated effort by a single gang of thieves. But there were so many people in the area that day that no one could track anything, and the thieves seemed to be very good at what they did. They may not have even been locals."

"And no one saw anything?"

"No, the town was all but empty. Folks thought nothing of locking up and going to the celebration. Those who remained were either occupied with something else and had no time to notice what was going on, or they were sick or sleeping."

"Or they could have been in on it," Cassie suggested. "It's not unusual for someone related to the people responsible to know about it and even offer help."

"True, but apparently no one has any leads."

Cassie glanced at his plate. "You'd better eat while it's hot."

The boys were back to making music, and Brandon handed her the newspaper. "The Republicans are asking for a recount on Wilson's win."

"What's happening in the war?"

"Not sure. Didn't get that far."

Cassie put the paper aside. "I've been writing down more stories." She opened her left desk drawer and pulled out a stack of typing paper an inch thick. "I've been typing them into book form."

He was busy shoveling food into his mouth but nodded. It was amazing that she'd taught herself so quickly to type. Even more amazing that she still found all these anecdotes to be so amusing.

She put the paper back in the drawer. "The boys were just telling me about the snake they found in one of the equipment barrels."

"Yeah, it was startling to say the least. They've gotten used to checking now. I kept telling them they needed to poke a stick around in places where snakes could hide, but they thought I was joking."

"We don't think that no more, Boss," Bruno said, bringing Brandon a glass of iced lemonade.

"Thanks." Brandon took the glass and downed about half of it in one gulp. "That hit the spot."

Cassie shook her head. "Better refill his glass," she said, reaching over to take it from Brandon. Bruno nodded and headed off to the kitchen.

The fiesta continued until about eight, when all at once the boys packed up their stuff and bid Cassie and Brandon good night. After they had gone, Cassie got to her feet.

"I'd better get those dishes washed."

"Give me a minute, and I'll help you," Brandon said. He'd grabbed a second piece of pie before Javier had taken the pan to the kitchen. "Just let me finish eating this. It's so good."

"I'm glad you like it," Cassie said. "I love coconut cream pie. Mama and I learned to make it years ago from a woman who has since passed on."

"I remember your mother making these pies. She was quite the cook, and she trained you well."

"Papa always liked it when you came by and kept him company. Mama liked it too. She said you were the son Papa never had."

Brandon remembered Bart saying the same to him. "He was a good man, your father."

"Well, to most. Melissa, of course, would say otherwise. Despite her agreeing to work on our relationship, she still blames Papa for all of her woes and miseries."

"She couldn't blame him more than he blamed himself." Brandon ate the last bite of the pie and leaned back in his chair to give his stomach more room to receive it. "Your father knew he'd done wrong by her."

"I've never heard you say much about it, Brandon." Cassie sat back down at the desk. "Please tell me what he said about Melissa, what he said about that time."

Brandon raised a brow. "Are you sure you want to hear it? It might cause you pain."

"It's important to know the truth. Melissa and I are trying to start over. Maybe it would help her to know the truth as well. She wants me to come visit sometime after Christmas, and I said I would. Maybe if you tell me about Papa's thoughts, I can share them with her, and it will help her to heal."

"What if it only stirs up more anger and hate?"

"If it seems like that kind of thing, then I won't tell her." Cassie frowned. "Is it that kind of thing?"

"Not to me. I doubt to you either, but I don't know your sister."

"I hardly know her myself," Cassie replied.

"Your father said she was very shy as a little one, so she clung to her mother and to you but wanted very little to do with him. That bothered him a lot. You were always all over him and wanted to spend all your time with him."

Cassie looked lost in memories for several moments. "I was devoted to Papa. Mama and I were close too, but Papa hung the moon as far as I was concerned."

"Your father said you used to look at him with such adoration. His day could have been nothing but trouble, but when he came home and you ran to him, he said all that went before disappeared. He knew you loved him unconditionally."

"I did. He was a wonderful father. He always made me laugh and feel safe. Mama told me he was capable of fighting off anything that might come along to hurt us. But he couldn't fight off sorrow. When Mama died, it overwhelmed us all."

Brandon remembered how broken his friend had been. Bart had said very little for months, and Brandon, being his student of sorts, didn't feel he could challenge the silence. When Bart did start talking about it, Brandon just listened, knowing he had nothing to offer to make the situation better. Bart had once commented several years later that Brandon's silence had been a balm to him.

"Bart said it was like he lost a part of himself. He'd go to work and do what was required more out of habit than actual focus. He said he knew in that first year he'd been rather dangerous. More than once he was taken to task. I remember he told me about one situation where the supervisor took him aside and said, 'You might not care about your own life, but I've got others on board who count their lives dear. Would you truly want to impose your pain on their loved ones by killing them?' Bart said he straightened up after that. He didn't want to be responsible for killing anyone."

"I've often thought about the fact that only he and Archie died," Cassie said. "So many others could have died if he'd been driving a passenger train. I know he would have hated causing pain even to one family, and Archie was a favorite of his."

"Your father cared deeply about others. It probably saved his life. I think he would have crawled off somewhere and died if it hadn't been for you and your sister. He knew he had to do what he could to be there for the two of you. Still, it wasn't easy for him. He told me he used to sit up at night, listening to Melissa cry until he was nearly crazy. She was able to mourn in a way he couldn't, and it tore at his heart."

"I knew it was hard on him, but I never thought about it that way. I suppose we would have been upset had he sat around displaying his feelings like that."

"No doubt. The worst of it was that Melissa would never come to him, and he felt that she blamed him for your mother's death. Like he somehow should have known her heart was bad. But your ma kept any discomfort from him, and he went off to his job, thinking everything was fine."

"She never told me either. There were a few times I saw her breathless after carrying in laundry or something heavy, but I had no idea it was anything more than that."

"He really hated that you lost out on marriage with that Beecher fellow."

Brandon wondered if that would strike a painful chord. He vaguely remembered Cassie courting Justin. Bart had been certain they would have married had it not been for the death of her mother.

"He wasn't responsible for that. Justin and I weren't meant to be." Cassie looked across the room and shook her head. "I didn't really love him. I suppose losing Mama and feeling obligated to take care of Melissa proved that to me because when he went away, I really wasn't that upset."

Brandon couldn't say why, but he felt a sense of relief. "Well, your father had a lot of regret over what happened. Not just that, but all of it. Even sending Melissa away. Maybe you can explain that to her. Tell her he was never happy with what he'd done and knew it was wrong."

"Then why did he let it go on?"

"He said it was the path of least resistance. By the time he came to understand just what he'd done by sending her away, she no longer wanted to come back. She'd chosen another family."

"Yes, but now I see a possibility to mend the past. To put it aside and forget about it."

"Don't count on it." Brandon could feel his forehead furrowing. "It may not be that easy."

"But if we both want it that way, then I think we can make it happen."

"There are always things in the past that refuse to be forgotten. I pray that you and Melissa can find peace together, but don't be anxious or sad if it doesn't happen right away. That's all I'm saying. These things often take a long time—if they happen at all."

"You speak as one who knows."

"I am." He looked at her a moment longer, then turned away.

"We'd better get to those dishes. It's getting late, and there's church tomorrow."

He picked up his plate and fork and walked into the kitchen. To his surprise, he found that everything had been cleaned and put away.

Cassie gasped. "Well, would you look at that. Those boys washed and dried the dishes. They cleaned up everything."

"Except for this," Brandon said, holding up his plate and fork.

"That's no problem. I'll see to it later." She took the pieces and put them in the sink. "Maybe even tomorrow."

Brandon headed for the front door. "I'll head out, then."

Cassie put her hand on his arm. "Thank you for telling me about Papa. I will share it with Melissa. She needs to know that he wasn't heartless about what happened. I think it will help her to know. If you think of anything else, please tell me."

He looked down at her and saw himself in her blue eyes. He felt a lump form in his throat and tried to clear it away. "I will," he managed to say, and then he turned and forced himself to walk away instead of run.

———

Cyrus watched Brandon DuBarko leave the small house. He was clearly preoccupied, as he didn't even look back to wave to the woman who stood in the doorway watching him go. He easily recognized Cassandra Barton. He had seen her back when he worked for the Santa Fe. She mended clothes for the men, and Cyrus had used her services on one or two occasions. Mostly he remembered her from the trial. Cyrus had raged against her and Barton after the verdict was read and he realized prison was his future. He had threatened to kill them both, along with DuBarko.

It seemed that DuBarko perhaps had a relationship with

Miss Barton. Cyrus smiled. She might come in handy with his plans for revenge. Maybe he could use her to lure DuBarko into a trap that would take his life.

Cyrus continued to watch until Brandon was out of sight. The door to the little house had long since closed, but Cyrus could imagine the woman inside moving about. It had only been her and her father at the other house, so unless she'd found another woman to share this house, Cassandra Barton most likely lived alone. That would be to his advantage.

# 15

I'm glad you were able to get back in time for the weekend, Brandon," his boss declared. He took some papers Brandon handed him and looked them over for several minutes.

It was good to be back in San Marcial. He and some of the boys, along with two other section gangs, had been two weeks helping with a new line of tracks in the southern part of the state. The trip had been without difficulty, and thankfully nothing had happened to slow their progress.

"This looks good, Brandon. I'm pleased you all were able to work out the details on the spur line. We'll have another new area to start up after Christmas." He looked up and smiled. "Meanwhile, I have something for you." He handed Brandon a check. "An early Christmas bonus."

Brandon took the check and glanced at it. "Thank you." The extra money would come in handy for the gift he wanted to give Cassie.

"I swear you never smile. A check like that would have me whooping."

It was a good amount of money, but Brandon so seldom smiled at anything that he had completely lost the habit of it. "I'm whooping on the inside," he said, forcing the slightest upturn of his lips.

The older man shrugged. "Either way, enjoy it."

"I will." Brandon stuffed the check in his pocket and left the building. Hopefully there was still enough time to go to the jewelry shop. He checked his pocket watch. Fifteen minutes until they closed. He picked up his pace.

He had deliberated for his entire trip south about whether or not to get Cassie a Christmas present. He knew his feelings for her had changed . . . that he wanted to make something more permanent with her than just friendship. Still, he couldn't be sure she felt the same way. She enjoyed his company—he was certain of that—but what if all she wanted from him was friendship? Worse still, he would have to come clean with her about his past. What if she wanted nothing to do with him after that?

Walking past the Harvey House, Brandon did a double take. Cassie was entering the establishment with someone who looked vaguely familiar. But it couldn't be the man Brandon thought it was. *Cyrus McCutchen?* The very possibility stopped Brandon in midstep.

Why would she be having dinner with McCutchen? Not only that, but why was he back in town? He had to know he wouldn't be welcome. It had only been five years since he was found guilty of stealing from the Santa Fe.

Brandon's frown deepened. He glanced up and caught his reflection in a nearby glass window. He looked angry. His fore-head was all wrinkled and his eyes pinched, with his brows coming together. Forcing himself to relax, Brandon wondered what in the world was going on. Cassie disliked McCutchen as much as he did. He had shouted all sorts of threats from the defense table at his trial. He had threatened harm to her father and Brandon, as well as herself. How could she be having dinner with him?

The jewelry shop would close in ten minutes, and if Brandon wanted to get that gift, he would have to hurry.

Still, he was torn between that and storming into the Harvey House to demand answers.

"Thank you." Cassie took the chair Cyrus McCutchen offered her, still rather stunned to find herself going to dinner with the man who had threatened at one time to kill her and her father.

"I'm just so grateful you agreed to come out with me. I've wanted to make amends for a long time," Cyrus said, taking a seat opposite her.

The Harvey House waitress gave them beautifully printed menus and took their drink orders. It was only moments before she returned with their coffee and cream, ready for the rest of their requests.

Cassie ordered roasted sirloin with whipped potatoes and asparagus. Cyrus chose broiled whitefish with candied sweet potatoes and creamed peas. Sipping her coffee, Cassie watched him as he flirted with the waitress about dessert.

When he finally turned his attention back to her, Cyrus beamed her a smile. "This is just the greatest blessing you could give me. I've prayed about this moment."

"Do tell." She put the coffee cup to her lips again, lest she feel the need to say more. Thankfully, Cyrus had plenty to say.

"Years in prison changes a man. I've seen them go for the worse or for the better. I chose the better and became a man of God. Read the Bible from cover to cover five times."

"How nice."

"Well, it taught me a lot. Seeing where crime and bad behavior took others, while being under my own punishment, taught me that it wasn't a life I wanted. Then I started reading about forgiveness and how important it was. Do you know that Jesus begged God to forgive the very people who killed Him?"

"I do."

"I didn't, and it so impressed me that I could scarcely sleep as I continued to ponder it. It was clear to me that I needed to make amends for what I'd done. I asked a preacher who came and preached to us every Sunday about forgiveness. If God could forgive me, perhaps others could as well. He encouraged me to make my way back to San Marcial and seek out those I had wronged."

"And did you?"

"Well, you're proof of that. I wronged you and your father. I threatened you with all sorts of bad things. I am so very sorry for that. I do hope you'll forgive me. You see, I've gone to the folks at the Santa Fe and asked their forgiveness. I asked if I might have my old job of fireman again to help pay them back. I suggested they could take a certain amount from each of my paychecks."

"And what did they say?" Cassie found his confession fascinating. She'd never known a man who seemed as evil as Cyrus McCutchen to seek forgiveness. He seemed sincere. After all, who would think of going to the people wronged and offering to pay them back?

"They were so amazed at my coming to seek forgiveness that they said yes. They are desperate for firemen and remembered I was very good at my job. I pledged that I would never steal from them again and that I would pay back the amount I'd stolen in goods. They said it wasn't necessary, though, since I had spent my time in prison, and insurance had covered the financial aspect of the theft."

"Well, it certainly sounds like you thought over everything." Cassie still wasn't sure what to make of it all. Her father had warned her about Cyrus and his inability to be honest or trustworthy. But Cyrus said he had made things right with God. He'd never brought God into the matter before . . . at least not as far as she knew. Still, she didn't feel entirely easy about the whole thing.

The waitress brought their food and refilled their coffee before leaving them to further discussion. Cyrus offered to pray a blessing, and Cassie bowed her head. He made a very short prayer of thanks and blessings and ended it appropriately in Jesus' name.

They dug into their food, which momentarily ended the need for conversation. Cassie found the roast a little dry and was grateful for the au jus that had been brought. She poured the liquid over the roast and began again. What did Cyrus want from her? Was it just forgiveness? He hadn't really wronged her, except to shout threats. It had been frightening at the time, but knowing he was locked up, Cassie had given him little thought.

"Is the meal to your liking?" Cyrus asked.

Cassie nodded. Now that the au jus was moistening the roast, it was perfect. "It's wonderful. And yours?"

"Delicious. I've always enjoyed fish. My father and I used to fish all the time when I was a boy back in Missouri. We ate fish at least five times a week."

That thought wasn't at all appealing, but Cassie said nothing and refocused her attention on the food in front of her.

"I always enjoyed working on the Santa Fe, especially with your father. He was a good man, and I was sorry to hear he'd died before I could make it back here to ask his forgiveness. Tell me, how did it happen?"

"It was a train derailment. Down south where that series of small ravines makes it necessary to have several bridges."

"Ah yes, I know it well. What caused the derailment?"

"Someone tampered with the line. They think it might have been Pancho Villa and his men because just after that, they raided Columbus. I think that convinced the Santa Fe that Villa was to blame."

"It's a pity that men like Villa are allowed to get away with such atrocities."

"I don't believe they're allowed to get away with it, Mr. McCutchen. I think it's more a matter of not being able to catch them. The soldiers have chased them from one place to another without success."

"Well, your father deserves better. How terrible to die such a death."

"The doctor said it was pretty instantaneous. He didn't suffer. That was all that mattered to me. He and Archie were good men, and they had a lot of years left to live. Especially Archie. He was supposed to get married in the summer. After Archie died, his fiancée moved to California to live with her sister. Archie's parents were so devastated that they moved back east. They couldn't bear to remain in the area."

"That is tragic. I had no idea."

"Apparently, Pancho Villa didn't care about such things." Cassie sighed and reached for her coffee.

When they were nearly done, the black-and-white-clad Harvey Girl reappeared to check on them and see what they'd like for dessert. Cassie declined to order, and Cyrus agreed just to have a little more coffee and cream.

As the meal concluded, Cassie said she needed to go, as she wanted to stop by the pastor's house, but as luck would have it, Myrtle and John showed up at the Harvey House for dinner. It was unusual for them to take a meal out, and Cassie flagged them down.

"Imagine seeing you here. I was just going to come to your house."

Myrtle and John looked at Cyrus as they approached the table. "And you," Myrtle said. "I'm surprised you aren't enjoying your evening with Brandon."

"Brandon DuBarko?" Cyrus asked.

Myrtle studied him for a moment, then nodded. "I don't believe we've had the pleasure of meeting you."

"Myrtle, John, this is Cyrus McCutchen. He used to live here and work for the Santa Fe."

Cyrus nodded. "I'm afraid I don't have a very good place

in the history of either the Santa Fe or Miss Cassie. I've come back to make amends."

John smiled. "I'm the pastor at the New Mexico Bible Church. We'd be happy to have you with us on Sunday."

"That would be wonderful. During my time in prison, I found church services to be quite a comfort."

"He read the Bible from cover to cover five times," Cassie offered, feeling suddenly uncomfortable.

"Well, we'd love to have you, Mr. McCutchen."

"I'll be there. But for now, I was just about to escort Miss Cassie home."

"Uh . . . that's all right, Cyrus. I have business with Myrtle, so I'll stay a little longer, if they don't mind the interruption."

"Not at all." Myrtle patted Cassie's arm with her gloved hand. "It was nice to meet you, Mr. McCutchen."

"Thank you for dinner, Cyrus," Cassie said as she stood to follow the Tylers. "I'm sorry to cut our evening short, but this won't keep."

"That's quite all right. I completely understand." He got to his feet. "I'm just grateful for your willingness to forgive me. Now, if I can convince Mr. DuBarko, I will be able to rest with a cleared conscience."

He paid the bill while Cassie made her way to a table with Myrtle and John. Once they were seated and Cyrus had gone, Cassie shook her head.

"That was such a strange ordeal. I'm sorry to have put you on the spot, but I was afraid he expected to come back to the house and be entertained."

"I didn't get a good feeling from that one," Pastor John said. "My discernment would suggest he is less than sincere."

"I had that feeling too," Cassie said. "I can't say why. He seemed to say all the right things, but none of it felt right."

"A man can say the right words, but it doesn't mean he's living and believing them."

"What do you suppose his purpose is?" Myrtle asked.

"I can't really say." Cassie thought back on the evening. "He showed up at my place about ten till five. He told me how sorry he was for the past and wanted to make amends. He said he'd taken Jesus as his Savior and knew that seeking my forgiveness was what God wanted him to do. Then he suggested we go to dinner somewhere public so I wouldn't be uncomfortable. I was so relieved he didn't expect me to invite him in that I immediately accepted, and we came here."

"And he asked you to forgive him for what, exactly?" John asked.

"The insults and threats he made in court during his trial. Papa and Brandon were the ones who testified against him, and he hated them. Threatened to kill us all." Cassie remembered it vividly. "I'd never known anyone filled with such anger and hate." She rose from her chair. "I'm sure he's gone by now. I'll just head home. Thanks for letting me interrupt your dinner. Oh, and for letting me use you as my excuse for sticking around. I suppose we should talk about something so that I wasn't out-and-out lying to Cyrus. I just didn't want him walking me home and then seeking to come inside."

"It's quite all right. I wouldn't have wanted that either," Myrtle replied. "See, we did have something to discuss." She smiled and looked to John and then back to Cassie. "But I don't want you to walk home alone. There's quite a bit of preholiday celebrating going on tonight. The bars were full to overflowing as we walked by them."

"You go ahead and order for me," John said, getting to his feet. "You know what I want. Come along, Cassie. I'll see you home."

They walked the few blocks talking about Christmas. Prior to Mama's death, Cassie had loved the holiday. After that, it had been a difficult time, and with Papa gone, it was all the harder. There would be no one.

"It certainly won't be the same without Papa here. My sister invited me to come visit after the holidays but couldn't have me until then. They will be in New York."

"I'd invite you to come be with us, but we're leaving right after Christmas services. Going to California to see my brother and his family."

"I'll be fine, I'm sure. Some of the boys who work with Brandon promised to come over and tell me more stories about their experiences on the railroad. I've got more than enough for my book, but they love telling their adventures."

They reached her picket fence. "Thank you again for bringing me home, Pastor John." She glanced at her dark house.

"See you at services."

Cassie watched him walk away for a moment, then went into the house. She searched for her matches and felt her way to the table where she knew there was an oil lamp waiting. She lit the lamp and sighed.

"You still aren't locking your door," Brandon said from across the room.

Cassie barely suppressed a scream and reached for the back of a chair to steady herself. "Brandon!"

He sat on her sofa, arms crossed against his chest. "Luckily it's me. But it could have been a lot of folks."

She drew in a deep breath to steady her nerves. "I'm sorry. I won't forget again."

Still his frown didn't lessen. "Why were you with Mc-Cutchen?"

"He asked me to dinner to seek my forgiveness. Apparently, he's looking to make amends with all those he wronged, including you."

"Why did you agree to go? You don't even know him." His tone edged on yelling.

"It seemed better than inviting him into the house and feeling obligated to feed him."

169

Cassie took a seat and felt her heart slow to a steady beat. It dawned on her that it really wasn't any of Brandon's concern that she'd been to dinner with Cyrus. Seeing him looking so angry was starting to make her angry as well.

"Now, if you're done, I have a few questions of my own to ask. Why are you here shouting at me, and what gave you the right to break into my house?"

Brandon's expression softened at this, and for a moment, he looked embarrassed. "I didn't mean to shout. I'm sorry, Cass. I was just worried about you."

"I appreciate your concern, but honestly, scaring me this way wasn't fair. I know I should have locked the door, and believe me, I won't make that mistake again. Although it's always nice to have you here." She smiled. "Would you like some coffee or lemonade?"

"No, I didn't mean to impose myself on you." He got to his feet.

"You aren't an imposition. At least not when you aren't scaring the wits out of me." She smiled again. "I baked some cookies. You might as well stick around and have some. I have cold milk too. Have you had supper?"

"I ate a couple of tamales." He shrugged. "I guess some cookies and milk would hit the spot."

"Good. It's been at least two weeks since I've seen you. You'll have to tell me all about your trip south."

He finally seemed to relax, and with that, Cassie did too. She knew he cared about her well-being, but the truth of how much she cared about him—how much she wanted to please him—was starting to surprise her.

# 16

With Cassie's cookies on a platter in the middle of the table and tall glasses of milk for each of them, Brandon took a seat and waited for Cassie to join him. He felt bad for having scared her. He wanted her to lock up and be safe, but he certainly hadn't meant to terrify her. He could still see the look on her face as she clamped her hand over her open mouth. He'd almost jumped up to wrap her in his arms. Almost.

"I made these Mexican cinnamon cookies as a favor to the boys. Maximo gave me the recipe from his mother. It wasn't at all difficult." She handed Brandon an empty dessert plate. "Help yourself."

He took three of the small cookies before settling back. "Look, Cassie, I'm really sorry about scaring you. It's just that the men have been talking about an increase in thefts and break-ins. I don't want to worry about your safety."

"I know you feel obligated to watch over me, and I do appreciate the concern you've shown." She bit into a cookie and seemed to ponder the flavors as she chewed.

"It's more than obligation. I care about your well-being." He suddenly felt very uncomfortable with the topic. "What did Cyrus have to say?"

"He told me he'd found God and needed to make amends for the past. He even went to the Santa Fe officials and apologized. He asked them to rehire him and take money out of his check until he'd paid back what he'd stolen."

Brandon frowned. "And did they rehire him?"

"Apparently so. He said they remembered what a good fireman he'd been. I guess they're shorthanded."

It seemed like a lot had happened in just two weeks. "I didn't know they'd taken him back. But then, I didn't know he was back in the area."

"I didn't either. He just showed up at the door." She smiled. "Maybe I need some sort of window to peek through before I unlock and open it next time."

Brandon shrugged. "It might not be a bad idea. But nothing big enough to break and get through to unlock the door."

Cassie laughed. "I was just teasing, Brandon."

"I wasn't. There are a lot of bad people in this world."

"Cyrus said he'd taken Jesus as his Savior and sought forgiveness. Don't you believe God can change the heart of even cruel and terrible men?"

Brandon considered this for quite a while. He could hear the ticking of a nearby clock and lost himself in the rhythmic sound.

"Aren't you going to answer?" Cassie finally asked. "Doesn't God have the power to change even the most heartless man? We're taught in church that God's love can transform anyone."

"Anyone who is willing. Cassie, a lot of people are unwilling. My father, for instance, was a bully and a vicious man. He took pride in belittling people and making them feel hopeless."

"I'm sorry to hear that, Brandon."

He hadn't meant to open that can of worms, but now that he had, he intended to use the example as far as he dared. "Some people pride themselves in their cruelty, and my father was one of those people—especially where his family was concerned. I think Cyrus is one of those people too. There's just something evil about him."

"Well, I know I felt very uncomfortable with him, and even Pastor John said he didn't have a good feeling about Cyrus. He said his 'discernment would suggest he is less than sincere.'"

"I've always known Pastor John to have good discernment. God's Spirit sometimes warns us through intuition. If you felt uneasy and Pastor John discerned a problem, then I would caution you to be careful. What did Cyrus want with you in regard to amends?"

"I don't know, except that he wanted to apologize and tell me how sorry he was for making threats toward me." She thought for a moment. "He said Papa was a good man, and he was sorry to hear he'd died. I talked about the derailment and the army seeking Pancho Villa, but honestly, there was nothing else he intended toward me. Not that I know of, anyway."

"Well, hopefully he'll keep his distance. I don't like the idea of him being back in town."

"And you truly don't think he could change? That God has changed him?"

"Jesus said in the Bible that many will say He's their Lord, but He'll say, 'away from me, I never knew you.' That says to me that a lot of folks will claim to have gotten right with God. Maybe just for show or to make an impression on someone. It takes much more, as you know. It's a yielding of the heart and of our will. It's turning from sin with the help of Jesus. It's all about Him and not about us. We have to be willing to surrender our ways and stop sinning. Cyrus McCutchen never struck me as the kind of man who thought he was capable of doing wrong, much less that he needed to stop."

"But he does now, or at least he said as much."

"A man can say a lot of things. Like I said, my father was especially good at putting people in their place—the place he felt they belonged. If he appeared overly cruel and the wrong people witnessed it, he would have some excuse and apologize, but he never meant it."

"How can you be the judge of that?" Cassie sounded almost accusing.

"Because he told me so. He wanted me to be just like him. He had visions of me working at his side with the same cruel and vicious nature. I told him that wasn't who I was. I despised his bullying. Especially toward my mother."

"Your mother?"

Brandon nodded, feeling control of the conversation getting away from him. "It's enough to say that he was determined to be in charge of his family, and he would brook no question or challenge to his will."

"He sounds terrible."

"He was, and because of him, I've avoided romantic entanglements. I plan never to marry or have children. I don't want to turn into the type of man he was. He was my example for how to be a man—how to be a husband and father."

"But you spent a lot of years with my father as a better example, Brandon. Despite losing himself in sorrow after Mama passed, he was a good man."

"He was still a good man after that. He just wasn't able to show it to your sister and maybe not even to you. You represented his loss. I didn't. I was someone completely removed from losing his wife. Someone he didn't have to comfort."

Cassie nodded. "Surely a man can make his own decisions regarding right and wrong. You know that your father's ways were cruel, so avoid being that man. It would be a pity to miss out on love because of fear."

Brandon had said too much. He had never meant to confide these things in her. He had spoken on many occasions to her father and even Pastor John, but he couldn't expect Cassie to understand. She thought everyone capable of good. She even considered the possibility that Cyrus McCutchen had changed.

Her gentle nature and innocence wouldn't allow her to realize that some men enjoyed being evil.

"If you were going to be like your father, don't you imagine it would already show in how you treat those boys you work with? Wouldn't your handling of them be similar to your father's handling of you and his employees? I don't think you have to worry about such things, Brandon. You are a different man. You placed your trust in God and sought to become like Jesus. Your father obviously never did."

Brandon hadn't thought about it that way. He'd only seen the dangers of taking a wife and having a family. Even thinking of his father made him uneasy, and he hurried to change the subject.

"So Cyrus said he'd been hired back on?"

Cassie watched him for a moment, then nodded. "Yes, I don't know much more than that. He saw it as a means to make amends and pay them back. They didn't want his money, though. They said his time in jail was enough and that insurance had reimbursed them."

Brandon took another cookie. "Well, I suppose we'll learn soon enough if he has really changed. We could use more firemen. Some of the boys are thinking about studying for it and seeing if they can apprentice for the position, but it's not an easy job. It's more than just shoveling in coal or wood."

"More milk?" She glanced at his nearly empty glass.

"No, I probably shouldn't stay. I don't want to hurt your reputation, and I've been here all evening, alone with you."

"People know us, Brandon. They know you look at me as a sister." Cassie's tone seemed resigned. Had he somehow offended her with talk of his father? "I think my reputation is safe."

Brandon glanced toward the door, hoping Cassie had no idea of the battle raging within him. He didn't think of her as a sister at all, and the very idea raised such a protest in him that he nearly told her the truth of his feelings.

"Still, I'd better go." He shot up from the table and didn't even wait for her to respond. "Thanks for the cookies and milk. They were very good."

"Wait! I didn't get a chance to tell you about the letter I had from Melissa."

Delaying his exit, Brandon paused at the door. "I hope it was good."

"It was. She said she's been praying and thinking about our talk and doesn't want us to be estranged anymore. She wants me to come for a visit after Christmas and maybe consider staying."

"For how long?"

"Forever." Cassie smiled. "She said if I liked it in Denver, I could perhaps live with them and help her with the twins. After all, if I'm to be a spinster, I might as well do it somewhere with family around me."

Brandon felt a band tighten around his heart. He didn't want her to go live with her sister. He wanted her to stay here, where he could see her . . . talk to her.

"What are you going to tell her?" he asked.

Cassie met his gaze. "I told her of course I'd love to visit. I didn't promise anything more yet." She seemed to search his face for an answer to some unspoken question.

He nodded. "I suppose it would be good to visit." He tried not to stress the final word. The truth was, he didn't want her to go for any reason. He wanted her to remain in San Marcial. "Let me know when you plan to head out."

Cassie couldn't understand Brandon's reaction to her news. She gathered their dishes and went to the kitchen. He had been in a strange mood tonight. First, he startled her to teach her a lesson about locking up, then he seemed consumed by Cyrus McCutchen—certain he couldn't have changed.

It wasn't clear to Cassie that the man had changed, but she hadn't really known him. She remembered her father's comments against him. When they had worked together, Papa had always had negative things to say. Cyrus seemed not to care much for authority and made his feelings evident in his words and deeds.

*But he says he found peace with God.* She quickly washed up the dirty dishes, then went back to the living room to make a fire in the hearth.

Perhaps she'd speak more with Pastor John and Myrtle. They always offered wise counsel. Then again, she really had no need to concern herself with Cyrus. Brandon was the only one who mattered to her. He seemed terribly troubled about his own past.

The thought of his father's being a mean man who had no good feelings for his family made her sad. Brandon was such a quiet soul. He seldom seemed to take pleasure in anything, but when he did enjoy something, it pleased Cassie more than she could say.

Straightening, she replaced the poker and went to her typewriter. The mending could wait. She wanted to type up some of the stories she'd been told recently. She took out her journal and opened it to a story from a dear old man who once worked in the shops. He had described a flood that came over twenty years ago.

She rolled paper into the typewriter and began to type, but her mind refused to let go of Brandon's comments about his homelife. It was no wonder he never smiled. Things must have been very bad, especially for a child to witness.

The rhythmic clicking of the keys stopped as Cassie considered how she might convince Brandon that he wasn't like his father. If she couldn't convince him, then there was no hope for a future together. Maybe there wasn't, anyway. Maybe she'd only allowed herself to give life to a girlish desire. She'd always wanted to marry and have children.

Cassie put her elbows on the desk and planted her chin in her hands. What was she to do? She could either pursue Brandon DuBarko and convince him he was nothing like his father, or she could continue as a spinster and head to Denver to play auntie to her nieces.

"What should I do, Lord?" She knew what she wanted, but what did God want?

# 17

"You like your old job?" Juan asked Cyrus.

"Not much, but it gives me some inside knowledge. For instance, I know of two locations where they plan to add to the tracks or put in new lines."

"What good does that do us?" one of the other men questioned.

Cyrus looked at him and shook his head. "Think about it. We know where the section gangs will be working, so it will be easier to cause problems elsewhere. If I'm working for the railroad, you can be assured I will get information that will be beneficial to us. Meanwhile, you can continue causing problems."

"But tearing up track doesn't put money in our pockets, jefe, and it's hard work."

"I thought we all had something against the Santa Fe," Cyrus countered. "I thought you men wanted revenge. We're costing them time and money, and while it's certain there are those I wish to see die, I'm also looking for ways to damage the railroad more permanently. We need some derailments where people actually die. We need to scare the public and stress the dangers of riding the train. We need to do whatever we can to ruin the Santa Fe's great reputation."

The men nodded, but Cyrus could tell they weren't all that interested. Money was far more appealing. And frankly, his pockets were pretty empty too.

"There's also the payroll. That will be delivered on the first. I've already got plans for taking it."

"That'll take too long," one of the men replied. "I'm out of money now."

"We could go up north of San Marcial and steal horses," Juan offered. "There's a big *rancho* there where some of the best horses are bred and raised. We could sneak in and steal some of them away."

Cyrus shook his head. "You'd have to go pretty far away to sell them, and no doubt the law will get out word to all the big stockyards where you would have the best luck."

"We could take them to Mexico. I know some wealthy people down there who would be happy to buy them," one of the men offered. The others started talking amongst themselves, seeming to agree.

Cyrus shrugged. "If that's what you want to do, do it. I will keep rethinking our plans. We probably won't dare risk taking the payroll after a big roundup of top horses. The law will be looking out for such things, perhaps even doubling their deputies."

Maybe it was time to rethink everything. These men weren't all that loyal to him. They had no reason to be. When they'd teamed up, they had a common enemy, but now all they ever talked about was really big jobs that would pay out like the day of the opening of Elephant Butte Dam.

Perhaps the time to part company had come. They could go steal their horses, and Cyrus could exact his revenge on Brandon DuBarko. Just as he had on Bart Barton. Everyone was so certain he'd been killed in the derailment, but Cyrus and Bart knew differently. They knew the truth.

He relived the moments of that derailment over and over as

one of the best things to have ever happened. He could still see Barton struggling to get to his feet after being thrown clear. He was bleeding badly from a head wound. Dazed and confused, he was hardly able to stand.

Cyrus had ridden down to the accident from his hiding place. The train had been moving at a good clip, and when they'd hit the damaged rails, the first eight cars had followed the engine off the tracks.

He had smiled at the destruction. It was easy to find Barton and his fireman. The boy was already dead, but Barton seemed determined to live. Cyrus took care of that easily enough. He'd bashed the man's head with the butt of his rifle. It knocked him unconscious, allowing Cyrus time to pick up a nearby piece of debris with which to hit him again and again until he was certain Barton was dead. He threw the older man's body into the wreckage, then mounted his horse and left the scene.

"Jefe, are you listening?"

Cyrus looked up. "Sorry, what did you say?"

"I said the boys understand, and we'll wait for the payroll. We're heading out for lunch and wondered if you wanted to come."

"No, I'm on a freight train tonight. If all works out well, I'll be in San Marcial for Christmas services." He laughed and jumped down from the fence rail where he sat. "Let's meet up after Christmas here in El Paso. I'm on a freight headed here late on Christmas Day. If you need me sooner, you can get word to me in San Marcial."

He headed for the depot, the memory of Barton's death still on his mind. There was still Brandon DuBarko to get even with. Wouldn't it be lovely if he could die in the same manner his mentor did? Derailments were so spectacular . . . so destructive . . . so satisfying. Cyrus frowned. But it would be harder to get Brandon on a train. There would have to be a good reason. It would have to be done in such a way to send Brandon hurrying on the rails to save the day.

Cyrus smiled. Let him be a hero. A much loved, much admired, *dead* hero.

Christmas Eve services at church were everything Cassie had come to expect. The children sang a song about baby Jesus, John spoke on the benefits of Christ's gift to the world, and the congregation sang some of her favorite hymns. But in truth, Cassie hadn't allowed herself to think much about Christmas. The holiday had been horrible that first year after Mama died, and even sadder when Melissa went away and refused to return. Cassie and her father had done their best to keep up their spirits, but Christmas had always been hard. Now, with Papa passed on, Cassie had no one to share Christmas dinner with, much less a true heart of celebration.

She did have a gift for Brandon. Years ago, she remembered him speaking of a book he had enjoyed in college. He had told her father the title, and Cassie had written it down, thinking she might like to read the book herself. This year, she'd finally managed to get a copy of the first two volumes of *An Essay Concerning Human Understanding* by John Locke. She hoped it would surprise and please Brandon to know she cared enough to keep track of something he enjoyed.

Aside from that, she had managed to make some embroidered tea towels for Myrtle and Sarah, but otherwise she'd not really given the holiday any consideration. Now, with Christmas to be celebrated the following day, Cassie was thinking she might just as well stay in bed all day.

The congregation finished singing and remained standing for the pastor's final benediction. Cassie noted that Brandon was just a few rows ahead of her on the opposite side of the room. She had hoped to talk to him about stopping by so she could give him her present.

"Let us pray," Pastor John announced.

Cassie bowed her head but thought little of the prayer. It was possible she could cook something simple for Brandon and herself, if he had nowhere to go for Christmas. Usually by now, however, the invitations were out. She had counted on Myrtle to invite her over, but they were catching a train immediately after the services on Christmas morning.

It would be all right. She could manage alone. She did it all the time, and this wasn't going to defeat her. She would offer an invitation to Brandon and any of the young men who'd helped her after the accident. She thought Brandon had said something about not all of them getting to go home for the holidays.

"Cassie?" Sarah nudged her. "Are you all right?"

Looking up, Cassie could see that the congregation was already leaving the sanctuary. "Yes." She smiled, feeling a little embarrassed. "I'm afraid my thoughts were sidetracked."

Sarah laughed. "It's not a problem, I was just worried about you. I know this is your first year alone for Christmas. We were hoping you might come for dinner tomorrow. We're going to invite Brandon too."

"I was planning to invite him as well as the boys who caused my accident. We've all grown quite close. Most of them are heading home, but Brandon mentioned some of them couldn't. I thought maybe I could fix a small ham. A couple of the men from the Santa Fe brought me one last week, and I baked it yesterday. It would be easy enough to reheat."

"Well, if you change your mind and want to join us for dinner, you'd be more than welcome. We'll eat at noon."

"Thank you so much." Cassie gave Sarah a hug, then pulled back and handed her a package. "Merry Christmas."

"Oh, Cassie, how sweet. I have something for you too. I'll bring it by tomorrow."

"Sounds good." Cassie turned to gather her things and was surprised to find Brandon waiting for her.

"Do you need help with anything?" he asked.

"No, but I'm glad you waited. I want to invite you to share Christmas dinner with me, and to bring any of the boys who couldn't make it home. It won't be a fancy celebration, but I have a ham and plan to bake a couple of pies."

"Sounds good. I'll let them know. What time would you want us there?"

"Noon would be fine. That way if you want to sleep late, you can."

Brandon helped her with her coat. It had turned cold, and many of the old-timers suggested they would see snow this year. Maybe not for Christmas but probably soon after. Cassie had been glad for her old wool coat, even though it had seen better days. She hoped no one would notice the worn edges of the cuffs and collar.

Cassie spied Myrtle. "I need to give Myrtle her gift. I'll see you tomorrow."

Christmas morning services were short and full of encouragement. The children were especially anxious to get home to open presents, so Pastor John took pity on them and kept things brief. Cassie had given Myrtle her gift the night before, as well as Sarah, so she had nothing more to concern herself with except feeding Brandon.

She exchanged words with him and learned that two of the boys might come with him, but they might not. Some of their family hoped to come up on the morning train, and he wouldn't know for sure until after that. Cassie assured him it didn't matter. She had more than enough food.

When she got home, she began preparations. She pulled her

best tablecloth from the drawer and spread it across her small table. Next, she built up the fire in the stove and waited for it to get hot. She hummed some of the Christmas carols they'd sung at church and did her best to put herself into a celebratory mood. She didn't feel much like celebrating, but for Brandon's sake and that of the others, she would do her best.

She had baked two pies the night before. One was pecan and the other custard. She knew Brandon was very fond of both. She pulled them from the icebox and placed them on the counter to warm to room temperature.

When the stove was finally warm enough, the ham went into the oven. Cassie basted it faithfully every half hour with a honey mixture she'd made from her mother's recipe. While that baked, she boiled potatoes and opened a can of green beans.

While the food cooked, she pulled dinner rolls from the warmer and placed them in a large bowl. She glanced around to see what else she might need to do. She noted the cloth-covered table empty of dishes and silver, but she wanted to see exactly how many showed up for dinner before setting the places.

A knock on the door sent Cassie's gaze to the clock on her mantel. It was ten minutes till twelve. Gracious, but the time had flown by. She wiped her hands on her apron and went to see if it was Brandon. Instead, she was surprised to find Sarah with a basket of goodies.

"Merry Christmas!"

"Oh my! How wonderful." Cassie opened the door to invite her in.

"I can't stay. I hope you enjoy this. I baked it all. There are cookies and brownies, and some empanadas my neighbor taught me to make. Oh, and some candy."

"It sounds amazing. I didn't do any holiday baking this year. Well, with exception to the two pies for dinner today."

Sarah winked. "Who knows, maybe you'll have a husband by this time next year."

185

Cassie didn't want to argue that this probably wasn't going to happen. She shrugged. "Could be."

They heard the gate open behind Sarah and turned to see Brandon coming up the path. He was alone.

"Merry Christmas, Brandon," Sarah said with a bit of laughter in her voice. "I was just bringing Cassie a basket of treats for Christmas. I'm sure she'll share with you if you ask her nicely." She giggled again and started past him and down the walk.

Cassie rolled her eyes and headed into the house with the basket. "Make yourself at home. Are the boys coming?"

"No, their families made it in. They're going to meet up at Roberto's home. His family has plenty of room, they said, and everyone's going to celebrate together after Mass."

"How nice. Well, I guess it'll just be you and me." She heard Brandon close the door and glanced over her shoulder. "Everything is just about ready. I still need to set the table."

"Let me take that basket. I can put it on your desk."

"Thank you." Cassie hurried to get the place settings, then she dished up the hot food and brought it to the table. "It's nothing special."

"It's special to me. I didn't have to cook it. We'd both be in trouble if I did." Normally, people might laugh at this, but Brandon maintained a serious expression and just shrugged.

She smiled just the same. "Go ahead and take your seat. I'll get the coffee and rolls."

When she returned, he was in his usual place. He'd sat there for years with her father. She had always thought of it as his place. He had so long been a part of her life that it didn't seem at all strange to have him here. It seemed right.

"Would you offer the blessing?"

"Of course," Brandon replied and immediately began praying. "Father, we thank you for Christmas and the blessing of a savior for sinful men. We praise you for your mercy and goodness and for the food we are about to eat. Bless the hands that prepared it, in Jesus' name, amen."

"Amen." Cassie smiled and took a dinner roll from the bowl while Brandon began to slice the ham.

"Pass your dish, and I'll serve you." He held up a large slice of ham.

"Not that big, please. I want to have room for pie." She laughed. "I gave serious thought to starting with dessert. We have pecan and custard pie."

He put the big piece of meat on his plate and sliced her a smaller portion. "I'll have room whether it comes at the end or the beginning. Your pies are delicious, and I wouldn't miss out for all the world."

"I thought the services yesterday and today were very nice," Cassie said, passing the potatoes.

"They were indeed." He helped himself to the potatoes and the green beans.

Finally, they were served and began to eat. For a long while, neither said a word. Cassie wanted to ask Brandon questions about their last conversation—about his family in particular. He knew all of the details of her family. He'd been there for all the important happenings, but she knew so little about him.

"Did you have Christmas dinners with family when you were a boy?"

He stopped with a forkful of potatoes halfway to his mouth. "We celebrated Christmas, if that's what you're asking."

"I just wondered if you had family gathered around. Grandparents and cousins, extended family besides just your mother and father. I know you're an only child, but I wondered if there were others."

"No, just us." He went back to eating.

Cassie cut her ham and tried to think how best to approach the matter. Maybe just being completely honest about it was the way to address it.

"You talked about your father's . . . meanness. I just wondered how your family celebrated Christmas."

"We had some festive decorations, even a party. My father was big on impressing society. My mother loved Christmas. She loved the snow when we had it and enjoyed the holiday spirit." Brandon never looked up but focused on buttering a roll.

"Well, I'm glad you had at least that much. We always made merry. My mother and father loved to amuse us children. They would celebrate the twelve days of Christmas. Every day, starting with Christmas, we had special stories about Jesus. First, they would start with the prophecies of His birth. My mother's father was a theologian, and he knew all sorts of interesting things. He would come and tell us all the wonderful stories about Jesus from the Bible."

Brandon paused and looked up as she continued.

"We had a spirit of merriment and of thanksgiving. Every day, Mama made some special treat to have with our teachings. We learned about the way everyone had to go back to the city of their ancestors and register. We learned about the way the shepherds took care of their animals and about the wise men. We celebrated every day from Christmas to Epiphany. It was amazing and wonderful. After my grandfather died, however, we mostly just celebrated Christmas and sometimes talked about all the other stuff. But I'll always remember those stories Grandpa told."

"Sounds nice. It really does. I loved learning in school about various traditions and ways that people celebrate Christmas," Brandon admitted.

"I remember when you used to talk to Papa about your days at college. It sounded like you really enjoyed learning."

"I did. I like what I do now too, but back then, getting away to school was a blessing."

"Because of your father?" She felt it was the perfect way to direct the conversation back to the things Brandon had talked about before. "Did he not like having you in school?"

Brandon ate for a moment, then took a long sip from his coffee cup. When he finished, he picked up his knife and fork as if he wouldn't speak of it, then finally answered. "He loved learning. He was the one who insisted I go to college as soon as I finished my secondary studies. I started university at sixteen."

"That doesn't surprise me." Cassie smiled. "You're very smart. Why did you quit?"

Brandon fixed his gaze on her. "Something happened when I was eighteen, and I had to."

"Can you tell me about it? I know it must have meant a lot to you."

"Remember when I talked about God not being able to fix some things? My family was one of those things. In order to fix a thing, everyone has to be willing. They have to recognize something is broken and needs to be fixed. My father didn't think there was anything wrong with our family."

Brandon put down his knife and fork again. Cassie could see by the look on his face that the topic was giving him great pain.

"We don't have to talk about it if you don't want to."

"I've never wanted to. I've always wished I could just forget it all. The pain, the misery . . . but it's my inheritance. The legacy left me by a heartless man who didn't care about the people he hurt."

Brandon threw his napkin on the table. "I'm sorry. I need to go." He got up and grabbed his hat and coat. He looked at Cassie, who remained sitting, too shocked to move. "I'm really sorry."

He left, and Cassie could only sit there, staring at the door. She felt terrible. She hadn't meant to hurt him. She just wanted to better understand him.

After a lot of contemplation, Cassie gathered up the dishes and food and put everything away. Christmas was already difficult, and now it had become impossibly painful. She built up the fire and sat in front of it to pray aloud.

"Father, you know it wasn't my heart to hurt Brandon. I suppose I was just too nosy, too curious. I thought if I knew more about him it would be . . . good. Even helpful. I didn't realize or stop to think that by prodding with all of my questions, I could be making his life worse. Please forgive me and help Brandon to forgive me as well." She wiped her eyes as tears came.

"I miss my family, Father. I miss them more than I could ever let myself admit, and now I've even pushed away the man I love."

She stopped. Did she love him? Wasn't that the question she'd been asking herself for weeks? Yet she had just confessed to God that she did, so it must be true. That made her cry all the more. She drew her knees up, wrapped her arms around them, and cried great sobs. She mourned her mother and father, mourned the troubles she had with her sister, mourned the love she might have had.

"Cassie."

She startled at the sound of Brandon's voice. She looked up to find he'd returned and stood just inside the front door.

She wiped her face with the back of her sleeve. "Sorry. I was just having a moment."

"I'm part of the reason for that, and I'm sorry. I'd like to say I can make it better, but I can't. I am, however, going to tell you everything, and then maybe you'll understand. That is . . . if you'll let me."

She nodded and got to her feet. "Of course. Do you want to sit here by the fire or at the table so you can finish your meal?"

"I'll join you where you are." He closed the door and crossed to the sofa. He studied her for a moment. He seemed to be wrestling with something.

"Please sit." She reclaimed her seat and waited for him to speak.

"My life at home wasn't just a matter of vicious words," he finally began. "My father was quite physical with my mother and me. He often gave me the back of his hand or hit me with a paddle. By the time I was sixteen, he realized I was too big for such punishments and changed his strategy. He told me I was nearly a man, and as such I needed to learn to fight back. He sometimes challenged me to strike him. Of course, I had no heart for it. I just wanted the violence to end. I didn't realize he was hitting my mother until I was nearly fourteen. I found out about it from the maid. When I came home from school one day, she had a bruise on her cheek and told me my father had done that and given my mother worse. I was horrified. I knew he hit me, but I had no idea he hit women."

He paused for several minutes, then began again. "I learned quickly that he had always been that way, and his father had been that way as well. Women were nothing more than property to command, as far as he was concerned. I tried to stop him once, when I was home from college, but instead he forced me to watch him punish my mother and say nothing, saying I was nearly a man and needed to learn to act like one."

"Oh, Brandon, I'm so sorry."

"I told him to stop. I told him I knew of no other man who would treat a woman, much less his wife, with such cruelty. He told me I was just naïve. That all men acted in this manner behind the closed doors of their homes. It made me sick."

"I can well imagine." She had never considered such people even existed. What a horrible thing for a boy to endure.

"I'm going to tell you something I've only ever shared with your father. I'm scarcely able to admit it, but you need to understand." His expression was one of pure agony.

"I want to know it all," Cassie said.

He looked at the fire. "I came home from university at the start of summer. I had just turned eighteen and had plans to travel abroad with some friends who were quite well placed socially.

My father was delighted. As a newspaper man, it wasn't likely that his son would rub elbows with Vanderbilts and Rockefellers, but I was enjoying the company of the very wealthy, and he was pleased and came up with the money for me to go to Europe in first-class service.

"I was to leave in just a couple of days but wanted to see my mother before I left. That night at dinner, things became difficult. Mother made a comment about worrying I would come to some sort of harm while traveling. My father began to criticize her for speaking. Soon he was shouting at her furiously. I got up to tend the dining room fire and heard my mother rise. She was crying, and the next thing I knew, my father had her up against the wall and was choking the life out of her. I couldn't call for the servants to help because they'd gone for the evening. I tried to get my father away from her, but as I approached, begging him to stop, he knocked me to the floor and started strangling her again."

"Oh, Brandon, how terrible." Cassie could see it all in her mind. How in the world could such violence be allowed to go on?

"I realized that I still had the fireplace poker in my hand, and in my anger and hatred of him, I raised it and brought it down on the back of his head."

Her hand flew to her mouth. She gasped, and Brandon turned to look at her.

"I killed my father. I dropped the poker and stood there, stunned, until my mother sent me for the doctor. When I came home, I ran to my room, unable to deal with anyone. I was so angry. I threw things in a rage. I knocked a hole in the wall. I realized I was just like him. I was just like the man I had hated for so long."

"No! No, you weren't!" Cassie took his hand. "You weren't. You were saving your mother."

"You don't understand. I wanted him to die."

192

"But not because you set out to see him dead. You were defending your mother. He would have killed her."

"Yes, he would have. He was so lost in his rage, and I was too."

"God knows what you felt in your heart. He knows the truth. You aren't a killer any more than I am, Brandon." She squeezed his hand. "What did my father say about it?"

Brandon shook his head and looked at the fire. "He said the same thing."

"See, that is confirmation. You didn't set out to commit murder, and obviously the law didn't think so either. You weren't sent to jail for it."

"No." He sat in silence for a long time. "I figured the police would come for me, so I just sat in my room, waiting. I never saw my father's body again, and the police never came. The doctor took care of everything, and we had a private funeral, despite my father's being a public figure."

"Then you need to rid yourself of the past, Brandon. Give this burden to God, and let yourself be forgiven. I certainly cannot hold such a thing against you. Let's put it all aside and forget about it. It's still Christmas." She let go of his hand. "Don't let the past rob you of the present . . . the future. Brandon, you are a wonderful man."

"But I never paid for what I did. No one ever knew what I did."

She came closer. "My father knew and didn't care, and now I know, and I don't care either. You had a reason for what you did. You saved your mother's life, and as far as I'm concerned, you are a hero."

# 18

Cassie typed the final page of her collection of stories and pulled the sheet from the typewriter to look it over. She was pleased and planned to talk to someone in the Santa Fe office as to what she might do next. She had no idea how to go about getting it put into book form. She put the page with the rest of the manuscript and smiled at the thick pile of papers. Tying the entire stack with a piece of twine, Cassie nodded in satisfaction.

She put the manuscript away and went to tend to her sewing. She had been contemplating how to manage all of this and still go to Denver to see Melissa. She knew there were several other women who could take on her clients, but they might not be so willing to give them back. Worse still, the clients might find they preferred the other seamstresses. This was Cassie's only means of making a living, and if she didn't prove available and faithful, it could lead to her ruination.

Of course, Melissa had spoken about having Cassie come live with them in Denver. She could help with the children, and Melissa might even be willing to hire her on as their full-time nanny. That relieved her worry a bit. It didn't, however, make the pain in her heart lessen. She hadn't seen Brandon since Christmas. He'd said he had work on another part of the division line. She knew that was no doubt true, but still there hadn't been any word at all. Even the young men who worked with him were gone.

It was a worry to imagine Brandon out there somewhere, bearing up under the weight of his past. She had hoped his telling her the truth would make it possible to let go of the nightmarish feelings he had been forced to live with. Imagine having to kill one parent in order to save the other. The thought was almost more than Cassie could fathom. Her parents had always been so loving and kind to each other. It was the kind of relationship Cassie had hoped she might one day find. She had no way of knowing her mother would die young and Cassie would need to take charge of her little sister and help her father through his time of mourning.

All her life, it seemed Cassie had put others first, and she couldn't even say she set out to do it that way. It was more or less imposed upon her, and she let it happen. But that was what God wanted a good Christian to do, wasn't it?

She didn't regret taking care of her father and sister. Putting them first had made her feel needed, and it was one way she could show them love. No, it wasn't wrong to have put others first. In so many ways, it had blessed her.

Picking up a pile of clean shirts, Cassie went to the table and sorted them into stacks based on which ones needed the most work. The men knew to have the clothes washed before showing up to her place with their request for repairs. Cassie made it clear she wouldn't work on dirty clothes.

She had pinned the name of the owner on each collar so she would know whom to return the articles to. This system not only made it easy to return the shirts, but also allowed her to mark each name tag with how much she would charge for that particular shirt's repair. She had it all arranged in such a way that when she finished with the sewing, she could iron the shirt and then ready it for return. With trousers and overalls, it was the same way. Once in a while, she got an order to make a new dress for one of the town's ladies. That was always quite pleasurable. Making something new and pretty allowed Cassie to be creative.

The wind blew against her windows, rattling them something fierce. The day had turned quite blustery, and Cassie wondered if they might get a blizzard. They'd had them before. At nearly forty-four hundred feet in elevation, San Marcial could sport all types of weather. She rubbed her arms and went to find her sweater. The thick wool immediately helped warm her. Cassie stopped to peer out the front window. Clouds had gathered, and streets were empty. No one wanted to be out in this weather.

She saw to the fire and then took up her sewing basket and went to the table once again. Sewing usually calmed her, but with the threat of a storm and not knowing whether Brandon was safe, she found no comfort in her duties.

By the time the mantel clock chimed six, Cassie decided it was time to put away her sewing and eat something for supper. She'd kept the stove hot just to help warm the house and allow for ready coffee, so it was easy to heat up the soup she'd made the day before. Myrtle had shared a nice piece of roast beef with her, and Cassie had chopped it up to add to an oxtail bone broth. She'd seasoned the rich soup with onion and celery, then added potatoes, carrots, corn, and green beans. It was delicious, if she did say so herself.

While the soup reheated, she whipped up a batch of corn bread and put that to baking. The aroma of the food made the house smell so good—so homey. And yet, it didn't feel like home anymore.

She looked at the empty table and remembered when it had been full with her family. She might live in another house, but having the family's old furniture around at least allowed Cassie to feel a tiny bit of their presence. Her mother had loved this table and chairs and polished them regularly. Cassie hadn't been as faithful but made herself a promise to see to it as soon as possible.

The sound of knocking startled Cassie, but as it grew more insistent, she worried that someone was in trouble. She hurried to open the door and found Brandon. He swept her into his arms and pushed her backward, then dropped his hold and battled the door. Once it was in place, he turned to face her.

"Sorry about my entry. I wasn't sure I could manage that wind any other way."

Cassie was still stunned by the feeling of being in his arms. She shook her head and met his gaze. "It's not a problem. I'm glad to see you. It's been far too long, and I was starting to worry about you, especially given the weather."

"We've had a lot of work. We barely got into town before the snow started."

She noticed the bits of snow on his coat. "Here, let me take that."

He pulled off the coat, revealing he'd hidden his hat inside. He handed the coat to Cassie and put the hat on a nearby table. "Sorry it's wet."

"It's not a problem." She gave it a little shake over the entry-way rug, then hung it on the coat tree. "Supper's nearly ready. Are you hungry?"

"I am, and it smells wonderful."

Cassie smiled. He looked so handsome with his wavy brown hair dampened by the storm. His blue eyes seemed to almost twinkle. She thought she saw a hint of a smile on his lips.

She wondered if he realized what she was thinking and suddenly felt embarrassed. "Uh, well, come on to the table. The corn bread should be done by now."

She hurried to the stove and pulled the corn bread from the oven. It was perfectly golden brown. She set it aside to cool and turned back to stir the soup. Sampling the broth, she was pleased with the flavor and glad that she'd made such a big pot.

The table was soon set for two and the food ready for eating. Cassie bowed her head, knowing Brandon would pray without being asked. He did, and it wasn't long until they were talking about his last two weeks and warming their insides with hot soup.

"We built an entire new line of track. The boys are getting so good at it that they hardly need any instruction. They're some of the best workers I've ever had."

"They seem to pay attention to details. Even when they were helping here, they were that way."

"I agree. You can almost always tell how men are going to be as workers within the first few hours. They always show themselves to have some attitude toward the job one way or another. All of these young men were glad to learn and eager to do what was asked of them. And they've become fast friends. They have a true spirit of unity."

Cassie was determined not to bring up the past or anything they'd spoken of related to Brandon and his father. But to her surprise, Brandon brought it up as he started in on his second bowl of soup.

"I want to thank you for not judging me too harshly. Telling you about what happened with my father was, strangely enough, a comfort to me. I didn't realize it completely until later, but it did help, and I wanted you to know that."

"I'm glad. I thought it helped me to better understand you. Why you're always so serious and never seem happy."

"I'm happy at times, but with that hanging around my neck like a millstone, it's hard to show it. At least now you know the truth."

The wind died down, and the silence it left behind was almost startling.

Cassie went to the window, but it was too dark to see much. "I think it's still snowing."

Brandon said nothing as he continued to eat. Cassie wished she could speak her heart. Tell him she had fallen in love with him and that she didn't care how many people he'd had to kill. Well, she supposed that wasn't true, but in the case of protecting his mother, she still saw it as the right thing to do. At least, it was right to intercede, and she found it hard to believe that Brandon had really wanted to end his father's life.

Just then she remembered the Christmas gift she still had for him. She went to her bedroom and fetched it from the bottom drawer of her dresser. She'd managed to wrap it and tie it with a green bow. It looked so festive that she hoped it might cheer Brandon.

"I forgot to give this to you when you were here at Christmas." She placed the gift on the table beside him.

Brandon put down his spoon and picked up the present. He undid the ribbon and opened the wrapping. His eyes widened at the sight of the title. "Cassie, how did you know?"

She laughed with delight. "I remembered you telling Papa how much you enjoyed reading this at the university. I wrote down the title and have been trying to find a copy for some time. I finally located a bookstore in California that took special orders and asked them to keep an eye open should they have any copies, and they finally did. Volumes one and two. I hope you'll enjoy it."

He looked at her with such a tender expression that Cassie sank to her chair, feeling weak in the knees.

"I don't know what to say. This is . . . well, it touches me that you remembered. I don't think I've ever known anyone like you."

Cassie wasn't sure what to say. A part of her wanted to break into a speech about how much she cared about him. The other part demanded her silence, lest she reveal her feelings and have them rejected.

"I'm glad you like it."

"I do. Very much." He put the book aside and fumbled in his pockets for something. After a moment, he produced a small box, the kind jewelry stores often used.

Cassie felt her mouth go dry. Had he bought her a ring? Were his feelings for her the same as hers for him?

"I hope you like it."

She reached out with trembling hands.

Brandon noticed and frowned. "Looks like we'd better stoke up the fire. You're cold."

Taking the box, Cassie could only nod. Brandon went to put wood on the fire, so she waited for him to return before opening her gift. When he was reseated, she drew a deep breath and lifted the box's lid.

Inside was a beautiful cameo—ivory carved against some sort of coral-colored stone. "It's . . . it's beautiful." She hoped her disappointment wasn't evident.

"I know you don't wear much jewelry, but you have that one pretty blouse with the high neck—you know, the one you wear to church sometimes?"

She nodded and pretended to examine the brooch. "I do. It will work perfectly with that." Finally, she managed to put her feelings in place and looked up with a smile. "Thank you, Brandon. It's lovely, and I will cherish it always."

He went back to eating, seeming quite satisfied with the turn of events. Cassie wondered if he had any idea of her feelings.

"I have some canned peaches, if you'd like dessert. I can pour cream over them."

"I'd just as soon have another bowl of soup. I can't remember when anything tasted quite this good."

Cassie was pleased he had enjoyed the soup, but she needed to get away from him for at least a few minutes.

"You go right ahead. I'm going to put this brooch away." She took the pin and went to her bedroom. She sat on the edge of the bed and heaved a sigh. Opening the box again, she stared at the cameo, still wishing it had been a ring—an engagement or wedding ring would have suited her just fine.

"Why couldn't he love me?" she whispered. "Love me as I love him?"

Knocking sounded at her front door, and Cassie regained her composure and put the box on her dresser. She smoothed her skirt and went to see who had come. By the time she got there, Brandon was staring down Cyrus McCutchen as if there was about to be a fight.

"Mr. McCutchen, what brings you here today?" she asked.

His narrow-eyed gaze relaxed a bit as he looked at Cassie. "I'm sorry. It seems I've interrupted something."

"Brandon's just sharing my supper table."

"That's what I was coming to see you about. I thought per-haps I could take you to dinner again."

Cassie shook her head. "I'm sorry, but no, I'm not inter-ested." She felt awkward with the two men staring at each other and then casting glances at her. "Uh, you could join us."

She hated making the offer the minute she spoke it, but thankfully, Cyrus had no desire to share Brandon's company. That much was clear. "That's all right. I'll just head over to the Harvey House. Thanks anyway." He turned to go without another word.

"Why would he come here?" Brandon asked when he had shut the door.

"I have no idea." Cassie went back to the table to collect her dishes. "I suppose the same reason other men ask me to dinner."

Brandon closed the door. "They what?"

Cassie wanted to laugh at the tone in his voice. If she wasn't mistaken, he totally disapproved.

"Well, you aren't the only one to seek my company for sup-per. Sometimes even the boys stop by. Honestly, Brandon, you look like someone just stepped on your toes."

He sat down, frowning, and picked up his spoon. For a minute, he moved it around the nearly empty bowl and offered no reply.

She took her dishes to the kitchen, then returned to find him still sitting that way. "Aren't you going to have another bowl of soup?"

"No . . . I guess I'm not as hungry as I thought."

"What's wrong?"

"I don't like McCutchen." He finally looked up. "I don't trust him."

"I don't either, if that helps." She sat back down. "I neither trust him nor like him."

"But you did go with him to dinner that one night."

"Yes, and I explained that was so I didn't feel obligated to invite him into my house." Cassie decided enough was enough. "If I'm not mistaken, I hear more jealousy than disapproval in your voice."

"I totally disapprove. Jealousy has nothing to do with it," he countered much too quickly. "Look, I just have my concerns. Someone mentioned to me that they think Cyrus had something to do with your father's death."

"What?" Cassie leaned forward, not even trying to hide her surprise. "What are you saying? Papa's train derailed."

"Yes, and it's not that hard to cause such a thing."

Her eyes widened. "You think Cyrus did something to the line that caused my father's train to derail."

"It's possible." He eased back in his seat. "I wasn't going to say anything to you until I knew something more. One of the brakemen and I were talking. He mentioned how odd it was that McCutchen was working again for the railroad. He said he knew the man hated the Santa Fe, and shortly after getting out of prison in March, he was heard boasting that he would do whatever it took to punish everyone responsible for seeing him in jail. Of course, he was drunk at the time and seemed to have a gang of men hanging on his every word. It could have just been him showing off, but I've had my concerns since your father's accident."

"I knew you wondered about the man on the hilltop, but I thought you decided that was one of Villa's men left behind to witness the accident's destruction."

"I said it was a possibility. It's a difficult topic. Burdening you with the details would have been cruel. I went out to the derailment right after it happened. I was expected to make any needed repairs to the line as another group cleared the debris and got the locomotive and cars upright again." He paused and shook his head. "There were a lot of people there. Some from the Santa Fe offices—folks trying to determine what had happened. Others were there to clear the tracks, and some were newspaper folks."

"You should have told me."

"Why?" His expression suggested confusion.

"Well . . . I don't know. I guess I would have liked to hear firsthand what had happened."

"I came and told you when we knew."

"Yes, but . . . well, I guess I would have liked to know more. Losing Papa like that was something that I always knew was possible, but I still felt overwhelmed, not knowing how it happened exactly. But that still doesn't explain why you think Cyrus was involved."

"The more I think about the man I saw up on the hillside, the more I'm convinced it was him. He just sat there, watching. I couldn't see for sure that it was Cyrus, but later, when I went up to see if the man was still there, I found an empty cigarette package. The same brand of Mexican cigarettes McCutchen always smoked. It was like a calling card, but I couldn't prove that it had belonged to him."

Cassie tried to take it all in. "What does it mean that he's back now, working for the railroad? He says he's making peace with God and those he's wronged."

"He hasn't come to make peace with me. He just had the perfect opportunity, yet he said nothing."

"Maybe he was embarrassed."

"Don't make excuses for him, Cassie. He doesn't deserve your pity. If I were you, I'd be very careful if he shows up again. I don't trust him. Not at all."

"You think he's still seeking revenge, don't you?" She swallowed the lump in her throat, but it refused to diminish.

"I think it's a good possibility, and I think we'd better watch our backs."

# 19

We still have no money, jefe. Some of the men have already headed south."

"I can see that for myself," Cyrus said. He knew they were angry. "I can't help that they brought the payroll in early because of the holidays. I had no way of finding out until it was too late. That doesn't mean we can't take the payroll on the first of next month."

"It does if it means waiting around without any money in our pockets," one of the other men said, slamming down his beer. "I've waited all I'm waiting. We did what we could to wreak havoc on the railroad, but we need money."

Another man piped up. "You have a paycheck from the railroad. We have nothing."

This made Cyrus mad. "Yes, and I'm working my backside off for that paycheck. Why don't you all take jobs until we can get that payroll? Then everyone will have a paycheck." He narrowed his eyes. "You obviously have no confidence in me, so just go your own way."

"Now, jefe, no one wants to leave who hasn't already gone."

"Good. I'll help you finish destroying the track near the mile marker we agreed on. After that, I don't care what you do. Just keep away from San Marcial. We need to be welcomed here without trouble from the law." Cyrus picked up his coat. "Come to the pool hall in San Marcial on the twentieth of the month if you want to help with the payroll." He fixed each man with a hard stare. "If you don't want to be a part of it—don't come."

He left the bar feeling mad enough to kill something . . . or someone. His plans were to kill Barton and DuBarko and be done with it. That was the only reason he'd come back to San Marcial. Now it seemed things were falling apart, and he'd never be able to manage what he'd come to do.

"I won't leave him alive," Cyrus muttered under his breath. "I won't."

The desert landscape was patchy, with a light covering of snow. Brandon inspected the rail work the boys had done and gave Javier a nod of approval. "This is perfect. You did excellent work. You fellas have learned fast."

"We had a good teacher, Boss." Javier grinned. "What's next?"

"We'll head back to San Marcial. Load up everything on the handcar." Brandon let Javier instruct the others. He'd become a natural leader, and Brandon knew in time he could recommend him for a leadership position.

Walking to where he'd left his things, Brandon spied something lying against the rail and reached down to pick it up. The empty package sent a chill up his spine. It was the same Mexican cigarettes he'd found the day of Bart's derailment. The same brand Cyrus McCutchen smoked. Could Cyrus be behind the destruction of the rail lines? Behind Bart's death?

*Don't be foolish. A lot of folks smoke these cigarettes.* He chided himself for jumping the gun. After all, Pancho Villa himself might very well smoke these cigarettes. He stuffed the empty package into his coat pocket.

"Come on, boys, let's get back to town and find a fire to sit in front of and thaw out."

The boys took turns pumping the handle to move the car, while the others balanced themselves on the edge of the platform and kept the tools from sliding off. It was only about eight miles to San Marcial, but by the time they got there, everyone except Brandon had their turn at the pump.

Once they were in the shop yards, Brandon instructed them to put things away and meet up with him at the usual place before they left for the day. Section hands kept all sorts of strange hours, especially with the way things were these days. Having marauders do their worst to interrupt train travel had the boys working around the clock to ensure the trains could run on time.

Brandon turned in the work order with notes as to what he had done and waited to see if there were further instructions.

When Bud came from his office, Brandon feared something was terribly wrong. He squared his shoulders and waited.

"We've got good news. There are going to be soldiers patrolling the track from now on. They will be placed along the line in teams of two. One will come from each end of the stretch they're assigned to. Each stretch will probably run eight to ten miles so they can reach either a water station or an actual town."

"That is good news. It's hard to imagine too much damage could be done with a guard like that on the job."

"We thought the same. The government finally decided, with us facing war, that the railroad is too important to lose. It's in the interest of national security to keep the rails up and running. They have a new interest in the lines along the border."

"They should." Brandon glanced around. "Is there anything else we need to do before I release the men? They've put in a lot of overtime."

"No, I think we're in a good place for them to have a couple of days off. Tell them to check in, though. Something might happen, despite the army's help. We'll have someone inspecting each stretch every day. I'll be in touch if we need something. See you Monday."

"Will do." Brandon knew there was always something the railroad could put them to work doing, but he was glad they recognized his crew had worked hard and deserved time off.

Brandon walked away, thinking of Cassie. After sharing the good news with the boys, he made his way to her house and knocked on the door. When no one came, he tried the handle. The door was locked.

"At least she's listening to me."

He started for his own place but saw Pastor John sweeping snow from his sidewalk. The older man gave a wave.

"Brandon, got time for a cup of coffee?"

"Sure, I was just going home to make a pot."

"Well, mine's already on the stove, keeping warm. You look frozen to the bone."

Brandon followed the pastor around the house to the back door. "I am. Been on the line for the past week."

"More damage to the rails?"

"I'm afraid so. I'm not sure we'll have to worry about it for long, though. The army is gonna start riding the line. The railroad is now an important national interest."

John took Brandon's coat and hung it on a peg alongside his own. Brandon took off his wool cap and stuffed it in the coat pocket before following John to the kitchen. The warmth of the stove felt amazing.

"I hope I'm not imposing."

John was already pulling down mugs for the coffee. "Not at all. The ladies are all gathered somewhere working on a quilt. I'm here alone."

"That must be why Cassie wasn't home."

"You're rather fond of her, aren't you?"

Brandon looked away, embarrassed by the question. "I . . . well, I suppose I am."

"It's nothing to be embarrassed by, son. Falling in love is the way God designed it. It's not good for man to be alone." John poured the coffee, then handed Brandon one of the cups. "We can sit in the living room in front of the fire so you can get warm."

"Thanks." Brandon waited until John had his cup of coffee, then followed him from the kitchen and dining room into the front room. True to his word, there was a nice large fire blazing in the hearth.

Brandon took a seat in one of the chairs by the fireplace. The heat felt so good as it penetrated his weary muscles.

"So why haven't you proposed to our Cassie yet?"

Brandon nearly choked on his coffee, which only made Pastor John laugh.

"I guess I've touched on a delicate subject."

Brandon steadied his cup and looked up to find John watching him. "I . . . I'm not sure. I mean, that is to say . . ."

"Good grief, man, we all know you care for her. You watch over her like she's a prize hog." John paused and shook his head. "That doesn't sound quite right, but you know what I mean. You care a lot about her."

"I promised her father I'd look out for her if anything happened to him."

"I think this is more than that."

Brandon set his coffee aside and drew a deep breath. He might as well be honest. John was a man of God and Brandon's own pastor. "It is more than that, but I don't feel like I can admit it."

"Why not? It's clear she has feelings for you."

"It is?"

John laughed. "For a man who has both life smarts and book smarts, I expected more out of you. Myrtle tells me she talks about you all the time. She never goes out with other men or has them to dinner at her place. Well, she did go to the Harvey House once with Cyrus McCutchen, but she didn't leave with him. I walked her home."

Brandon nodded. "I remember. I was in her house when you did. I'd been after her to lock her door, since there'd been a lot of thefts reported. She kept forgetting, so I went into her house and waited for her to come home. I saw from the streetlight that it was you who was with her. It liked to scare the wits right out of her when she came inside and found me."

John chuckled. "I'll bet she locks her doors now."

"She does."

"So why can't you just tell her how you feel? As far as I can see, you both feel the same way."

"It's a long story." Brandon picked up his coffee and took a drink.

"I've got time. Like I said, the ladies are occupied for the afternoon."

It dawned on Brandon that perhaps it was time to confess to his pastor what had happened and get his advice on what to do about it. There had to be a way to put it from him once and for all.

He began telling the story of his childhood. Pastor John listened and made no comment as the story grew darker. Remembering his father was never easy. Brandon had gone out of his way for a great many years to forget the man even existed. He spared John no detail, even telling him about the beatings he had taken as a child. When he reached the part where he had found out about his mother enduring the same kinds of punishment, Brandon had to stop.

John still didn't speak. Instead, he got up and retrieved the coffeepot. He poured himself a cup, then refilled Brandon's before setting the pot on the edge of the hearth and reclaiming his seat.

Brandon knew he had to continue and began again. It seemed every time he talked about it, the burden grew a little lighter. He concluded the story with all that had happened on that final evening.

"I killed him. I'm not sure how Mother explained it to the doctor, but no one ever said a word to me. No one questioned his death at all. There was a small private funeral, and then Mother and I returned home and said very little about it. It was as if it had never happened."

"But not for you," John stated more than questioned.

"No, I've carried it inside all these years. I told Cassie's father. He was the first one I ever talked to about it. Then, a few weeks back, I told Cassie. I don't know why."

"I think I do. You know you've developed feelings for her but also that this might stand in the way of your feeling free enough to ask her to be your wife."

"I can't strap her with a murderer. I mean, what if they come after me?"

"You think that's possible after all these years?"

"I'm still guilty. I still cost a man his life."

John nodded. "Then perhaps the only thing you can do is go home and confess."

Brandon looked at him for several moments. He was right. That was the only thing left to do. If he wanted to clear his conscience and rid himself of the past, the only thing he could do was turn himself in. But what if they didn't understand? What if they decided to have a trial and convicted him of murder?

"I think you will never be free until you do," John said. "I doubt anything will come of it with regard to the law. Once they hear what happened, I believe they'll call it self-defense. You said yourself you were afraid you were next, and in the frenzy of everything, what else could you do?"

Brandon nodded. "You're right. I suppose I've always known that I'd one day have to account for it."

"I'd start with the doctor who tended to everything. He obviously didn't believe it to be murder, or if he did and your mother told him what had happened, he would make a good character witness for you."

"All right. I'll do that." The doctor had been only ten years or so older than he was. Surely he was still alive.

"Are you going to tell Cassie? I think you should."

Brandon nodded. "I will."

Cassie opened the door to find Brandon preparing to knock again. "Sorry it took me so long. I was in the back room. Come on in. Supper isn't ready. In fact, I haven't even started it." She gave a shrug and smiled. "But it won't take that long, if you aren't picky."

"I didn't come for supper. I came to tell you something."

She heard the seriousness in his tone. "Well then, have a seat by the fire, and I'll be right there."

Brandon did as she asked while Cassie went to the kitchen and slipped a casserole in the oven to warm, praying as she did that all was well. She rejoined Brandon and took a seat on the sofa.

"What did you want to tell me?"

"I had a long talk with Pastor John. I told him about the past—about my father."

"That's good. I'm sure he offered you sound counsel."

Brandon stretched his legs toward the fire. "He suggested I go back to Virginia and confess what happened."

Cassie felt her chest tighten. She could hardly breathe. "For what purpose?"

"He thought the situation was such that the law would see it as self-defense. If not, then I suppose there would be a trial, and I might very well end up in prison or hanged."

"No!" She forced herself to calm down. "Surely they wouldn't see it that way. You aren't a murderer."

"No, I'm not. But I did take a life, and I deserve my just punishment."

"It seems to me you already endured that." She drew a deep breath and let it go. "But nevertheless, I will support you no matter what."

"I think this is the only way to clear my conscience once and for all. I feel that I'm forever bound to the past until I find a way to do that." He got to his feet and leaned against the fireplace mantel. "I hope you understand. Maybe you could even go see your sister while I'm gone."

Cassie nodded. "I want you to do what you feel you must. It takes a lot of bravery to even consider such a thing."

"I don't feel brave—just determined to loosen these chains."

Cassie stood and walked to where he stood. She didn't care what he thought, she needed to do this for herself. She embraced him. Hugging him tightly, she fought back tears. "You must know how much I care about you. I will pray every day for you."

Brandon's arms went around her, and he returned her embrace. Then, just as suddenly, he stepped back, forcing Cassie to let go.

"I care about you, Cassie. Maybe that's why it's so important I do this."

She met his gaze and nodded. "We can't have a future until we lay the past to rest."

⁓

Two days later, Brandon was gone, and Cassie was on a train for Denver. She had wired her sister about coming and received a reply urging her to do so. Cassie could occupy herself with the visit and seeing her nieces for the first time rather than sit around dwelling on Brandon and what the outcome of his trip might mean.

Myrtle had assured Cassie this was a smart thing to do. Getting away would help her clear her mind—help her figure out what she wanted in life.

But Cassie already knew what she wanted. She wanted Brandon DuBarko for her husband. She wanted him to love her as much as she loved him.

# 20

Brandon stood outside the office of Dr. William David-son, MD. He gazed up at the brass plate that bore the man's name for a long time. He wanted very much to go inside, but at the same time, he wanted no part of it.

The door opened, and an older woman came out. She smiled and nodded at Brandon but said nothing. He tipped his hat and took advantage of the open door to go inside. He glanced around the small room, then cleared his throat. He wasn't sure what else to do. There was nobody to be seen.

The door to the waiting area opened, and a tall man stepped into the room. "I'm Dr. Davidson. How can I help you?"

Brandon studied the man for a moment. Yes, this was the same doctor who'd tended his father's murder. His face was older by twenty-four years, but he was the same person.

"I'm . . ."

"Brandon DuBarko, if I'm not mistaken," the doctor inter-jected. "I've expected—hoped, really—to see you ever since your father's death."

"I need to talk to you about that."

"I thought you might someday. Let me close things down." The older man went to the door and locked it. He put a sign in the window, then directed Brandon to follow him.

Brandon and the doctor walked to the back room and through a doorway that led into the doctor's office.

"Have a seat, Mr. DuBarko."

"Please call me Brandon."

The doctor smiled. "I will, thanks." He took a seat behind his large oak desk. "And you must call me Bill. You certainly haven't changed much."

Brandon took a seat. "I was thinking the same of you."

"Have you come to ask me about that night?"

"No, I've come to confess and see what you think I should do."

The doctor looked confused. "Confess?"

"I don't know what my mother told you. That night . . . my father . . . well, there was a horrible fight between him and my mother. He lost control and—and . . . tried to kill her. I was certain he would succeed if I didn't stop him. I've hardly been able to live with myself all these years, and I'm not sure why you protected me, but I have appreciated the freedom it allowed me. However, I find that my secret is a burden I can no longer carry." Brandon eased back in the chair. "I took the fireplace poker and hit my father in the back of the head to stop him from killing my mother. I killed my father."

The doctor's expression relaxed. "No, you didn't."

"Yes, I did. No matter what my mother told you, it was me."

"Brandon, you really don't know, do you?"

"Know what?"

"You didn't kill your father. That blow just knocked him out. It was the three blows to the side of his head that did him in."

Brandon shook his head vehemently. "I didn't hit the side of his head three times. Just the once on the back."

"I know." The doctor leaned forward. "Your mother hit him after she sent you to fetch me. She took a brass bookend and hit him repeatedly. She explained it all to me."

"My mother?" Brandon could scarcely believe what he was

being told. "No, I don't believe it. She wouldn't have done that. She was much too gentle a person."

"She did. When I arrived, she sent you upstairs. Do you remember that?"

"Of course, she met us at the door and whispered to me that she would take care of everything." Brandon remembered it as if it were yesterday.

"Exactly. She sent you upstairs and bade me to follow her to the dining room. When I got there, I found your father—his head bashed in on the right side. She told me everything. Showed me the bruises on her neck. She said you'd hit him once across the back of the head, and she sent you to get me to come to the house. Meanwhile, your father started to revive. She couldn't bear the thought of his living to commit his vicious deeds again and again. She said she grabbed the nearest object and hit him until he was dead."

"My mother?" Brandon repeated. He couldn't believe the demure and petite woman he'd known had been capable of anything like that.

"I sent for the police chief. You remember he lived just two doors down?"

"Yes."

"I told him what had happened, and we both agreed to call it an accident. We both knew what kind of man he was. We knew the way he treated your mother. We couldn't blame her for what she had done. She was probably half out of her mind from fighting for her life. We had a little conspiracy with the undertaker, and your father was quietly buried and forgotten. We were all pledged to secrecy for your mother's sake and told her never to speak of it again. As far as the public was concerned, your father took a fall and hit his head. He died from those wounds. There was nothing more to report."

"I had no idea. I left so quickly after the funeral . . . at my mother's insistence. I thought she was trying to protect me."

"In a sense, I believe she was. Protecting you from learning the truth about what she had done. I was with her when she fell ill and knew her time was short. She told me she had no regrets in ending her husband's life. He had been violent toward her since before she married him, but she had had little say in her marriage. Her father insisted she marry your father, and he had beaten her since their wedding night. She hated his punishment of you, as well, but there was never an opportunity to leave. He watched her carefully. She begged me not to tell you the truth about what happened, but the truth can't hurt her now, nor you."

All of these years, Brandon had been certain he killed his father. He had borne the guilt but no regret, which only added to his guilt. "I came here to confess what I did. I was never sure what my mother told you had happened. I thought perhaps she made up some story about Father interrupting a burglar. I knew she hadn't told anyone else that I'd hit and killed him. Now I guess I know why."

"She was a good woman, and I think being nearly killed herself, she was determined to finally fight back. But I don't consider it murder, and neither did the police chief. We both agreed it was a form of self-defense. We learned soon enough that no one really cared what had happened, they were just glad he was gone. Your mother encouraged you to leave and find a new life, while she went to live with her sister across town."

"Yes, she was happy with her sister. She wrote me several letters, and I could tell her entire demeanor had changed. She sold the newspaper, and they bought a bigger house near the river, in the country. I saw it when I came home for her funeral. It was so different from the home I grew up in. It was on a farm and was cozy and comfortable. My aunt said it was exactly the home my mother and she had always wanted when they were children."

"She lived those last three years in happiness, Brandon. I

know she'd be beyond grief to think you were still living with the burden of what happened. I hope you'll be able to give it over to God. The past is dead and gone."

"Just like my mother and father." Brandon shook his head and got to his feet. "I'm glad I listened to my pastor and came to see you. Here I wondered if I'd be arrested or if I'd at least have to detail all that had happened for the police." He paused and reached his hand out to the doctor. "Thank you for protecting my mother. She was a good woman."

The doctor nodded and shook Brandon's hand. "She deserved much better. I'm glad we could help her have a few years of true happiness."

Nothing had gone right. Nothing at all. Cyrus had made plans with his remaining band of thieves, and everything was set for robbing the Santa Fe of its payroll. The best time, they figured, was while the money was still on the train. Two men could easily knock out the paymaster and then throw the payroll box from the train. They could have riders ready and waiting to pick up the money, and they'd all ride to meet at an appointed place.

But instead, the men he sent came face-to-face with a dozen soldiers. They were quickly taken into custody, and that was that. Cyrus had acted as fireman on the train and saw everything once they arrived in San Marcial. The soldiers had marched his men off in shackles and immediately taken them to jail. He could do nothing to help them. He could only hope they wouldn't talk.

When he arrived at the rundown house north of Old Town, where the others were waiting to find out what had happened, Cyrus could only shrug.

"Apparently they are putting guards on the payroll now." He sat down on a rickety chair. "They took the others to jail."

"We have to get them out," Juan declared. "A few of us can manage the job. There won't be soldiers guarding the jail."

"We don't know that. I didn't figure on soldiers joining the train in Albuquerque. It could be they're gonna have soldiers guarding them." Cyrus's hands fisted and relaxed. "We'll do what we can."

"Frank and I can scout it out, jefe," Juan said, looking at Frank. The younger man nodded in agreement, and Juan turned back to Cyrus. "We can manage it. You stay out of trouble."

Cyrus appreciated Juan's concern that he not be tied to the situation. Perhaps his loyalty was due to their friendship. They'd known each other from before Cyrus went to prison and had shared many a beer together. On the other hand, Cyrus had often lent Juan money in his times of need, so maybe it was nothing more than that.

"If you can get them out without too much trouble, do so and get to Mexico. I'll send word when it's safe to come back."

Juan smiled. "With any luck at all, there won't be a need for that. We'll just go to El Paso and wait for you at the usual place."

Cyrus nodded. It was all on them. If they only went as far as El Paso and got caught, that would be their problem. Unless, of course, they talked.

His eyes narrowed. If they talked, Cyrus would never escape. Maybe when Juan and Frank came for the others, Cyrus should kill them all. Then no one would be talking about anything.

---

The cold wind whipped at Brandon's coat as he stood looking down at his mother's grave. His father was buried some fifty feet away—his mother's choice. Here she was laid to rest, and later her sister had joined her. They had each other but wanted nothing to do with the man who had made his mother so miserable.

He squatted down and swept snow and old decaying leaves from around the headstone. He remained there, just thinking about the past and all they had endured.

"Mama, I'm sorry for what happened. Including that you felt your only choice was to end what I started. You were a good woman, and I loved you more than life. I wish we could have those last three years back to spend together, but I know you were happy, and that makes me happy."

Tears came to Brandon's eyes. He couldn't remember the last time that had happened. It seemed his ability to express emotions had died with his childhood.

"I miss you, Mama. You always made me feel good about myself, even when Father told me I was worthless. He said he only told me those things to make me stronger, but I think he believed them. Even when I was able to go to college at sixteen, I think he felt I should have managed it sooner. But not you. You always believed in me—always encouraged me to stay close to God. And I did."

He wiped at the tears on his cheeks. There was such a feeling of release in knowing the truth about his father. "I know what you did for me—for us." He touched the stone and traced her name.

*Maryanne DuBarko*
*1849–1895*

Only her name and the years of her life were given. It was much too simple a monument to an extraordinary woman, but Brandon knew it was all she wanted. She'd made that clear when they buried Father.

It suddenly came to Brandon that she had only been four years older than he was currently when she died. Much too young. The doctor said she'd had an infection—a fever. Brandon wondered if her guilt over what she'd done had taken its toll on her instead.

"I hope you didn't feel guilty. You did what you had to in order to stay alive. You deserved a good life, Mama. I pray that you are at peace in God's forgiveness."

He straightened. It still amazed him to know the truth. His mother had always been so soft-spoken and amiable. That was one of the reasons it was so shocking to learn of his father's treatment of her.

Cassie came to mind. She was just like his mother. He'd never heard her lose her temper. Never had he seen her treat another person harshly. She was the perfect woman, as far as he was concerned, and he intended to marry her when he returned to New Mexico. If she'd have him.

His lips twitched at the edges. Of course she'd have him. They were both people of few words, but even the unspoken words were clear. She loved him. Of that Brandon was certain. And he loved her. More than he'd thought possible after all he'd been through.

A smile formed on his lips. An honest-to-goodness smile of happiness.

Cassie looked at the numerous dresses Melissa had had the maid bring.

"I knew you wouldn't have much to wear that would fit into our society. These are old gowns of mine I had packed away. Some of them only got worn once or twice." Melissa held up her hand. "Before you condemn me for that, just understand it's the way things are here. After I'm through with a dress, I usually give it to one of the maids or to the poor. There's a group of women at our church who take the gowns and remake them in a less opulent manner to give to the poor."

"That's a brilliant idea." Cassie couldn't imagine how the silk fabrics could be made into anything very enduring, but it was a kind and thoughtful idea. She fingered one of the velvet cloaks. "These are lovely."

"Terry wants me to have the best, and in his family's society, to have less would embarrass them—even though his mother and father are very down-to-earth people. They have never fully recognized the societal rungs created by others. They are just good godly folks." She met Cassie's gaze. "I hope you like them."

"I'm sure I will. I know they have to be nice people—amazing people—to draw you into their fold in such a loving manner."

"They are." Melissa's gaze grew distant. "It was so hard when I came here. I was so alone. They were good to me and made me feel like I was part of their family."

Cassie smiled. "I'm so glad you had that, especially since we weren't able to provide it."

Melissa looked at her. "I never considered how difficult things must have been for you. I only thought of myself."

"You were only a child. How could I ever hold that against you?"

Her sister moved to the window and pulled back the heavy paneled draperies to gaze outside. "I'm sorry I've been so hateful. I have to admit I still feel angry toward our father. I know you loved him dearly, but I don't remember ever having that kind of feeling for him. Oh, I know before Mama died that we were all very close, but . . . frankly, Papa sometimes scared me. He was so big and loud. After Mama died, he got so quiet, and that was even more frightening."

"You mustn't let it harden you, Melissa." Cassie joined her at the window. "Papa never knew how to accept Mama's passing. He was so lost without her. I'm not making an excuse for him . . . not really." She paused, shaking her head. "Maybe I am. But I can honestly say that he wasn't the man I'd known before Mama passed away. He never let me get close again. We merely existed, never really thriving."

Melissa turned to face Cassie. "It will take time for me to care about how he felt. It will take time to feel something other than anger and betrayal. Please be patient with me. I want this to work. I want us all to be close."

Cassie nodded. "I will be as patient as you need me to be. The goal is much desired, and therefore, I find I can be quite long-suffering."

Her sister smiled. "You were always much better at that than I."

"Well, we each have those things God has called us to. I suppose a part of my life has been molded around the loss of those I love."

"Like that young man you were going to marry. I feel terrible knowing I was part of the reason you let love slip away."

Moving back to sit on the edge of the bed, Cassie folded her hands. "That wasn't really love. I know the difference now."

"Brandon?" her sister asked, leaving the window. She came to the bed but didn't sit. "Are you in love with him?"

"I am. And if it all works out, I intend to marry him. I've never been quite so determined to make a thing happen as I am that."

"I'm glad. I really am. For all my anger at you, I truly want only good for your future."

She really did look so much like their mother. Cassie got to her feet and hugged Melissa close. As she dropped her hold, Melissa looked perplexed.

"What was that for?"

Cassie smiled. "Just because."

A young maid popped in through the open door. "Madam, the babies are awake."

Melissa took Cassie's arm. "Come and meet your nieces. I just know you will love them."

"I'm sure I will."

Cassie followed her sister to the opposite side of the house, where the nursery and master chambers were located. Inside the nursery, the décor had been arranged in hues of pale lilac and green. There was a nursemaid's bed on one side of the room and then a large crib situated not far from the fire.

The babies, now nearly eight months old, were sitting up, and upon seeing their mother, they maneuvered to the railing of the crib and pulled themselves to their feet.

Cassie gasped. "Oh, look what they can do."

"This is something new they started a week or so ago," Melissa replied. She reached into the crib and drew out one of the twins. "This is Annabella." She handed the baby to Cassie.

The infant looked up at Cassie as if to assess her. Cassie smiled, which made the baby smile in turn. Annabella reached up to touch Cassie's face.

"Oh, she's precious. Such a dear."

"And this is Lily Mae. She was born second, although barely three minutes later."

Cassie looked from Annabella to Lily Mae and shook her head. "They're identical. How do you tell them apart?"

"So far I've found little ways. Annabella is very forward in her behavior, while Lily Mae is quiet and less pushy. Annabella will squeal and cry out for attention, while Lily Mae seems content to let her sister manage the affair for them both. And, as you can see, we've dressed them differently. Annabella wears yellows and blues, and Lily Mae wears pinks and whites. Sometimes we do dress them alike, and when that happens, we use specially marked diapers with their names embroidered on them."

Cassie laughed. "What an adventure this will be. I can just imagine the girls trying to change places and fool everyone."

"I have imagined that myself," Melissa said, smiling. "It seemed like a thing I might have done had I a twin."

"I'd say Annabella favors you more than Lily Mae in personality. You were quite capable of drawing attention to yourself as an infant."

"Terry says he guessed the same thing. His mother tells us Lily Mae is far more like her father. He was always very quiet." Melissa hugged Lily Mae close. "I hope that doesn't cause me to love her more than Annabella."

"Oh, I don't see how it could. These babies are the very best of you both. How precious and dear. I wish I'd been here sooner."

"Well, you're here now," Melissa declared as Annabella began to fuss. "They're hungry. We must let their nurse see to them. Besides, Terry is waiting for us downstairs. I promised him we'd return as soon as I got you settled in, and here we are playing with the children."

Two older women appeared at the sound of Annabella's cries. Lily Mae whimpered, joining in, but never quite gave as heartfelt a showing.

Melissa guided Cassie to the stairs. "They make me so happy. I hope you'll have children of your own one day, Cassie."

Terrance Bridgestone awaited them with tea and refreshments in the large front parlor. Cassie could see through the open draperies that it had begun to snow. Melissa said that was quite normal for Denver, despite there being six inches of the stuff already on the lawn. There were times, she declared, when they had several feet of snow rather than just inches.

A huge arched stone fireplace was the focus of the room with a log as big as a man centered in the massive iron grate. There were smaller pieces of wood piled around it, and the flames climbed high as they consumed the dry pine.

Cassie loved the fireplace. It was big enough for a person to stand in, and it put out a lot of heat. She stood there only a moment before she was sufficiently warmed to the bone.

"Did you tell her about the ball?" Terry asked Melissa.

Cassie took a seat to the right of where Melissa had joined her husband on the beautiful blue sofa. "What ball?"

"I suppose that answers my question," Terry said, laughing.

228

"My folks are giving a ball in celebration of their thirtieth wedding anniversary. It will be next Friday at their house."

"How nice. Thirty years of marriage is a long time." Cassie couldn't imagine. Even if she married Brandon tomorrow, she'd be in her sixties before reaching such a celebration.

"We're very much looking forward to it and want you to be our guest. Mother was adamant that we invite you to the party."

"But I haven't the clothes for such an affair," Cassie said. "It's one thing to get by in dresses my sister has lent me, but a ball is much too important. I can just stay home with the twins."

"Nonsense. My mother has already arranged for a gown. It should be delivered tomorrow, and you can see what it needs to fit properly." Terry put his arm around Melissa. "We both very much want you to be there."

Cassie wasn't at all excited about the idea. She couldn't dance very well and certainly had no interest in learning. "Well, if it makes you happy, I suppose I can hardly refuse."

She forced a smile, wondering what kind of gown Terry's mother had chosen for her. At least Cassie was handy with a needle and thread. She could most likely adjust any part of the dress that needed attention.

"Good. It's settled then." Terry smiled, and Melissa did as well.

# 21

The night of the ball was clear. The weather had, in fact, warmed a bit. Still, the carriage ride was slow going as the horses picked their way through the plowed and drifted snow.

There was a definite sense of excitement in the air. Cassie had never been to a ball and certainly had never worn such finery. Her blue silk gown was overlaid with the most extravagant sleeveless mantelet. The creation must have weighed twenty pounds, with all the gold and silver beading and sparkling trim. It wasn't created to sit in comfortably, as Cassie was finding out, but it was incredibly beautiful. The main portion of the gown was robin's-egg blue, while the mantelet had a darker blue base. The bodice was open to reveal intricately designed ivory lace, so fine and delicate that Cassie wasn't sure how it came together to form the low-cut bodice. Thankfully, she'd been able to remove a couple of the folds in the lace to draw it up higher on the neckline. Otherwise, she might have had to leave on the fox-trimmed cloak her sister had lent her.

Having already met Terry's family days before, Cassie felt immediately welcome when they arrived at the house. She was greeted as one of the family by Terry's mother, who not only embraced her but offered her a kiss on the cheek. All of the family's friends stopped to stare at Cassie as her cloak was removed and taken away. She felt like a china doll being inspected for flaws.

She touched a gloved hand to her hair, hoping everything had stayed in place. The maid had loosely pulled it into a soft roll at the back of her head and trimmed it with feathers and more gold and silver in the form of decorative combs. Cassie had scarcely recognized herself, and no doubt these people were just as fascinated by the creature who had come to join them.

"Are you nervous?" Melissa whispered.

"A bit, but I keep reminding myself that if I stay close to you, no one will even notice me. You are so beautiful, Melissa. I am so impressed with the way you look in that gown."

Melissa smiled. "You're the one who is stealing the show. Everyone is curious to know you, and I'm sure the men are dying to dance with you."

"I can't really dance," Cassie replied. "You well know I've had no need of it."

"So we'll tell them you aren't dancing this evening. Perhaps a twisted ankle."

Cassie shook her head. "I hardly see the need to lie. Just say I won't be dancing and leave it at that."

Melissa laughed. "You were always very straightforward."

"Well, if I'm not going to lie about the big things in my life, why would I about something like this?"

Her sister nodded and took Cassie's elbow. "Come along. I want to introduce you to some of my friends."

Cassie did as she was bidden. It was apparent, however, that Melissa's friends were less impressed with meeting her than Melissa had hoped.

"Mrs. Burton, Mrs. Hill, this is my sister, Miss Cassandra Barton," Melissa introduced.

"Charmed, my dear," Mrs. Hill replied. She looked at Cassie for a long moment. "She looks nothing like you, Melissa."

"She takes after our father with her lighter hair and eyes," Melissa explained.

Mrs. Burton raised her chin a degree and looked down her nose at Cassie. It wouldn't be the last time such a pose was struck that evening, she was sure. Cassie felt as if she were a specimen under glass—observed and reviewed for its value and acceptability.

Melissa whisked her away as soon as the ladies had their say. "You mustn't let them bother you in the least. Mrs. Burton drinks something terrible, and Mrs. Hill is having an affair with a married man. Worse yet, her husband knows it and tolerates it. She even has paintings of her lover hanging in their home."

"Goodness, that's rather bold." Cassie looked around at all the beautiful people.

"They've all got their secrets. I'm the poor orphan who came to wealth by attaching myself to the Bridgestone family."

"Orphan?" Cassie asked, remembering that the newspaper article about the wedding had said Melissa had no living family.

Melissa frowned. "Yes, well, I let that rumor spread so I didn't have to explain the past."

"And how do you explain my being here now?"

Laughter escaped her sister's lips. "I have enough money and social standing that I don't have to explain anything. I'm part of the Sacred Thirty-Six."

Cassie shook her head, mystified. "Whatever is that?"

"It's something Louise Hill put together, and if you're invited to participate, you're the cream of Denver society. Even New York society accepts you if you're one of the Thirty-Six. Now, come on, I must introduce you around. Terry and I will be expected to be at his parents' side throughout the evening. I'll make sure you know everyone, and then you can happily mingle as you will."

After a whirlwind of names and faces, Cassie wasn't sure she'd be able to remember who anyone was, with the exception of Louise Hill. She had made a great impression on Cassie for her scheming and appointing who was socially acceptable.

Around ten, Cassie was ready to go home, but according to a brief encounter with her brother-in-law, the party had barely started. The Duchess of Canton had just arrived to join the fun, and no one would dare leave before she did. He pointed, and Cassie found the grand old lady only a few feet away, being received by his parents.

"I know the duchess," Cassie told her brother-in-law. This brought snide laughter from a group of women nearby. They were supposedly good friends of Melissa, so Cassie turned slightly to include them in the conversation. "I met her at the opening of the Elephant Butte Dam in New Mexico and rode in her private train car. She was very charming."

It was clear, by the women's expressions, that they didn't believe her. They began whispering to one another, and Cassie looked back at Terry.

"I don't suppose it matters"—she lowered her voice to a whisper only he could hear—"but I mended one of her gowns. She was quite grateful."

He chuckled. "I'm sure she was grateful. Now, I must go do my duty."

Cassie followed him, deciding it was better to escape the snobbish women and their comments. After he found Melissa, Cassie diverted to the table where punch and refreshments were being served. It wasn't but a few moments, however, before the group of women who'd laughed at her reappeared to taunt her some more.

"So you know the Duchess of Canton," one of the younger women commented. "I can scarcely imagine how that came about."

Cassie had a cup of punch in her hands and took a sip before answering. "As I said, I met her at a celebration. They were opening a new dam in New Mexico."

"And the duchess was there? I find that hard to believe," one of the older ladies said, looking down her nose at Cassie. "Goodness, what would an English duchess be doing at an inconsequential event such as that?"

"I'm sure I don't know why she came, but I assure you she was there. She also invited me to share her private car as we rode back from the celebration." Cassie smiled. "It was so grand. I very much enjoyed my time there."

The women looked at one another and shared sneers. The older woman spoke again. "One thing you will find is that we do not brook liars, Miss Barton. We have no tolerance for it."

"Excuse me, miss," a uniformed man announced rather formally, joining their group and directing his words to Cassie.

For a moment, she thought he was going to ask her to leave. "Yes?"

"The duchess would like you to join her in the grand salon."

The other women gasped.

Cassie nodded. "I'm not sure I know the way."

"I will take you there myself," the man replied.

As she passed them, Cassie found each of the women speechless. She couldn't help giving them a smile.

In the grand salon, the duchess was already seated and speaking to a variety of people as they came and went. She was the very center of attention, and Cassie wondered how the great lady even knew she was there.

"Ah, Miss Barton," the duchess said as the footman brought Cassie forward. "I'm so glad you could join me. Come sit beside me. It will be a comfort to have you near."

Cassie did as she was instructed, still in awe of the woman in all of her splendor. She was dripping with diamonds and other jewels, and her gown was of the finest silk and design. It looked, if Cassie wasn't mistaken, to be another creation by Worth. Not that she was an authority on such things, but she had come to notice certain stylistic trademarks by the House of Worth.

Sitting beside the duchess, Cassie was privy to all of the introductions and brief conversations. It wasn't long before the same women who had laughed and sneered at Cassie appeared to be introduced.

It was hard not to stiffen in discomfort when the women came forward. The duchess's servant announced the names of the women and the fact that Her Grace had requested their appearance. She looked rather critically at each one.

"I asked you to meet me because I overheard you giving my friend a most difficult time." The duchess looked at Cassie and took her hand. "This woman has become quite dear to me, and I find it rather appalling that you should treat her so poorly. Has she done something to offend you?"

The women were speechless. They looked at one another and then at the duchess. The oldest of the quartet stepped forward. "It was all a misunderstanding, Your Grace. Nothing more."

The duchess gave her a hard look. "It seemed a great deal more. Cassie, my dear, what say you?"

Cassie couldn't hide her surprise. She looked at the four women and shook her head. "I don't really know them, Your Grace. They are friends of my sister."

"Well, it certainly seems they might treat you better."

"Of course we will," the older woman said, interrupting the duchess. This was met with a raised brow from the grand old lady. The woman stepped back, realizing she had made a terrible social mistake.

The duchess dismissed the women and turned to Cassie with a devilish smile. "There, now they are sufficiently in their place and will let everyone else know that you are to be treated with due respect. I cannot abide belittling others, especially when you hardly know them."

"You are too kind, Your Grace."

"I am still hoping I can convince you to join me on my trip and eventually in England."

Cassie shook her head. "If not for the fact that I'm in love, I might well take you up on such an exciting proposition."

"Love, eh?" The old lady smiled all the more. "Well, let it never be said that I interfered in that marvelous comfort."

---

"Oh, Cassie, you should have heard them. They were terrified and overcome with regret all at the same time," Melissa told her at brunch the next day. "You've got the Thirty-Six quivering in their diamond-buttoned boots."

Melissa's mother-in-law had come to join them in order to announce that Cassie was a complete success. "I was simply inundated with requests to call upon you."

"As was I," Melissa declared. "Goodness, but you made a very big impression on everyone."

Cassie couldn't hold back her laughter. "They would think twice about their invitations if they knew my act of endearment to the duchess was as her temporary seamstress."

"They don't need to know that," Melissa countered. "They need to learn their lesson about snobbery and thinking of themselves as better than everyone else."

"The Bible says to esteem others as better than ourselves," Mrs. Bridgestone said, accepting eggs in hollandaise sauce from the footman. "Of course, many of these women never bother to open the beautiful Bibles that sit on grand and glorious stands in their homes. Should they do so, they would have to face up to the truth, and that would change everything."

"I hope you didn't accept any invitations for me," Cassie said, slicing into the ham on her plate. "I think the time for me to return home is upon us."

"I suppose you must go back and find out what Brandon's intentions are," Melissa replied. She poured cream into her coffee, then added sugar.

Cassie smiled. "Yes, I must, for I believe they are the same as mine. And if that's the case, you shall very soon receive an invitation to my wedding."

Mrs. Bridgestone smiled in approval. "Then we shall add one more to our family, for surely we have already added you, Cassie dear."

Brandon looked at the newspaper in his hand. Some new political intrigue related to the war had captured all of the headlines. Glancing at the story, it sounded as though the Germans had sent a telegram to Mexico, announcing unrestricted submarine warfare in the Atlantic. It also said something about Mexico being allowed to reclaim lands they'd lost to the United States if they would assist Germany. Those lands included New Mexico.

"This will definitely mean war," a man reading over his shoulder announced. "It's about time. We needed to come to the aid of the English long ago. After all, most of us are descended from those folks."

Brandon said nothing. He turned away, folding the paper as he walked toward the approaching train. He was headed home and nearly there. Albuquerque was the last place he'd have to change trains, thankfully. He climbed into the car and made his way to an empty seat by the window. Sitting, he pulled out the paper again and continued to read.

He wondered what this new announcement would mean. The leadership of the United States would never allow for part of the country to be ripped away.

"Have you heard the news?" a man asked him, coming to sit beside Brandon on the train. "We're sure to go to war."

Brandon pulled the paper closer. "Only time will tell," he muttered, hoping the man would understand his disinterest in discussion.

"Wilson's been a fool to avoid it," the man continued. "We have to get involved and put an end to it. The rest of the world needs us to take charge. Only America can resolve this matter. I know I'll sign up to go."

With a sigh, Brandon focused on another column that spoke of President Wilson's thoughts and actions. Brandon knew that soon his world would be turned upside down, but for now, he wasn't going to second-guess anything. Whether he would need to put on a uniform and travel across the ocean or remain in New Mexico to defend and maintain the railroad, that decision could come after he saw Cassie again. His desire was to return home and marry the woman he loved. Together, they could figure out what the future held.

# 22

Cyrus McCutchen sat waiting for his supper at one of the local cafés. He had just returned from working a lengthy trip and was anxious to eat and go to bed. Exhaustion was giving him serious second thoughts about even waiting to eat.

Having worked the last few weeks, he was already making plans to quit. First, he had to figure out a way to punish Brandon DuBarko before he cut out of the area altogether. It wasn't easy to figure out what could be done. Not working full-time. That had been a mistake, to be sure. Why he had thought it would prove useful to him was now a mystery. The truth was, working as a fireman for the Santa Fe took all his time and energy. He supposed the five years in prison had aged him more than he'd realized. Still, he wasn't about to let DuBarko get away with having put him there. The man needed to be punished.

The food finally arrived, and Cyrus settled in to eating beans and tortillas with cold beer to wash it down. From time to time, someone he knew came into the place and gave him a wave, but he showed as little interest as possible, and they took the hint and left him alone. He was in no mood for small talk or discussions about going to war, yet that seemed to be all anyone wanted to talk about.

Thankfully, he was too old to be expected to go to war. However, there would no doubt be other things they would expect of him, like guarding the borders or at least keeping the railroad working. They could expect all they wanted of him, but that didn't mean they would get it. Cyrus was his own man, and if nothing else, prison had taught him to keep a precious guard on his freedom. Maybe he'd go to South America. He'd heard there were a great many possibilities for an industrious man there.

"You in for the night, Cyrus?" an older man asked as he passed his table.

"I am. What about you?"

"Heading out on the 8:10." He looked at his pocket watch. "Came to get a couple of tamales to take with me."

Cyrus gave a nod. "We didn't have any trouble coming up from El Paso, so you should have it clear going down. Unless, of course, someone was able to get in there and make quick work of tearing up track. I doubt it, though. They've got the army riding defense on the track from Albuquerque to El Paso. Shouldn't be a problem."

With the death of his two men who'd tried to rob the payroll train, as well as Juan and Frank, Cyrus was glad they were no longer trying to tear up track. Glad too that the guards at the jail had been the ones to kill the four men instead of Cyrus having to do the job. It was just fortuitous the way some things worked out.

"That's good to know. I heard they were gonna start shooting folks on sight, since we're practically at war. It seems like the Mexicans are joining up with the Germans."

The war again. Cyrus would have thrown his glass, but it still held plenty of beer. "Yeah, I heard something about that. I doubt Mexico has the nerve to do it. They know they'd have to face us sooner or later, and we aren't going to take kindly to them trying to take over a piece of ground we've improved."

"Yeah, the Mexicans best not mess with the United States. It'd be a hard lesson to learn." The older man noticed the cashier waving him forward. "Looks like my tamales are ready. See ya, Cyrus."

"Later."

It was purely coincidence that Cyrus finished his meal in time to walk past the depot when the 8:10 got in. He spied DuBarko stepping down from the train. Cyrus paused in the shadows to see what he intended to do.

DuBarko walked in the general direction of Cassie's house but was stopped by a man who came out of the Harvey House. It was dark, but in the streetlamp light, Cyrus could tell it was the pastor.

The two men talked for a time, then started walking toward the church and parsonage. Cyrus wondered what they were up to. They seemed pretty chummy, just like Bart Barton and the pastor used to be. He followed them at a leisurely pace, knowing that if anyone asked, he could easily point out that he was headed home. The Santa Fe employee housing was just beyond the New Mexico Bible Church, where John Tyler preached.

"I want to hear all about it, Brandon. Come on, we can have some coffee and cake. Myrtle just made a pumpkin-apple cake. It's got nuts, raisins, and coconut. I think you'd like it."

"Sounds delicious," DuBarko said.

Cyrus was nearly upon them when the two men stopped and turned.

Spying him, DuBarko frowned. "McCutchen, what do you want?"

"Me?" Cyrus smiled. It was rather enjoyable, knowing that his presence was disconcerting to Brandon. "Headed home. Just finished up a run in from El Paso a few hours ago. Had me some supper, now heading to bed. What about you? I saw you just got in on the 8:10." He pulled a package of cigarettes from his coat pocket.

DuBarko watched him unwrap the top and take out one of the smokes.

"Want one?" Cyrus asked.

"No, I was just noticing your brand. It seems you've smoked that one a long time."

"I have." Cyrus looked at the package and shrugged. "They're cheap, and a lot of the boys get them across the border and bring them back. Some even sell them. There's good money to be made if you know the right folks."

"I wouldn't know." DuBarko offered nothing more, and Cyrus nearly laughed out loud. The man was going to hold his cards close to the vest.

Cyrus stuck the cigarette in his mouth, then found a match in the same pocket and flicked it on his thumbnail to light it. He lit the cigarette and drew long on it before letting out a stream of smoke with a satisfied sigh.

"Well, evening to you both. Seems like the weather is warming up a bit, so maybe I'll sleep with my windows open." Cyrus didn't wait for their response but headed on past them.

Neither man seemed at all interested in having him around, and while that didn't really matter to Cyrus, he couldn't help but wonder what was going on in their minds. They almost seemed to be up to something.

Even after he went to bed, he kept thinking of DuBarko's look of contempt and his unusual interest in Cyrus's cigarettes. Why should he care what brand of cigarettes he smoked?

Cyrus rolled over on his side. He was very nearly on his own now. He could scrounge up some of his men, but most were gone, and with the army guarding the rails, it was almost impossible to do the damage they had before.

*It's not the rails I want to damage.* Cyrus couldn't stop seeing DuBarko's expression. He acted as though he were better than Cyrus. He always had. Most everyone did, but DuBarko managed to make Cyrus feel useless. Once he got rid of him, Cyrus could leave the area and start his life over elsewhere. *I just need to get him alone.*

~

"Come in and have a seat, Bran." John went past him into the kitchen. "I'll put the coffeepot within reach."

"Brandon, how good to see you," Myrtle said, coming to give him a hug. "Did John tell you Cassie is still in Denver? She's due back tomorrow."

"He was just telling me. I hope she had a nice trip." Brandon knew how important it was to Cassie to mend fences with her sister.

"I had one short note from her after she first made it up there. She said the train ride was nice. A bit scary near Raton. Apparently, there was a lot of slippage, and sand was necessary to get them up and over."

"Sounds about right."

"I promised our boy some coffee and cake," John said, already looking for a knife.

"Well, why don't you both sit, and I'll bring it to you," Myrtle declared. She went to the cupboard and took down a couple of plates.

Brandon took a seat at the kitchen table. It was good to be home. He was tired and ready to head to bed, but he felt the need to explain the full story to John since the pastor had been instrumental in his decision to go east and seek the truth.

He wondered if Myrtle knew anything about his trip, but after she made several more comments about Cassie and the weather, Brandon figured John had kept his secret. He was glad for that. No need to have everyone know about his past. Especially now.

Myrtle had them served up in no time at all. She left cream and sugar on the table, and after making sure there was plenty of coffee, she kissed John on the top of the head. "I'll go to our room, John. I have some sewing I want to get a head start on."

"Sounds good, darlin'. Thanks for everything."

She smiled. "Brandon, it's good to have you home. I know Cassie will be anxious to see you." She didn't say why but instead turned and headed to the back of the house.

Brandon picked up his fork and dove right in to the cake. It was heavenly. The spices were a pleasant blend that made him think of cider and pumpkin pie.

"Well, you're here, which means you weren't arrested," John said.

"No, in fact, the entire matter was so completely different from what I expected that I'm still in a state of surprise."

John picked up his coffee mug. "Let's hear it, then."

"I didn't do it. I wasn't responsible for my father's death." He lowered his voice on the last word, still unable to make an open confession without feeling someone would appear to arrest him.

"So what happened?"

"My mother happened. She sent me to get the doctor, and while I was gone, my father regained consciousness. . . . She hit him several more times. She killed him."

John nodded. "Doesn't surprise me. Poor woman had probably taken all she could stand."

"That's what the doctor said too. Her abuse was well-known by him, as well as by the police chief. The doctor sent for him as well. When I got home, my mother sent me directly upstairs. I didn't see my father again. The casket was closed for the funeral. From what the doctor said, if I'd seen him, I would have realized that he'd been hit more than just what I had done."

"So they decided to keep your mother's secret."

"Yes, they figured she'd been through enough. They coordinated with the undertaker, and Father was buried without much pomp. Even though he owned one of the largest newspapers in town, people simply didn't care that he was dead. I never knew how much he was hated until talking to the doctor." Brandon sipped his coffee and leaned back in the chair. "I suppose a man like that can't help but make folks want to avoid him. They didn't even want to make sure he got buried."

"I've dealt with men like that in my lifetime." John drank another swig of coffee, then put down the cup. "I guess this frees you from your guilt."

"It's like a huge weight has been lifted from my shoulders. But at the same time, I feel bad for my mother. She should never have been made to feel that was her only choice. I hate that she lived for years in fear with no one to confide in—no one to help her."

"There are a lot of women who endure such things. They definitely need to speak up, but so often nobody wants to listen even when they do. You know the laws. They are kept by their husband's will and purpose. Few judges interfere."

"I know. I thought a lot about that. Had the doctor and police chief not been kindhearted, she would have gone to prison."

"And she would have deserved to go." John held up his hand at Brandon's deepening frown. "Wrong is wrong. Killing is still wrong."

"I know that, but my mother didn't set out to kill him. She didn't plan it. She clearly feared for her life."

"I figure the same, and no doubt that's what the others thought to be true. My point, Brandon, is this: what happened was tragic and sad. It was a horrible price to pay for both you and your mother, but also for your father. His nature led him to destruction and death. Now you must decide where your nature will lead you to. The past needs to be laid to rest. You cannot do one thing to help your mother or father, but you can help yourself. You and Cassie could have a future."

"I want that future." Brandon picked up his fork. "And I intend to have it. I'm going to ask her to marry me when she gets back."

John grinned. "I like the sound of that. Do you think she'll say yes?"

Brandon nodded. "I do."

"Just keep practicing that phrase over and over, and soon enough I'll ask for it and join you with your lady love."

A smile tugged at the corner of Brandon's lips. He hadn't felt this free and happy in years. "I won't have to practice. It's gonna come quite natural."

The next morning, Brandon reported to work. The day was overcast and looked like it might actually rain. He found his supervisor and was happy to hear that things were going well.

"Since the army has been helping us with track security, we're doing much better. There was some questionable activity near the dam, but that turned out to be curious children," Bud explained.

"I'm glad it was nothing important."

"You and me both. You heard, I'm sure, about the problems with Germany and Mexico?"

"I did. Has it caused problems for the Santa Fe?"

"Not exactly. We're mostly concerned with the border. We have to keep an eye on everything from Texas to California. If Mexico is gonna strike at us, they'll no doubt make it someplace that's poorly guarded and seemingly inconsequential. We'll need to be careful, Brandon. Don't take any chances. I figure you and I need to make a trip up and down the line in our division. Let's make sure everyone knows what's expected and that they have what they need for protection. We were told that most likely the army is going to get pulled out and sent overseas if we join up with this war."

"Maybe we won't join up." Brandon didn't think there was much hope of staying out, but it was worth throwing it out there.

"Yeah, that'd be nice, but I think Germany's gone too far. They've killed an awful lot of good people, and Americans aren't likely to just sit by and let that go. I have a feeling we'll be in the war before much longer."

"Sadly, I think you're probably right."

"There's an unscheduled freight coming in at nine. I want you on it with me."

Brandon nodded. "Should I pack a bag?"

"Yeah, I doubt we'll be home for a week or more."

He glanced at the clock. There was only about half an hour before the train would arrive. "I'll go right now. But there is something I want to say—something that's been bothering me for a while now."

"What is it?"

"I think Cyrus McCutchen is trouble."

"I don't doubt you feel that way, given that you were responsible for sending him to prison."

"It's not just that. I've a suspicion that he might even be responsible for the track tampering that killed Bart Barton."

"How can you say that? You know Pancho Villa and his men were active in the area when that train derailed."

"I know, but I also know a man watched the cleanup of that accident from up in the hills. He had the right build for Cyrus, though he was too far for me to see clearly. He left behind an empty package of Cyrus's brand of cigarettes. I don't know, but it just seems awfully coincidental that Bart's train should derail a week after Cyrus got out of prison."

"I've heard all of this before. General consensus is that the man you saw was one of Villa's watching to see what the end result of their work had been. He left quickly enough after that and no doubt caught up with Villa to report what had happened. Sounds like you have it in for McCutchen and want it to be him." Brandon's boss raised his brows in question. "Do you still hold a grudge against him?"

"It's not a grudge. It's a desire for justice. I can't say exactly why I believe he's here to cause trouble, but I do. I feel like he's only here to settle scores, and it worries me. It threatens the safety of the railroad, and that's a little closer to home than the Mexicans or Germans causing us trouble."

"Do you have any proof at all? Anything other than the bad feelings you hold toward the man?"

Brandon considered this for a moment. "No, I suppose I don't, but I can't help but think he's been responsible for a lot of the trouble along the line."

"Well, he's not going to be able to cause much trouble while he's busy shoveling coal into a firebox. Unless you have some other proof, I'd suggest you keep this to yourself and do your job. We have far too many enemies out there to go making up new ones."

Brandon nodded, but in his heart he knew Cyrus was going to show his hand sooner or later. "I'll get my stuff. See you on the train."

Keeping hidden to overhear DuBarko and his supervisor, Cyrus seethed at the fact that DuBarko had figured out the truth. He would have to step up his plans and see DuBarko dead at the first opportunity. He'd contemplated all sorts of ideas, from sneaking into his house and cutting his throat to causing some sort of accident, but nothing seemed likely to work. He needed to get DuBarko out alone—away from town and his section hands.

He thought of Cassie Barton. If he were able to take her, DuBarko would follow, but that too had its issues. Cassie was beloved by most of the town, and everyone looked out for her. Plus, she was out of town visiting her sister. He frowned. Why was this so hard to figure out?

Walking away, Cyrus decided that no matter how hard it was, Brandon DuBarko was going to die—and soon. DuBarko was trying to get him fired, and that wasn't going to happen. When Cyrus left the Santa Fe this time, it was going to be on his own terms.

# 23

Traveling had been fun, but Cassie was so happy to be back in her own little house. She'd returned almost a week ago, and she knew from things she'd heard that Brandon was back in town too. She supposed the new troubles and the threat of the country going to war had kept him busy, but oh, how she longed to see him and hear what had happened back east. Obviously, he hadn't been arrested, so that was a positive thing. At least as far as she was concerned. If everyone agreed it was self-defense and that Brandon's actions were justified in order to save his mother's life, then hopefully there would be no legal consequences for the choice he'd made. God knew the poor man had borne a lifetime of guilt for what had happened already.

She finished her washing and ironing and was just considering what she might put together for supper when there was a loud pounding on her front door. She headed to answer it, but before she got a chance, Brandon burst in. With great purpose, he crossed the small entryway and living room and came to where she stood.

Cassie opened her mouth to bid him hello, but Brandon swept her into his arms and kissed her soundly. Having never been kissed, Cassie pondered the act for just a moment, but as Brandon pulled her tighter, she found she could scarcely breathe. Then her heart began to beat faster, and as if they had a mind of their own, her arms encircled his neck.

Brandon pulled away and looked at her with a boyish grin. "I came to tell you how I feel about you."

Cassie blinked. "I think you just did."

He laughed, something Cassie had never heard before. He seemed overjoyed, delighted in every way.

She gave him an apprehensive smile. "I suppose the fact that you're here and in such a good mood means you didn't get arrested and haven't any need to continue worrying about the past."

"That supposition is correct." He took her hand. "Come sit with me. I have so much to tell you."

"Would you like me to fix something to eat while you talk?"

"No, we'll go out after this and celebrate."

She wasn't sure what they'd be celebrating, but she was too nervous to ask. She was still reeling from the kiss and even more so from the fact that Brandon had laughed and smiled.

"Everything is good, Cassie. It wasn't at all what I expected, but it has freed me from my guilt and fears."

She joined him on the sofa. "Tell me everything."

And he did. He revealed to her every detail about the trip. When Brandon explained how the doctor and the chief of police knew all about the abuse his mother endured, she grew angry.

"Why was she left to suffer if people knew what was going on? Why did no one come to your poor mother's rescue?"

"It's mostly the fault of the law. Women and children are basically property to be treated however their men desire. My father was a big name in town, and people wanted to keep on his good side, I suppose. He had power that folks dreaded—the power to put their name in print and shame them or humble them, bring public opinion against them. Of course, they could sue, but that just made the accusations all the more public, and people of means hate to be involved in scandal."

"So everyone just looked the other way."

"They did for a time, but then they also did the same for my mother."

"What do you mean?" Cassie could see there was more to the story than he'd already shared.

"My mother is the one who actually ended my father's life."

She gasped and put her hand to her throat. "Your mother?"

"Yes, my father started to rally after my blow to his head. I was gone by then, and Mother probably never even considered the consequences. She just acted on her fears and hit him several times in the head with a bookend. The doctor said it was never a question of whether or not she had defended herself. He figures she was so caught up in the shock of nearly dying at his hand that she hit my father as a means of stopping the attack."

"I can definitely understand that," Cassie said, rubbing her arms. Her father had always been such a loving and good man. She could barely imagine the feeling of needing such a defense.

Brandon scooted closer and put his arm around her. "I visited the cemetery where she's buried and thought of all the years she suffered and struggled. But she had the last three years of her life to live as she desired with her sister. The doc said they were good years, and I know from what she wrote to me that she was happy."

"I hope she was at peace with all that happened, though I'm surprised she encouraged you to leave."

"I think she knew there was nothing there for me. She probably feared if I remained in my father's shadow, I might become like him. But, Cassie, I will never be like him. I promise you that."

"What are you saying?"

"I'm saying I want to marry you. I want to have a family with you and grow old together. You once pointed out that

I'm nothing like my father, and I can finally agree with you. For the most part. I have a similar temper, but over the years, I've learned to let God control it—to help me not to give in to it. Now, when situations come up, I reason through the matter. I'm quiet and thoughtful about things, and when there are problems, I don't just fly off the handle and do whatever comes to mind. I think through situations, knowing there are good solutions and bad."

She smiled, familiar with that side of him. "I'm glad you can finally see that for yourself. The rest of us have known what a good man you are for ages."

"Once we're married, you never have to worry about me resorting to my father's type of behavior. I promise."

She looked at him, searching his face for answers. "Is that your roundabout way of proposing?"

He chuckled. "I suppose it is."

"I see." She got up and walked to the fireplace. "Well, before I can respond, I have to have an answer to one question."

He got up as well and came to where she stood. "I'll answer anything. You already know everything about me. What more could I possibly share with you?"

"Why do you want to marry me?"

A look of relief washed over his face. "Because I love you."

It was Cassie's turn to laugh. "That is a perfectly good answer, because the truth is I love you too. I just wanted to make sure I knew what your motivation was."

He took her in his arms and kissed her again. This time he was very gentle, and the tenderness he showed brought tears to Cassie's eyes.

"I hope those are tears of happiness," he murmured against her cheek.

"They are. They are tears I never thought would be mine to cry. I never even dared to dream of this until the last few weeks. When I realized how much I cared for you—loved you—I was almost paralyzed with fear. I was afraid you would be arrested and jailed, and I might never see you again."

"Yet here I stand."

"Yes. With the promise of a future and the love that has been so sorely missing in my life."

"How about we go to dinner to celebrate our engagement and make plans for our wedding?"

"I'd like that," she said. "Let me grab my jacket."

She had just started for the bedroom when a horrible ruckus started at the front door. It sounded as if a dozen or more people had arrived in protest. Cassie stopped short of her bedroom, and Brandon opened the door to find his section gang all talking at once.

"They're going to destroy the tracks," one of the young men said in Spanish.

Javier gave an enthusiastic nod. "And cause a derailment."

"They're gonna do that first, so that everyone is busy at the accident site, and then they're gonna blow up the dam," Max said, huffing and puffing as if he'd run a long way to bring the news.

"Hold on, boys. Hold on." Brandon held up his hands. "Come inside and tell me calmly what's going on."

The young men filed in, and Cassie drew near to see what was happening.

"Who did you say is going to do these things?" Brandon asked.

"We don't know the man. He's new. He has reddish hair and a big mustache. He works for the Santa Fe," Zorro declared.

"I think he's a fireman," Bruno added.

"Cyrus McCutchen," Brandon muttered. "It couldn't be anyone else." He looked at Cassie, and she nodded. It certainly sounded like him.

"Where did you hear him say that he was going to derail a train?"

"We were at the pool hall," Javier said, taking charge. "We went there after work, and we were all busy playing when some men came in. They went to the bar to get their drinks, and then that man came in and motioned for them to follow him to the side of the room closest to the pool tables.

"I didn't pay him much attention, but he was acting strange. Trying to be all secretive and quiet," Javier continued in rapid-fire Spanish. "He told them the time had come that they could complete what they'd started, and . . ." He looked at the others, who nodded as if giving him permission to continue.

"And?" Brandon said.

"And he said he would find a way to make sure you were taken care of."

"Me?"

"Sí, he said he held you a grudge. He said you had caused him trouble, and he was going to get back what you owed him."

Cassie came to Brandon's side and took his arm. "That has to be Cyrus."

"Where are these men now?"

"Another man came in and said the horses were ready. The man doing all the talking said they needed to set everything in motion tonight."

"Did they say where they were headed?" Brandon asked.

"Just that they were going to make another derailment, bigger than the one they set last year, near that series of dry washes where the tracks go over the trellis bridges. Apparently, they have some other men coming up from the south. They're already at work on the line."

"Oh, Brandon." Cassie felt her knees go weak. This time last year her father had been killed. Could it be that Cyrus McCutchen was truly the villain behind her father's death? Was Brandon right?

"I knew it," he said grimly.

She nodded. "And now he figures to kill you as well."

"We won't let him," Max said, puffing out his chest. "We will guard you, Boss. We won't let anyone hurt you."

"We need to call down the line and keep the nine o'clock freight from coming through," Brandon said, shaking his head.

"We can track them. They had a lot of horses. It should be easy to follow them," Angel, the shyest of the bunch, spoke up.

"We've got to go speak with the Santa Fe officials first. They need to get word out," Brandon said. "Come with me, boys, and you can tell them what you know. We can send a wire down to the dam and make sure they're on the lookout. How long ago did they leave?"

"Just a few minutes before we came here," Javier replied.

Brandon looked at Cassie. "I have to go."

She knew he did, and despite the worry that he might get hurt or perhaps even killed, she put up a brave front. "Of course you do. Hurry, before Cyrus hurts someone else."

---

"Are you boys sure about this?" Bud Wilkes asked.

"Sí. We're very sure. We heard them at the pool hall. They did not know we were listening," Javier said, looking to the others. They all nodded.

"I told you I was worried about McCutchen. He just seemed to be up to something with his hollow apologies and eagerness to work for the railroad again." Brandon hoped the man wouldn't delay contacting the army.

Bud picked up the phone. He tried to raise the operator, but the line was dead. "Looks like they've cut the line," he said, putting the phone aside. "That means they will have cut all of the lines—telegraph too."

"Get the repair engine warmed up and ready to go," Brandon said. "We'll load it with everything we need to fix the track and plenty of wood. We'll make two-mile signal fires on either side of the place where the tracks have been destroyed. We'll put out torpedoes so that when the nine o'clock gets close, they'll hear the warning and stop the train." Torpedoes were small dynamite charges that could be fixed to the rail. When the train's wheel passed over it, the charge would fire and give off a small explosion as a warning to the engineer. When the engineer heard the explosion, he would know danger was imminent. Of course, they would have to get them set up on the other side of the damaged track and do so well before the evening freight came through.

Brandon looked at his watch. "We don't have much time to find the area they've torn up, but we'll get at it." He looked to Javier. "Which of you boys are the best horseback riders?"

Javier grinned. "Me and Zorro. We ride like the wind."

"Good. Go to the livery and tell them this is an emergency and that we need their two fastest horses. Better yet, I'll come with you so there's no mix-up. They know me over there." Brandon headed for the door. "We'll get the horses, then grab you some torpedoes."

"We'll have everything ready when you get back, Bran," Wilkes promised. "The rest of you gather the supplies needed for the repairs and get it on the flatcar. I'll get the orders set to get the repair train out of here in twenty minutes. You boys will need to work fast."

Brandon took Javier and Zorro and raced for the livery stables. If he could get Javier and Zorro in place on the opposite side of the track damage, they could hopefully save the nine o'clock freight.

# 24

Brandon paced the gravel area around the track, waiting for the engine's boilers to be heated sufficiently to pull out of the roundhouse. He had been afraid McCutchen would pull something like this. He'd never trusted the man to have found God and be desiring to make amends. It just seemed too convenient.

He'd instructed Javier and Zorro as to what they needed to do, but the boys already knew. They were well trained and eager to please. They didn't want to see the freight derail, possibly killing the engineer and fireman. Brandon knew they would put their own lives on the line rather than let someone else die. They were young men of integrity.

Bud approached Brandon. "I've sent riders down the track to see if they can figure out where the telephone and telegraph lines have been cut. My guess is it'll be somewhere fairly close to town. Once those are repaired, I'll get word to the army."

Brandon nodded. He prayed they'd be fixed in time.

"We're ready, Brandon," the engineer called down. "Let's go."

Brandon signaled his other workers to take their places on the train car. They had loaded the flatcar in record time, throwing on items that would certainly be needed along with a few that probably wouldn't. But better safe than sorry. "Let's go, boys."

They rushed for the train, easily jumped the distance from the ground to the car, and took their places alongside the repair supplies.

Brandon had already told them he was going to ride in the engine just to keep an extra eye out for problems. He hoisted himself up the steps and inside the toasty box.

"We're ready," the engineer announced. Dave had only been with the Santa Fe for about two months, but he'd driven trains most of the last twenty years.

Wes, the fireman, gave a nod. "Steam's up full."

Dave pulled the whistle, giving signal to those on the tracks. The train gave a jolt and moved forward a fraction. Then another jolt was felt, and another. They lurched out of the service yard and made their way to the main track headed south.

Brandon was anxious to get to where the damage had been done. That series of bridges was some fifty miles away. They would have to give it all they had to make it there within the hour.

With all lines of communication cut, Brandon knew it was soon to be a matter of life and death. He wondered at Cyrus's carelessness and the fact that he would make such a secret thing a very public announcement. The town was full of Santa Fe men.

That thought started doubt stirring within. Cyrus was no fool. He knew there would be plenty of Santa Fe men to overhear his plans in such a public place. Why would he make the announcement unless he *wanted* word to get out? But why would he want word to get out? He had to know it would result in someone trying to fix the situation.

Then again, maybe Brandon was giving Cyrus too much credit. If the man was in a hurry, perhaps he'd gotten careless. He had his men around him and might not have given much consideration to anyone else hearing or understanding what was going on.

"Can't we go any faster, Dave?"

"I've got her wide open, Brandon. We're doing the best we can. This little engine ain't as powerful as a full-size one. You know that."

Why hadn't they thought to get one of the engines from the roundhouse? Brandon knew most were there for repairs, but one of the larger engines might have been ready for service.

He kept his gaze ahead on the track. The pitch-black night was broken only by the light of the engine. The locomotive's lamp was helpful, but far from perfect, and only allowed for a short distance of light. They would have to stop shortly and load water. Maybe there would be some word of the lines being repaired.

They stopped and took on water, then proceeded down the track, increasing speed until the train was moving at a good clip. Brandon was certain that by the time they reached the area Cyrus had mentioned, Zorro and Javier would have been able to secure the torpedoes. Still, there was something not quite right about all of this. He couldn't put his finger on it, but something didn't set well.

He thought back over what the boys had told him. The derailment was to be a diversion for Cyrus and his men to blow up the dam. Cyrus had to know the army was still there, offering protection.

"But maybe they're not," Brandon murmured.

"What'd you say?" Dave asked, keeping his eyes on the road ahead.

"Nothing. Just thinking out loud. Say, Dave, do you know if the army has been pulled from the dam? I know I heard something about them having to withdraw from patrols on the tracks. Did they already do that?"

"Yeah, they took the patrols off yesterday. The army is being called back to their various forts. They're preparing for war. I don't know about the dam. I figure if they're pulling the troops out, they'll take them all."

"What about protecting the border?"

Dave shrugged. "Not sure. There might be some staying on. I haven't heard."

Brandon looked back down the long track ahead. There was a flash of light in the distance. He looked again. It flashed just like a man waving a lantern. Maybe it was one of the boys.

"I see a light ahead. Better stop," he told Dave.

The engineer looked at him like he was crazy. "I didn't see anything. We're coming up on the grade, and if I stop, it will be hard to get up it without backing up and making another run. Usually I put on a little more power here."

"I know I saw a light." Brandon narrowed his eyes. "There it is again. Didn't you see it?"

Dave shook his head. "I didn't."

"I still want you to stop. If we have to back up all the way to San Marcial to get up enough speed to make the grade, then so be it. This is too important. Javier or Zorro may be waiting there with word."

The engineer shrugged and signaled to Wes. The train slowed, and Brandon continued to watch ahead for the lamplight. He was certain someone was out there.

---

Cassie knew there was nothing she could do but pray. It seemed so little, and yet she knew prayer was the very tool given to Christians that could change the entire world. It was so often overlooked and disregarded, but she had learned, especially of late, that it really did make a difference.

Taking her Bible, she sat down by the fire in her mother's old rocking chair and began to pray for Brandon and the boys' safety. She had no idea what they would find once they got out there in the desert.

"Father, please watch over them. Help Brandon find the place where the track has been destroyed. Let them be able to make the repairs so that no one gets hurt."

She tried not to fret or think about the past, but her father's death came to mind without her bidding. She thought of Cyrus McCutchen getting out of prison with the sole purpose of killing her father and exacting revenge. If he was truly the one responsible for the derailment, how could they prove it? How could they make him pay for what he'd done?

Papa had loved his work for the railroad—loved the Santa Fe. He had only turned McCutchen in because it was the right thing to do. He wasn't seeking revenge or retribution. Papa just wanted justice and safety for all of the employees. McCutchen, he had once told her, made life difficult for everyone with his lack of concern for safety and his inability to abide by the rules.

Cassie shivered at the thought of how she'd gone to dinner with McCutchen. Who knew what kind of danger she'd been in? The nerve of the man, to talk about how he'd found God's forgiveness and wanted to make amends for the past. And if he was the one responsible for killing Papa, all the worse.

The clock on the mantel ticked painfully loudly. It was the only sound in the house other than Cassie's breathing. She opened the Bible to the Psalms and tried to read.

"'Fret not thyself because of evildoers, neither be thou envious against the workers of iniquity. For they shall soon be cut down like the grass, and wither as the green herb. Trust in the Lord, and do good,'" she read from Psalm 37. She smiled and closed her eyes. "Fret not and trust in the Lord."

It sounded like the kind of message her mother would have given her when Cassie was a child.

"I miss you so much, Mama. You always had a way to calm

my fears. You promised me God was ever near and would never let me face trials on my own."

She opened her eyes and looked down at the Word of God. "'Delight thyself also in the Lord: and he shall give thee the desires of thine heart.'"

Mama had explained that this verse was powerful, with definite direction for the reader: delight in the Lord.

*"How do I do that, Mama?"* Cassie remembered asking.

*"It's a matter of putting your mind on Him who has given you everything, and taking joy and true happiness in who He is, what He is going to do for you, what He has already done, and what you can do for Him. It's all-encompassing and goes well beyond mere feelings, Cassie."*

*"And then God will give me whatever I ask for?"* Cassie had posed the question in childish innocence. *"Like that porcelain doll at Mr. Brickman's store?"*

*"It's about so much more than that."* Mama hadn't been angry at her wrong assumption, nor chastising. *"The desires you have will be ones God puts there. It won't be about wanting dolls or trinkets. It will be about helping others, loving others. It will be about desiring God's will over your own."*

It had been hard for Cassie to understand at the tender age of seven, but as she grew older, she had come to see the real meaning of that verse. It wasn't that God wouldn't give desires for personal things that were beneficial and good. He was a generous and loving Father who wanted to give His children good gifts. But He also longed for His children to desire more than selfish ambitions.

Cassie could see that now. She understood it was God who had put a desire in her heart to give of her time and effort to benefit others. It was God who had convinced her that even when it came to business dealings, she could rest in Him and not fear for tomorrow. Look at how He had provided for her when she broke her wrist.

There were times when she had helped folks who couldn't afford to pay. She knew such projects were ones God had sent her way, and she did her best on each one—just as if she'd be paid handsomely for each piece. She had learned to give her best, even if there wasn't a guarantee of reward or even acknowledgment.

For some reason, the Duchess of Canton came to mind. Cassie had been so careful with her expensive Worth gown, but if it had been her maid's outfit, Cassie knew she would have treated the piece with the same care. This was the desire of her heart that God had placed there. To treat each person as if they were the most important person in the world. After all, they were all God's children.

She looked at the clock. It had hardly moved, and it brought a heavy sigh from her lips. She'd barely gotten to tell Brandon she'd marry him before they'd received the news about Mc-Cutchen. Now she feared that evil man might take Brandon from her, as he had her father.

"Lord, please intercede. Keep Brandon safe and provide angels of protection for him this night."

"There's nothing here," Dave said, looking at the length of track ahead. He had climbed down from the engine and walked a ways with Brandon. "It all looks just fine. Come on, we're wasting time."

Brandon shook his head. "There must be something here. I'm positive I saw a light."

He pressed on toward the ravine and the bridge that crossed the dangerous gulch. He hadn't taken but two steps when there was a cracking sound, and he sank into the sand up to his knee. He looked beyond his position and watched as the sand shifted.

"Bring the light, Wes."

The younger man was there in a heartbeat, shining the lantern so they could all see that the place beneath the track was far from solid. Someone had undermined the support system and managed to put everything back in place to look as if there were nothing wrong.

Brandon pulled himself out of the hole. He walked back to where the boys were milling about and asked for a tamp bar. He returned to the place where the earth had given way and began tamping along the ground. He found a thin piece of board only strong enough to support a façade of sand to make it appear the rail was fully supported by gravel and ties.

As the sand gave way, Dave whistled. "If we'd hit that, we would have derailed and gone into the ravine." He looked at Brandon in the dim glow. "We'd be dead if not for you seeing some phantom lamp on the track."

"Perhaps that light was of heavenly origin," Brandon said, glancing upward.

"Moonlight on the rails?" Dave questioned, following Brandon's skyward gaze.

Except there was no moon that night.

"I hear horses approaching," Wes said, cocking his head.

"Boys," Brandon called, "take cover. Someone's coming."

Cyrus had been delighted by the way Brandon's section gang raced from the pool hall to find him. It was going just as he'd hoped. Brandon would be so focused on playing the hero—keeping the train coming up from El Paso from meeting with a serious fate—that he would give little thought to his own safety.

And just as Cyrus had anticipated, Brandon had gathered his people and gotten the repair engine headed out as quickly as he could. But Brandon would be expecting the damaged tracks to be another thirty miles down the track, so he'd be pushing the engineer to drive the repair train at a high speed, knowing there would barely be enough time for him to get someone down the track to set warning torpedoes.

But this time, rushing to the rescue would work for Cyrus. Brandon and the others would hit that place just before the ravine, and the entire train would go plunging into the gulch.

Cyrus and his men rode after Brandon and the others. With any luck, they'd arrive just after the derailment. They could kill any survivors and leave it all to be further complicated by the El Paso train. Cyrus delighted at the thought of that freight plowing into the wreckage and causing further destruction.

There wasn't a bit of light to go by, but Cyrus and his men knew this area. There were a few houses along the way—a few landmarks. They kept the rails to their right and pressed on. It wasn't far now.

He saw the glow of the locomotive headlamp first. He couldn't tell by the light's position if the engine was upright or on its side.

"Slow," he called to the men.

The horses were slowed and then halted as Cyrus listened for any sound of chaos or trouble. Perhaps they were all dead, and he wouldn't have to kill anyone.

They pressed forward, still uncertain as to what had happened. Either the train had derailed, or it hadn't. At the very least, they might have slowed to a crawl and caved in the rails where Cyrus and the others had weakened the section of track.

Cyrus reached the back car. He could see it was upright, as was the next one. The darkness shared very little, but he could see the outline of the engine against the starry sky. He cursed, wishing the accident had been more dramatic.

"Halt where you are," a voice called out. "The US Army has you surrounded."

Cyrus tried to turn his horse to ride in the opposite direction, but someone had a hold of the bridle. He pulled at the reins to force the horse back, but the man held the animal in place.

"You aren't going anywhere, Cyrus, except back to jail."

DuBarko's voice left him seething. He wasn't giving up that easily. Cyrus threw himself over the horse's neck toward DuBarko, but the younger man was ready for him. They fell to the ground, and the horse made a mad dash to get away from the commotion. Cyrus knew it was over, but going back to jail wasn't an option he wanted to face. He pulled the gun from his holster as DuBarko tried to wrestle him to the ground. Although he tried to aim at DuBarko, Cyrus found it impossible, and soon he lost his grip on the gun altogether as one of the other men pulled it from his hand.

Cyrus felt himself being forced to his feet. He wasn't sure who had hold of him, but it felt like at least four sets of hands. He growled in anger and discomfort. This wasn't how he'd seen the future at all.

"Good thing Javier found the army heading back to the fort, eh, Boss?" one of the kids asked as they managed to get the last of Cyrus's men in hand.

By now they had several lanterns lit, and seeing the men involved in his capture left Cyrus little doubt that he was completely done in.

"Yep," DuBarko said, still holding fast to Cyrus's upper arm. He looked Cyrus in the eye. "This little stunt ought to see you spending the rest of your life in prison."

---

Cassie was waiting with Myrtle and John when the army filed into San Marcial with Cyrus and his men. Brandon and his crew had stayed out to repair the track and didn't return to town until nearly two in the morning. Nevertheless, Cassie, Myrtle, and John were waiting with food and drink.

Brandon had eyes for no one else and made a beeline to where Cassie stood at Myrtle's stove, pouring cups of coffee. He carefully took the pot from her and placed it on the stove, then pulled her into his arms for a long embrace.

Neither spoke, they just held each other as if the world had come to an end and they were the only ones left.

"Are you hurt?" she murmured against his ear.

"Not a bit. Although I would be, if McCutchen had his way."

She pulled back. "I was so afraid, but I just kept praying."

"Wait until you hear what God did," he said, smiling. "You'll never doubt the power of prayer again."

"I never doubted it," Cassie replied. "God's been far too faithful to start doubting Him now."

"I agree." Brandon nodded. "So when are you going to marry me?"

"Whenever you say the word."

"Well, it's not all up to him," John said, poking his head into the kitchen. "I like to meet with my couples a few times and help them get to know some of the secrets of how to deal with married life."

Brandon let Cassie go. "Such as?"

"How to work through arguments. How to overcome things from the past. How to agree on things to do with the future."

Brandon shook his head. "After all we've been through, don't you think we've figured that out for ourselves?"

"If you have, then you won't mind going over it again. Four meetings at my house. Myrtle will cook the most amazing meals for you, and then I'll happily wed you in any fashion of your choosing. In the church, on the train, in the desert. Whatever you say."

Brandon rolled his gaze to the ceiling. "I thought we'd already dealt with the hard part."

John laughed. "Oh, son, you're just beginning."

# 25

The entire town of San Marcial declared Friday, April 6, 1917, a day of fiesta on behalf of Cassie and Brandon's wedding. It was only happenstance that Congress also approved President Wilson's request to declare war on Germany.

At first, Cassie thought they should change the date. A declaration of war and a wedding seemed so completely at odds with each other that she feared it would be bad luck to force the two together. However, the plans had already been put in motion, and her sister and brother-in-law had made a special trip to San Marcial to be part of the festivities.

So many people knew Cassie from her sewing and mending, and just as many knew Brandon from his training of what they estimated to be over one hundred Santa Fe employees. It was as if the entire town wanted to join one last celebration before giving themselves over to the grim duties of war, and Cassie couldn't fault them for that. Let them all celebrate and enjoy life while it was theirs to enjoy. The dark days of war would soon be upon them, and God alone knew how many lives would be required.

Cassie studied her reflection in the mirror one last time, certain that the simple wedding gown of white muslin and lace would be more than adequate for the day. A last-minute surprise had come on the train from the Duchess of Canton in the form of a stunning headpiece and veil. Cassie had been shocked to learn the duchess even knew of her wedding plans.

Melissa revealed that her mother-in-law had kept the old woman informed. Apparently, once she'd found out that Cassie was in love, she had insisted on being kept abreast of the wedding plans. Cassie was deeply touched that the duchess had even cared. No doubt, with the war raging on, she had plenty to keep her busy.

"Are you ready?" Melissa asked as she came into the bedroom. She was dressed in a sage green gown with four tiers of ruffled lace and a bodice that was fashioned in a shawl-type style of ruffled lace and fitted sleeves.

"You look beautiful," Cassie said, noting her sister's upswept hair. "Seeing you is sometimes like having Mama here with me once again."

Melissa smiled. "I wish I were half as good and kind as she was. It's definitely something I want to strive for but know I miss the mark on."

"Nonsense. You are good and kind, and you will always be an inspiration to her memory."

Melissa hugged her sister tightly. "And just look at you. Every bit the radiant bride with your diamonds and lace. I wonder if your guests will know there are thirty diamonds in that headpiece."

"What?" Cassie turned back to the mirror. "These aren't real . . . are they?"

"Can you imagine a duchess sending you paste jewels?"

"I can't wear this." Cassie reached up to pull the headpiece from her carefully styled hair.

Melissa barely stopped her in time. "Cassie, leave it be. You are beautiful. It's just as it should be."

"But I had no idea they were real." She felt her heart skip a beat. "I've never worn anything worth the kind of money this must have cost."

"My guess is it is a family piece, and she was happy to share it with you. The duchess has no children, so why not let her enjoy herself? We'll make sure there are plenty of pictures taken so you can send her a photograph of you wearing it. She'll be so pleased."

Cassie bit her lower lip. She wanted to wear the piece. She truly did. But what if someone tried to steal it? What if she dropped it or lost one of the diamonds?

Melissa took hold of her hands. "This is your special day. Don't make it a day about the duchess's jewelry. Despite all of the problems the world could throw at you, you've won the love of your life. Be glad and enjoy the moment. There will never be another like it."

The words had a calming effect, and Cassie gave a brief nod. She and Brandon deserved this day with their friends. There would never be another one like it. War or no war, she was marrying the love of her life, and they would face the problems of the future together.

With Melissa on one side of her and Terry on the other, they walked the short distance to the crowded church. Melissa was to stand up with Cassie, while Terry had agreed to walk her down the aisle. To Cassie's surprise, Brandon had picked Javier to be his best man, and the two stood waiting at the front of the church as the organ began to play.

Melissa made her way in graceful order down the aisle. Someone placed a bouquet of flowers in Cassie's arms. She looked up and found Myrtle smiling like a doting mother.

"I hope you don't mind my stepping in like this, but I wanted you to have something special from John and me."

"They're beautiful. Thank you." Cassie pulled the bouquet of roses to her face and inhaled. The sweet scent was strong and pure. "Just perfect," she murmured.

Myrtle kissed Cassie's cheek, then hurried to claim her seat at the front of the church. Finally, it was Cassie's turn to go forward. She was glad for Terry's steady arm as she felt her knees begin to quiver. She glanced up and found Brandon watching her, and his gaze calmed her unlike anything else could. He had always been there for her, even when she didn't realize it. She smiled, and he returned it. Just months ago, he would never have considered such a thing. Now it seemed he smiled quite often.

The closer she came to where he stood, the faster Cassie wanted to move. She wanted to reach him—to touch his arm—to know that nothing would ever separate them again. But, of course, there was the war. That fear lingered for just a moment in her mind. What if he was forced to join the army? Worse still, what if he decided joining was his duty, and he wanted to go? Could she be brave enough to let him leave? Could she support him going off to fight?

*Oh, God, please give me strength to face the future.* She breathed the prayer in silence as she came to stand beside Brandon.

It was as if Brandon could read her thoughts. He squeezed her fingers in encouragement. There would be plenty of time for such worries later. Right now, in this moment, they needed only to focus on each other and the love God had given them.

"Dearly beloved," John began, and Cassie drew a deep breath and squared her shoulders.

Later, under the starry skies with music playing all around them, Cassie and Brandon held each other and swayed. It was their own version of dancing, as neither had ever really learned how.

"Do you suppose we shall ever learn to do a proper waltz or two-step?" Cassie asked as Brandon held her close.

"Do you really think we'll have need of it?" he asked, looking down at her with one brow raised.

"Who can say? I never thought I'd need to learn a lot of things that have come in handy. Spanish. Fancy stitches. How to wear a diamond headpiece."

"A diamond headpiece?" He studied the stones reflecting the dim light.

"The duchess sent me this headpiece, and Melissa assures me it contains thirty diamonds."

"And here you are just wearing it out in the street, dancing away as if it were nothing."

Cassie laughed. "I almost fainted when she told me. Apparently, it's something from the duchess's family heirlooms. She has no children."

Brandon looked around at the other couples dancing in the street. "Do they all know it's real diamonds?"

"I have no idea. I've certainly said nothing about it, and it isn't the kind of thing Melissa would mention. In her circle of friends, it's always assumed that things are exactly as they are represented to be, even though I've never seen a setting with fewer true and honest people."

"Perhaps the jewels and furs are all real so they can disguise the fake people."

Cassie nodded. "I believe that's well put, Brandon."

He pulled her to one side, and they stood looking back at the street of dancers. Most of the older folks had long given up dancing for sitting and chatting. Some were eating, and a few seemed to be caught up in discussions.

"It was quite the affair," Brandon said, pulling Cassie close.

"I think everyone needed this. With the war upon us now, they needed one last party before they set their mind to serious matters."

"Are you afraid?"

She looked up and gave a nod. "A little. I can't bear the thought of you leaving, of wondering if you're safe."

"Then don't worry about it. My supervisor said I am urgently needed here to keep the Santa Fe Railway capable of transporting equipment and troops. I won't be going anywhere except along the rail. Oh, and Mr. Mackie wants to see that book of yours."

"Of stories about the Santa Fe?"

Brandon nodded. "When he heard about it, he thought it would be a great thing to offer encouragement and a sense of American spirit. He wants to see it as soon as possible."

Cassie hugged him tightly. "Oh, Brandon, both of those things are all that I want in the world, but especially for you to stay here. I know I can face anything with you by my side."

# Epilogue

Cassie sat holding her sleeping six-month-old son, Wesley, and listening to the speech given by one of the Santa Fe officials to mark the end of the Great War. Brandon had been honored only a few minutes earlier with several other men, including Javier, for their service to the Santa Fe in keeping the district rails in perfect working order and being available for whatever work was demanded of them. They hadn't missed a single day of work since war had been declared, and their efforts were lauded as keeping America's railroad systems running.

Brandon, never one to want attention, had been less than pleased to have to sit on the stage and face the crowds gathered to celebrate the war's end, but Cassie had encouraged him to endure it. Then they could disappear back to their room at the Alvarado, a beautiful Harvey hotel so finely appointed and fashioned that Cassie could have spent several weeks there and never tired of its grandeur.

"We are especially thankful for the hard work and dedication of all of our Santa Fe workers. These brave men and women put their lives on the line as surely as if they had gone to the battlefront. It is often forgotten that a war is not won only on the battlefield, but also in the hearts and minds of the people back home who keep materials moving to the front, who fill in for the brave men called to service. We at the Santa Fe salute and applaud your faithful work and honor you today as we celebrate the end of this tragic and horrible war."

The audience applauded as the man took his seat and another came to the podium. Cassie felt Wesley stir at the loud clapping and cheers. She hoped he might remain sleeping, but as he opened his eyes and looked up at her, she knew it wasn't to be.

While people were still preoccupied with shouting their approval, she got to her feet and slipped to the back of the room. Wesley began to fuss, so she waited just a moment to catch Brandon's attention. He finally saw her and gave a nod as she pointed to the door.

Outside, Cassie bounced the baby and murmured soothingly to him. He was the joy of her life—a gift from God she hadn't been sure she'd ever have.

"Wesley, you dear boy, you don't need to fuss. That noisy group will soon calm down."

The celebration continued as she made her way back to the hotel suite they'd been given as part of Brandon's reward for all he'd done. As Cassie entered the room, she found a young maid working to lay a fire in the hearth. It was rather cold, and Cassie was grateful that such a thing had been considered.

She spoke in Spanish to the girl, thanking her for her kindness. The girl seemed surprised at Cassie's ability.

"You speak Spanish. Most Americans do not."

Cassie smiled and shifted Wesley in her arms. "I've lived in New Mexico for a long time. Spanish is the language most people speak. It seemed important to learn."

"Yes," the girl said, shifting to English. "And I learn English. I'm not speaking good."

"You are doing very well."

"You would like the fire, yes?"

"Yes, please, it's rather cold today, and I don't want the baby to catch a chill," Cassie said, switching back to Spanish.

The young woman lit the fire and made certain it was well underway before leaving Cassie and Wesley.

Cassie took a seat by the fire and held Wesley up to stand on her lap. He bounced up and down, now fully awake and ready for action. His blue eyes and wavy hair were very much like his father's, and Cassie could see a bit of her own father's nose and mouth in her son's features.

"You, tiny sir, are very much loved."

The baby gave a gurgling sound and offered his mother a smile. She thought of how few of those smiles she'd seen from Brandon over the years, but that would not be the case with his son. Wesley smiled all the time, much to the delight of Cassie and Brandon. He was the joy of their lives.

The door to the hotel opened, and Brandon came striding in with the hotel maid following close behind.

"Sabrina is going to watch Wesley while you join me at the superintendent's private party. I was told this was most important and that you were not allowed to say no."

"What in the world does the superintendent want with me?"

Brandon smiled. "It's a surprise, and I think you'll be glad you came."

Sabrina went to Cassie and smiled. "I take good care of your baby."

"His name is Wesley," Cassie said, handing him to the girl. "He just woke up after a very short nap, so he'll probably want to play."

Sabrina nodded. "I will play with him. I have many brothers and know very well how to keep a baby happy."

Cassie was reluctant to leave Wesley. She'd only ever let Myrtle babysit for her when Brandon planned a dinner out. Sabrina, although a nice girl, was a complete stranger.

Looking at Brandon, Cassie couldn't help but worry. Brandon smiled. "It'll be all right. Sabrina came highly recommended, and I trust that she'll do a good job."

"Very well." Cassie moved to Brandon's side. "Lead the way."

They stepped outside the room, and Brandon startled Cassie by sweeping her into his arms for a passionate kiss. When he let her go just as abruptly as he'd taken her into his arms, Cassie nearly stumbled to the floor. Brandon righted her and gave her a grin.

"Glad to know I can still make you go weak in the knees."

She laughed and wrapped her arm around his. "You will always have that effect on me. Now, tell me what this is all about."

"It's a surprise. I'm not allowed to speak a word of it."

"Not even a hint?"

"Not a word," he said, grinning. "But it's a good surprise. I'll say that much."

Cassie was truly intrigued. What could the superintendent of the district possibly want with her?

They entered a private dining room where refreshments had been laid out in a lavish spectacle. Red, white, and blue banners and streamers were hanging throughout the room, and the tables were festooned with eagles holding America's and New Mexico's flags.

The food caught her eye immediately. There was every kind of delicacy, but it was the pastries that intrigued Cassie most. Hopefully she'd get a chance to sample a few before returning to their room.

Brandon led her straight to the front of the room, where she recognized the superintendent and his entourage from earlier in the day.

"Ah, Mrs. DuBarko. I'm so glad you decided to join us," the tall man declared, reaching out to take her hand. He shook it firmly, then looked at Brandon. "Your wife is quite the woman."

"I agree," Brandon replied. He glanced at Cassie and gave her a wink.

She had no idea what was going on, but everyone seemed happy and more than congenial, so she simply went along with the spirit of things.

"Come and stand here. I will get everyone's attention, as I know you have a young baby waiting for you." He turned away from her. "Ladies and gentlemen, could I have your attention, please!"

People from all over the room came and gathered directly in front of Cassie and Brandon. The superintendent waited until everyone quieted and then reached behind him for a red book with gold lettering that lay on the table and held it high.

"I asked you all here to make an announcement. Mrs. DuBarko, as many of you know, compiled a collection of stories told by our workers regarding their experiences on the Santa Fe Railway. Today I am proud to hold a copy of that book in my hands and present it to Mrs. DuBarko in congratulations. This is book number fifty thousand."

There were gasps of surprise around the room, but no one gasped louder than Cassie.

"*Another Day on the Santa Fe* has proven to be a top seller among our souvenir shops and depots. Folks have responded very positively to reading about our workers and the various trials and adventures that have been a part of their daily working lives. Mrs. DuBarko, we are so pleased with what you've accomplished in the telling of these stories that the Santa Fe would like to offer you the opportunity to write a second volume of stories." He extended the book. "We are very pleased to have you as a part of our Santa Fe family."

Everyone clapped as Cassie took the book. She'd seen it before in the shops, of course, and she even had several copies back at the house in San Marcial, but this was number fifty thousand. She had hoped that the book would sell a few hundred copies, even a few thousand, but to learn it had done so well was a shock.

"Tell us, Mrs. DuBarko, what gave you the idea for this collection of stories?" the superintendent asked.

Cassie glanced at Brandon, who gave her a nod of encouragement. "My father worked for the Santa Fe. He was an engineer. He told me amazing stories of his days on the rails. I thought they were the kind of stories others might appreciate hearing. As I began to write them down, it occurred to me that other Santa Fe workers might have their own stories to tell."

"Is it true that you began this project while injured from a fall?" the man asked.

Cassie nodded. "Yes, I was a seamstress in San Marcial. Most of my work was for the men of the Santa Fe and their families. I took a bad fall and broke my wrist and two fingers, which made sewing impossible. It was during my recovery that I began to write down the stories."

"And we are very glad that you did." The superintendent reached inside his coat pocket. "I believe you will be equally glad when you see this royalty check." He handed the check to Cassie, and her eyes grew wide. She handed it to Brandon, and his eyes widened as well.

"I can see I've stunned you both, but there is more to come. Let's give Mrs. DuBarko a round of applause, and then I'm sure we can talk her into autographing a copy of her book for each of you, compliments of the Santa Fe Railway."

The people began to clap, but all Cassie could do was look at her husband.

It was a wonderful surprise, unlike anything she had imagined, and later that night as she reflected on the day, Cassie could only whisper a prayer of gratitude at all that God had done in her life. She thought of Job and how after he had lost so much, God restored and blessed him beyond all that he had known. Cassie, too, suffered many losses, but God had given again and again, blessing her in ways that had not only been unexpected, but frankly . . . unimaginable.

As she stood watching Wesley sleep, Brandon slipped in behind her and wrapped her in his arms. He pulled her back against him and whispered, "Are you happy?"

"More than happy. I was just thinking of how much God has blessed me. Despite the things I wish were different, He has given me a life of abundance." She sighed and turned to face her husband. "Are you happy?"

"Do you have to ask?" He smiled and kissed her lightly on the forehead. "I am beyond happy. There is a contentment and joy in my heart that I never hoped to have, Cassie. I thought the past and my mistakes had forever robbed me of such things, but God has redeemed it all."

She remembered her morning Scripture reading. "'My lips shall greatly rejoice when I sing unto thee; and my soul, which thou hast redeemed.'" She smiled, meeting her husband's gaze. "We are redeemed, Brandon. Redeemed in His love."

Look for
Tracie Peterson's next historical series,
PICTURES OF THE HEART, debuting with

*Remember Me*

**in March 2023!**

After escaping a horrible past, Addie Bryant hopes for a fresh start and that she can forever hide what she left behind. Years later, she has found peace in her new life as a photographer. But when she is reunited with her old beau, Addie must decide whether to run or stay and face her wounds in order to embrace her life, her future, and hope in her God.

Read on for an excerpt from *Waiting on Love* from Tracie's bestselling series, LADIES OF THE LAKE, available wherever books are sold.

# Chapter 1

Elise Wright watched her sister, Caroline, as she greeted the wedding guests. Caroline was five years her junior, and Elise wanted to be happy for her but found it difficult. Caroline hadn't sought their father's advice, or even Elise's, about her marriage. Of course, her sister was so distanced from the family that when Mama died the year before, Caroline hardly even seemed upset. Elise had tried not to hate her for her callous attitude, but it required a great deal of prayer. Now Caroline wanted Elise and their father to be happy about her marrying into New York society to a man none of them really knew.

Still, Caroline seemed happy as she moved effortlessly in her ivory wedding gown of satin ruching and lace upon lace. The long train didn't seem to slow her in the least, nor did the trailing tulle veil. She was radiant and full of energy. Maybe she truly had married for love rather than money and position.

"She is beautiful, isn't she?" their father whispered against Elise's ear.

"She is. And she seems so happy. Nelson must be the right man for her." They'd met Nelson Worthington only a few days ago.

Her father nodded. "I had my doubts, but your uncle James assured me he was from a good family. They're in church every Sunday. Your mama would be happy to know that."

"I don't know that it would be enough. Mama used to say that Satan himself is in church every Sunday. The purpose in being there is what really matters."

Her father smiled. "You're so like her. How I miss her." His joy seemed to fade.

"I do too, Papa." She let him hug her close despite her very tight corset and uncomfortable clothes. She knew her father was just as miserable in the fancy suit that Uncle James let him borrow. As if reading her thoughts, Papa loosened his tie.

"It's been a little more than a year, and yet it seems like she was here just yesterday," her father whispered. "Other days it feels like she's been gone forever."

"I know, Papa. It's that way for me too."

He gazed out across the garden reception. "She would love seeing your sister get what she wanted for her wedding."

"It would have been nice if Caroline had given more consideration to what you and Mama wanted." Elise struggled with the anger she felt toward her sister. Caroline had hurt their parents so much with her choices. She never seemed to think of anyone but herself.

"We used to talk about you girls getting married. We worried about having enough money to give you a nice wedding. I regret that your uncle is paying for this. I offered him money—what I could—but he said it was their delight to give this wedding to Caroline. What could I say?"

"Well, you won't have to worry about giving me this kind of wedding. I can scarcely breathe, much less enjoy myself, in restrictive gowns like this." She looked down at the lavender creation she wore. "I feel completely out of sorts. Especially with this bustle. Goodness, whoever created such a thing?" She glanced over her shoulder and then gave her father a smile. "Besides, I don't intend to marry. I'm married to the *Mary Elise*," she said, referencing their ship.

Her father roared with laughter, causing many of Oswego's social elite to look their way. It would no doubt be a terrible embarrassment to Caroline, who hated that she was from a ship captain's family and spoke very little of it. Elise had heard from her cousins that Caroline told people their father was quite wealthy and chose to captain a ship for pure pleasure. Elise herself had heard her sister say their father took to sailing because it was his favorite thing to do, and he was very eccentric.

The truth was, however, that Elise and her sister had both grown up on ships, and money was often scarce. When Uncle James got into the shipping business six years ago, he had helped Papa buy the *Mary Elise*—a three-masted schooner named after Elise and Caroline's mother and grandmother. Elise loved life on the lakes and had helped their mother in the galley, but Caroline had enjoyed when they stayed with Uncle James and his family. She had taken to the life of a wealthy socialite and never wanted to return to their shipboard life. More than once, Caroline had made their mother cry, and Elise hated that Caroline had been so heartless. Her sister was only a child at the time, so Mama had encouraged everyone to be patient with her, but as the years passed, the tantrums only increased. Caroline would cry for hours. She would take to her bed and swear that ship life was killing her. By the time she was fifteen, Mama and Papa had given up. They allowed her to live with Mama's wealthy brother and his family.

Uncle James had been Mama's support throughout the years. Even when she ran away to elope with Papa, he had been the one to make it possible. When he'd offered to let the girls come live with him and his family, it wasn't a surprise. He had told his sister that the girls would never get good husbands if they weren't trained properly. Mama and Papa left it up to Elise as to whether she wanted to join her sister. She didn't.

"Are you enjoying yourselves?" her cousin Louis asked, interrupting her thoughts.

"It's everything I expected it would be." Elise gave him a smile. "What about you?"

"I'd rather be anywhere else in the world," he answered, returning the smile.

"You mean you don't like dressing up in tight-fitting suits?" Papa asked.

"As much as any fellow ever has at these occasions. Being here just reminds every would-be bride that I'm eligible to marry." Even though he was three years younger than Elise, at twenty-two, Louis seemed to have a very stable outlook on life.

Elise giggled. She had watched a bevy of frilly young ladies flock around her male cousins all day.

"Go ahead and laugh, but it's torment for me. At least Caroline and her young man seem happy. A father could hardly ask for more." Louis looked at Elise. "She did, however, step out of line and marry before her older sister."

"Oh, I am not finding her position enviable," Elise replied, hugging her father's arm. "Besides, being married hasn't seemed harmful to your brother Randolph. He looks quite content." She nodded toward the tall, handsome man who stood smiling into the face of his wife.

"They're absolutely gone over each other. It's so embarrassing, but our mother's greatest triumph. Well, at least until now, with Caroline. Mother just loves pairing us all up." Louis grinned. "If Elise sticks around, Mother is convinced she can get her married off as well. She loves having people to fuss over. I suppose they're like china dolls to dress up and arrange."

"Well, I'd just as soon Elise stay with me awhile longer," her father declared. "After all, if she were gone, who would cook for the men on the *Mary Elise*?" He winked at her.

"Also," Elise said, trying to keep her tone sweet, "I'm afraid

I would make a very poor china doll. Besides, the *Mary Elise* is my life. I don't intend to add a man to that equation."

"You are a strange one, just as Mother said." Louis bit his lip. "I didn't mean to say that. It's not exactly what Mother meant."

"It's all right. I know I'm not what passes for a normal female in her world." Elise did her best not to reveal the hurt his words had caused. Why should her aunt call her strange just because she enjoyed life on the lakes with her parents? Since Mama died the year before, however, Aunt Martha had nagged Elise to come and live with them.

"It looks like that dashing Mr. Casper is coming our way," her father whispered. "No doubt he wants to dance, Elise."

"Oh, please send him away. He stepped on my foot three times in our first dance. I have no desire to repeat the performance, and I'm sick of dancing."

"I'll take care of it," Louis declared. "I know Charlie. I'll take him to see my new horse. He loves horses more than anything else on earth. Charlie! Wait until you see my new mare." He headed off to intercept the man, whose face lit up as Louis explained his plan.

"What a sweetheart." Elise would have to find a way to pay Louis back. "How much longer will this go on?"

Her father shrugged. "I have no idea. In my experience, the party's over when the liquor runs out, but since these folks have enough money to keep that flow steady, I'm not sure what will bring things to an end."

"Perhaps someone will announce it, as they do for dinner." Elise smiled, imagining a well-dressed butler announcing that the party was over and everyone needed to vacate the property.

"They seem to have announcements for just about everything else. Why not the end of a party?" her father replied.

"Do you suppose if we just sneak off to our rooms to change, they will leave us to our rat-killing?" Elise asked with a grin. *Rat-killing* was her mother's favorite phrase for any odd task that needed to be done. "We could slip upstairs when no one is looking."

"I honestly don't expect we'll be missed. Not even by your sister." There was an edge of regret in Papa's voice. "Besides, I need to check on Joe and see what the doc said about his leg."

Neither of them expected the news to be good. The *Mary Elise*'s first mate had injured his leg nearly a month ago, but no one had known about the wound until he started limping. By that time, the leg was putrid, and red streaks were moving up the thigh.

"Let's just go, then. We can tell Caroline good-bye and pray with her on our way out the door."

Elise pulled Papa in the direction of her sister. She didn't want to give him a chance to refuse. He didn't even try.

Elise waited for her sister to finish speaking to some guests before tapping her shoulder. "Caroline, we must be on our way."

"But you can't! Not until you help me change. I was already looking for an excuse. Nelson said we had to keep to our schedule."

Elise looked at her father with a shrug. "I guess Caroline needs my help. I'll be back as soon as possible, and then we can go."

Caroline all but dragged Elise up the stairs. "Everything was beautiful, wasn't it?"

"Yes. Quite lovely."

"The garden was perfect for the reception. I was so afraid there'd be no roses because of the cold spring, but they were in full bloom, and the gardeners were able to buy additional flowers to weave in." Caroline opened the door to her bedroom suite.

Elise gazed around the large room. There was a sitting area by the fireplace, a dressing area, and, of course, a beautiful four-poster bed with elegant gossamer curtains draped from its frame. It was hard to imagine calling such a place home.

"Unfasten the buttons in back," Caroline commanded as she removed her veil.

"What about *please*?"

"I'm used to servants, and you don't say *please* or *thank you*. It's their job."

"But Mama always encouraged us to be polite, even to the lowliest servant."

"Well, you aren't Mama," Caroline snapped.

"I'm also not a servant."

Silence hung heavy for a moment. Caroline gave a little huff. "Would you please undo my buttons?"

Elise began the task of unfastening thirty-six pearl buttons. "Why did you make that comment about Mama?"

"Well, ever since you and Papa arrived, you've done nothing but mother me. You've even talked to me like Mama. I'm sure you must feel the need to step into her shoes, and while that might be acceptable regarding cooking for Papa and the boys on the ship, it's not for me. I'm perfectly capable of seeing to myself."

"Including your back buttons?"

Caroline sighed. "Very well. Etta!" she called, not seeming to notice whether Elise continued with the buttons.

The uniformed maid appeared. "Ma'am." She gave a curtsy.

"Bring my new traveling suit and help me dress." Caroline glanced over her shoulder as Elise finished with the last of the buttons. "Please."

Elise smiled and watched the maid hurry away. "That wasn't so hard, was it?"

Caroline rolled her eyes. She worked at undoing the buttons on her sleeves. "Etta can help me now. Why don't you go downstairs and wait with the others? I know they plan to throw rice."

Elise waited as Caroline finished with her buttons. Stepping close, she surprised Caroline with an embrace. "I just want you to know that I love you. I hope you have a wonderful trip . . . and marriage."

Caroline hesitated, then finally returned Elise's hug. "I'm certain I will, so you can stop fretting." She stiffened and gave a little push. "Now, let me get back to this."

"We were close once." Elise hadn't meant to whisper the words aloud.

"We were children," Caroline countered. "And we had no choice. There was no other person to confide in or play with. We had only each other."

In that moment, Elise saw her sister not as a wealthy bride but as a little girl. "I liked it that way. We knew we could always count on each other to be there. Now you have other obligations. I will continue to miss you."

"Oh, bother. Where is that girl?" Caroline went to the open door that led to her bathing room. "Etta?"

"Coming, ma'am." Etta returned carrying a forest-green traveling suit. She placed the outfit carefully at the end of the bed, then went immediately to Caroline and helped rid her of the ivory gown.

Elise slipped from the room, knowing that neither woman needed her nor cared for her company. Her sister's attitude only stirred her anger. How could she be so cold? Didn't Caroline have any feelings of love toward her family? Maybe money and prestige were all she loved now.

An hour later, Elise waited in her uncle's borrowed carriage outside of Joseph Brett's apartment. Her father's first mate lived in a modest part of town. Elise knew that despite Joe being a better-paid seaman who didn't drink or gamble, he was still hard-pressed to keep his family fed and clothed, so the tiny duplex came as no surprise.

Joe had a family of five children and a wife who had once been quite pretty. Since Mrs. Brett had been on her way out the door when they'd pulled up to the curb, Elise had decided to wait outside and let her father and Joe visit privately. The two women had exchanged hellos, but then Joe's wife had to be on her way to retrieve her children from her sister's house.

Mrs. Brett had at least shared the news that Joe was doing better. The doctor had given him medication for his wound and strict orders for tending it. She was certain he'd be back on his feet soon.

It was good to hear. Joe had been her father's first mate for as long as Elise could remember. Papa relied on him heavily. It was hard enough to be without Mama on board, but losing Joe would be sheer misery. Her father would be relieved to hear the good news.

While she waited in the carriage, Elise fidgeted with the bodice of her gown. At least it wasn't as fancy as her wedding clothes, but it was just as snug. Probably much smaller than she usually wore, thanks to the tightly tied corset beneath it. She could scarcely draw breath, and given the day's heat and humidity, she worried she might faint dead away. How ridiculous! Why did women put themselves through such torment? A well-fitted corset tied in a reasonable manner was a useful thing, but the practice of securing them as tightly as possible was absurd.

There was some sort of commotion going on down the street, and Elise looked up just in time to see a freight wagon veering out of control. The horses pulling the wagon were driverless and headed straight for her. All she could do was brace herself for impact as her uncle's driver struggled to get the carriage out of the way.

**Tracie Peterson** is the award-winning author of over one hundred novels, both historical and contemporary. She is often referred to as the "Queen of Historical Christian Fiction," and her avid research resonates in her stories, as seen in her bestselling HEIRS OF MONTANA and ALASKAN QUEST series. Tracie considers her writing a ministry for God to share the Gospel and biblical application. She and her family make their home in Montana. Visit her website at traciepeterson.com or on Facebook at facebook.com/AuthorTraciePeterson.

# Sign Up for Tracie's Newsletter

Keep up to date with Tracie's news on book releases and events by signing up for her email list at traciepeterson.com.

# More from Tracie Peterson

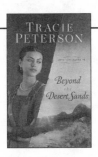

After living an opulent life with her aunt, the last thing Isabella Garcia wants is to celebrate Christmas in a small mining town with her parents. But she's surprised to see how much the town—and an old rival—have changed and how fragile her father's health has become. Faced with many changes, can she sort through her future and decide who she wants to be?

*Beyond the Desert Sands* • Love on the Santa Fe

# You May Also Like . . .

When bankruptcy forces widow Susanna Jenkins to follow her family to New Mexico, what they see as a failure she sees as a fresh start. Owen Turner is immediately attracted to Susanna, but he's afraid of opening up his heart again, especially as painful memories are stirred up. But if Owen can't face the past, he'll miss out on his greatest chance at love.

*Along the Rio Grande* by Tracie Peterson
LOVE ON THE SANTA FE
traciepeterson.com

On the surface, Whitney Powell is happy working with her sled dogs, but her life is full of complications that push her to the edge. When sickness spreads in outlying villages, Dr. Peter Cameron turns to Whitney and her dogs for help navigating the deep snow, and together they discover that sometimes it's only in weakness you can find strength.

*Ever Constant* by Tracie Peterson and Kimberley Woodhouse
THE TREASURES OF NOME #3
traciepeterson.com; kimberleywoodhouse.com

When Madysen Powell's supposedly dead father shows up, her gift for forgiveness is tested and she's left searching for answers. Daniel Beaufort arrives in Nome and finds employment at the Powell dairy, longing to start fresh after the gold rush leaves him with only empty pockets. Will deceptions from the past tear apart their hopes for a better future?

*Endless Mercy* by Tracie Peterson and Kimberley Woodhouse
THE TREASURES OF NOME #2
traciepeterson.com; kimberleywoodhouse.com

◊ BETHANYHOUSE

# More from Bethany House

Longing for a fresh start, Julia Schultz takes a job as a Harvey Girl at the El Tovar hotel, where she's challenged to be her true self. United by the discovery of a legendary treasure, Julie and master jeweler Christopher Miller find hope in each other. But when Julia's past catches up with her, will she lose everyone's trust?

*A Gem of Truth* by Kimberley Woodhouse
SECRETS OF THE CANYON #2
kimberleywoodhouse.com

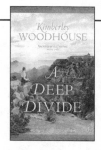

When her father's greedy corruption goes too far, heiress Emma Grace McMurray sneaks away to be a Harvey Girl at the El Tovar Grand Canyon Hotel, planning to stay hidden forever. There she uncovers mysteries, secrets, and a love beyond anything she could imagine—leaving her to question all she thought to be true.

*A Deep Divide* by Kimberley Woodhouse
SECRETS OF THE CANYON #1
kimberleywoodhouse.com

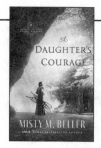

Charlotte Durand sets out on an expedition in search of a skilled artisan who can repair a treasured chalice—but her hike becomes much more daunting when a treacherous snowstorm sets in. When Damien Levette finds Charlotte stranded, they must work together to survive the peril of the mountains against all odds.

*A Daughter's Courage* by Misty M. Beller
BRIDES OF LAURENT #3
mistymbeller.com

◊ BETHANY HOUSE